Civil Warrior

Stewart's Journey

J.W. Jones

Civil Warrior: Stewart's Journey

First Printing March 2014

ISBN-13: 978-1494276164 (CreateSpace-Assigned)

ISBN-10: 149427616X

Dedicated to the memory of Sergeant Gregory Dean Stewart, Marine, Soldier, Police Officer, and one of the finest men I have ever known, and to his parents and son who keep his memory alive. It is further dedicated to all veterans of the United States Armed Forces from all generations who, during both peace and war, have secured and ensured the blessings of liberty for all Americans, past, present, and future.

Chapter One

May 15, 1865, somewhere near the Kentucky/Tennessee state line...

Captain Stewart looked up at the sun briefly. It was getting late in the afternoon and it was hot. The stale sweat dripped down from under his hat. He felt tired. No, he thought, that wasn't an adequate description of how he felt. He'd never felt so completely worn thin in all of his life. Four years of war had made him feel like he was over a hundred years old. He was ready to quit but quitting wasn't something that was in his nature. So here he was on yet another mission trying to win a war that had started off so well but had become so convoluted over time that he wasn't really sure about much of anything anymore.

It had all seemed so clear at the beginning; the South was fighting for their independence from Northern tyranny. The severe tariffs and sanctions on southern states had reached an intolerable level in the federal effort to dictate state law. It just wasn't American to tell other folks how to live their lives and what they could and couldn't own or what private enterprises were legitimate or not. Stewart was certainly no proponent of slavery, but it wasn't like it was a southern invention. Humanity had been enslaving each other since the beginning of time. Even the bible was full of references to slaves and even told them to obey their masters, like the entire book of Philemon. The Yanks conveniently seemed to ignore those particular passages.

The damn Yankee fools didn't even really want to free the slaves anyway, they wanted to send them all back to Africa and completely destroy the South financially in the process. Not that the war hadn't done that anyway. He just didn't understand the hypocrisy of these "republicans" who claimed exclusive rights to the bible and morality while using both to destroy their financial enemies. It wasn't right any way he looked at it. The whole issue had just become an awful bloody mess. Maybe a million Americans were dead now. All of his friends were either dead or sent home missing parts or pieces. He also wanted to go home now too, only as a whole man. The trouble was that he didn't *have* a home anymore. There was nothing left for him back in Texas. He looked back down the road.

The Yanks weren't far away; about six miles east up the creek. His mission was to gather intelligence on the enemy and capture some prisoners for interrogation. He looked at his men hiding in the tree line. They looked like hell. Like gaunt, half-starved wraiths from some nightmare as they crouched quietly in the woods waiting for an enemy patrol. The only thing that looked alive about them was the grim determination in their eyes. He vaguely wondered if he looked just like them but with a slightly better looking uniform.

There were only twenty four men left in his company and they were all in bad shape. He couldn't think of any of them that weren't nursing a wound of some kind. Even he had a mini-ball stuck in his left shoulder that he'd have to have taken out when he got the chance to see a real doctor. The butchers they had in camp would just cut off the whole arm, he was sure. It wasn't hurting right now so he pushed it out of his mind.

His senior enlisted man, First Sergeant Curtis, waved to him from the south end of the bend in the road. He'd heard something coming. Stewart signaled back, 'horses or wagons?' Curtis made the sign for 'horses' and stepped back a little more into creek bank's defilade.

"Great," muttered Stewart, "Cavalry. We're gonna have us a fight."

Curtis passed the signal down the ranks and Stewart noted the men making their weapons ready as expected. Stewart pulled out his two big 1858 Remington .44s and cocked both hammers. He thought about reminding the men to take prisoners but immediately dismissed the thought. They were all seasoned men who fully understood the mission and would do all they could to accomplish it. More men would die today, that he knew. When they would stop dying was the real question. He set his jaw and prepared to do battle.

The sound of trotting hoofs came hard now. Hurried, but cautiously, they were making their way to the Yankee camp. Their commander must be pretty smart and was most certainly looking for just such an ambush as the one that Stewart was setting for him. This wasn't going neat or easy. It could even be a trap. He would worry about that later if it turned out that way. There really weren't too many ways to plan for a trap. A man just had to trust his gut and roll with it.

He felt his tired muscles tense as he prepared for the coming battle. The first troops came into view over the slight rise in the road. The blue uniforms looked clean and new, especially on the lead man. His buttons and brass twinkled as they caught brief traces of sunlight through the heavy tree cover. The bend that Stewart had chosen was a low spot in the road near the creek and under heavy shadow. The Yanks would have just come under the trees about a hundred yards back so hopefully their eyes would still be adjusting. Just then, their leader seemed to sense this problem and slowed the pace to try and see his way ahead.

Stewart watched him as he grew closer and realized that the man on the horse wasn't an experienced veteran officer, but a brand-new second lieutenant. Apparently he'd had some good instructors. He was probably a young rich kid, whose daddy bought him a commission for his 21st birthday. The lieutenant was scanning the area intensely as if he knew that Stewart and his men were waiting in the woods for his patrol. He looked back behind the young fair-haired lieutenant at the Yankee troops. They were mostly German or Dutch immigrants from the looks of them. Stewart had known many Germans back in Texas and respected their fighting ability. A few had even served with him and distinguished themselves in battle. This would be a hard-won fight.

The blond lieutenant was almost up to his position now. Stewart took a deep breath and stepped out in front of him on the road. He aimed both pistols at the lieutenant's face and said, "You're surrounded, young man. You'd best surrender."

Shots rang out instantly and men began to fall behind the lieutenant as his men began to shoot wildly into the trees. The Rebels fired deliberately and accurately and the forty man platoon was quickly reduced to twenty.

The lieutenant froze only for an instant and then reacted. He shifted in his saddle to his right, which was the side away from Stewart, drew his saber, and landed on the ground, all in one smooth move. He then charged Stewart while his horse cantered away. Stewart analyzed his move and fired all in a split second.

9

But he'd done something he hadn't done in a very long time. He'd missed! Shocked, he realized that the kid had calculated his shots and slid off the horse to the right just as he'd fired. The horse then hit Stewart, knocking him to his knees and leaving him staring at the falling blade of the saber when he looked up.

Stewart was in battle mode now so his mind was intently focused on the quickly changing situation. He smoothly rolled right, kicking the lieutenant's leg as the blade came down. At the same time, he parried the blade with his left pistol and though he'd successfully blocked it, it took the pistol out of his hand. The lieutenant went down on his leg and sprang back up instantly, but found himself staring right into the barrel of Stewart's other Remington. The hammer was cocked and Stewart was tensing on the trigger. The lieutenant glared back, red-faced with intense defiance. Captain Stewart could tell that the boy's mind was churning like a locomotive.

It was quieter now, with only a few screams of "Mine Gott! Mine Gott!" coming from the immigrant soldiers every now and then. Without taking his eyes off of the lieutenant, Stewart called back over his shoulder, "First Sergeant! What's our situation?"

"First Sergeant Curtis is dead, Sir."

"Well then, Sergeant Danner, what's our situation?

"We got six killed, Sir."

"And the enemy?" Captain Stewart calmly asked.

"They gots about twenty three killed, Sir". Sergeant Danner's voice was deadpan as if he were giving a list of supplies to his commander.

"Wounded?"

"Yes, Sir. Pretty much all of us here are. 'Cept you and the Yank butter-bar there."

"Well, young man, this is what happens when you don't surrender when you're surrounded. Are you ready to do so now? I'm really tired of killin' you young boys in blue, but that don't mean that I won't. Ya got ten seconds."

The lieutenant seemed to finally find his words and yelled in a high-pitched, cracking voice, "This is a criminal action! It is illegal and a clear violation of the terms of your surrender! You men are all guilty of murder and I will see that you all hang!"

"Two seconds, boy," Captain Stewart pushed the muzzle closer to the lieutenant's face, which instantly went white. The blade clattered to the ground. Apparently he finally realized that he really was about to die.

"That's better, son. Now drop the pistol belt and tell your men to do the same. Now, if don't try nothin' stupid you might yet live to see your twenty-second birthday."

Stewart slowly shifted his position so that he had the lieutenant in view and he could see the battle scene. It was a bloody mess. Those who were still standing stood as if frozen, many at the point of firearms and bayonets. The Rebels definitely had the upper hand as most of the Yanks were either dead or seriously wounded. First Sergeant Curtis was lying on his back beside the Yankee who was holding Curtis' bayonet deep in his chest. It looked like they'd traded steel as Sergeant Curtis was keeping one warm as well. Both men had startled looks on their dead faces, although Curtis' expression was mixed with an obvious disgust with the situation.

"Drop your weapons, men" said the young lieutenant as he carefully lowered his pistol belt to the ground. His voice still trembled but was slightly calmer now and his men began to drop their weapons. He was trying to maintain his military bearing as the unit's commander. Stewart noted that it wasn't a bad effort considering that the boy had lost over half his platoon in his first combat action.

"Sergeant Danner, clean this mess up. Take all weapons and ammunition. Have them clear their dead from the road and then tie them all up." Danner nodded and started moving men around to comply with the captain's orders. "Come here, son." Stewart picked up the dropped pistol belt with his left hand and led the boy and his horse farther up the road and away from the men.

"I can't believe I missed you from that range, you're lucky to be alive, boy. Okay, so what's this nonsense about our 'surrender,' young man?" Stewart kept his guard up just in case the boy got stupid.

"It's true. Lee surrendered all southern forces to General Grant almost five weeks ago. The war's over." He swallowed slightly. "We won, you lost… and you didn't miss." He leaned to the right to show the crease below his left ear and a similar one on

11

his left forearm. Stewart nodded at the wounds, looking slightly relieved.

"So the war's over, huh? Prove it, kid." Stewart's eyes narrowed at the lieutenant. "Your boys have been trying that 'surrender' trick since Gettysburg."

"It's true, Sir." The lieutenant tried a more tactful approach now. Respect went a long way with Rebs. It was pretty sincere respect at this point anyway. This man had all but destroyed his first command in less than a minute. "I have an official dispatch in my saddle bags, as well as a couple of newspapers. That is, if you can read them."

Stewart's look got even harder suddenly and the lieutenant quickly realized the insult he'd just made. "Sorry, Sir, I didn't mean anything by that." This large man scared him to death. He looked the rebel captain over closely. He was over six feet tall with wavy dark brown hair sticking out from under his kepi hat. The hair flowed down to a dark close-cropped beard and mustache. The lieutenant was a little surprised by the kepi as most rebel officers wore more elaborate hats similar to his own cavalry hat laying in the ditch now. Some even put feathers in them. This man did not look like the feather type. The big man was thin, wearing a well tailored but now dirty and threadbare uniform that probably fit him quite well when he was 30 pounds heavier. It sagged on his lean frame now, much like the expression on his face. He was obviously a war-weary man of the type that the young lieutenant had seen returning from the war back in Philadelphia just a few months ago.

He looked the captain in the eye and quickly looked away. His eyes were intense, steel-gray daggers staring back at him. His were the eyes of a killer. If they truly were the window to the soul then this rebel's soul was full of pure death.

Stewart's look softened just a bit. "Okay, son, I can read just fine. That's the whole reason that they made me an officer almost three years ago. I wouldn't be much of an officer if I couldn't read my orders now, would I?" The young man shook his head quickly in agreement. "Now, you just slowly reach up there and get those papers out of your saddlebags. Move *very* slowly now, ya hear?"

"Here they are." The lieutenant brought them slowly and deliberately out of the left saddle bag, keeping himself in full view of the rebel captain. "Your president Davis is still running around trying to keep the war going but the South has generally acknowledged Lee's surrender and the end of the war. President Johnson has announced the reconstruction of the Union. All southern states are now occupied by Union forces and will remain under martial law until proper civil law and the loyalty of the south can be restored. It's all there, Sir."

"Johnson? So we really did capture Lincoln after all?" Stewart inquired.

"Captured Lincoln?" The lieutenant almost laughed but stopped himself when he looked at Stewart's face. He replied in a more serious tone, "No, Sir, he was assassinated at a theater last month, just about a week after Lee's surrender at Appomattox."

"Appomattox, huh? We'd heard a rumor that Lincoln was captured and taken out to sea on the CSS Texas in early April." Stewart eyed him suspiciously, looking for some sign of deception in the young man.

"No, Sir! He was definitely shot by one John Wilkes Booth at Ford's Theater in Washington. Shot him right in the back of the head with a Derringer .44. He died about nine hours later. It was a sad day for the Union." He shook his head slowly. He appeared to fully believe what he was saying and Stewart nodded slightly in acknowledgment.

Stewart hooked the lieutenant's pistol belt onto the saddle horn and took the papers in his left hand. The boy stepped back slightly and put his hands up, giving Stewart the ability to relax his guard somewhat so he could read the papers. He read through them briskly. A small look of triumph came over the young man's face as he saw the truth dawn in Stewart's eyes. Stewart looked up at him and simply stared. He was speechless.

"You see, Captain, it is you who should be surrendering to me," the lieutenant said quietly. He maintained a respectful tone in his voice. He knew he wasn't out of the woods just yet.

"What's your name, son?" Stewart finally asked him.

"Second Lieutenant Brian D. Foster, Sir, Fifth United States Cavalry." The lieutenant snapped to attention as he introduced himself.

"Well, Lieutenant Brian D. Foster, it would seem that I may owe you something of an apology. I'm not really one to apologize much though so just put your hands behind you and I'll take it from there." Stewart turned him around and began to bind his hands together.

"But you know it's true, Sir; I saw it in your eyes."

"No, you saw me think that it might be true, young man. This only changes the situation slightly. Now I'm just going to try just a little harder not to kill you and I won't be needin' any prisoners. You men can stay here with your dead until more Yanks get here, which should be in about fifteen or twenty minutes." Stewart spoke while his hands worked and the lieutenant's hands were quickly bound tight.

"That is a finely tailored uniform you have there, Lieutenant. Where did you have it made?" Stewart's tone was almost conversational as he admired the well-tailored jacket and trousers. Foster was a bit taken aback by the friendlier tone of the scruffy Rebel Captain.

"Philadelphia, Sir. A little shop called Stein Brothers."

"Nice work. Nice material. A man should always try to look his best, regardless of the circumstances. I had three sets of these made in Richmond after they commissioned me in '62. This one's pretty rough now and another got ruined at Wilderness. I've saved one in the original paper to wear home for the victory celebration. I guess that probably won't be happening now." A sad look filled his eyes as he looked toward Foster's horse.

"That's a fine steed ya got there, son. You must come from some money, Foster."

"A bit." Foster looked uncomfortable. "You're going take my black stallion, aren't you?"

"Sure am."

"Do you have any idea what that horse cost me?" Foster was getting angry again.

"A whole bunch, I'm sure."

"You seem to like my things a lot, you thieving bastard!" Stewart shot him glance that made him gulp. Foster tried a different tack.

"Look, we have a camp just two miles up the road, Captain. They'll be here any minute now." Foster was feeling a little more

14

confident now but didn't want to be left helplessly bound either. There were Indians in this area after all, which was what he had really been expecting.

"I appreciate nice things, Lieutenant. You're obviously a man of good taste and I respect that. Oh, and it's more like six miles, son. We checked this mornin'. I got about fifteen minutes left before they get here, unless they were already on the way. Them's mostly colored boys over there anyway so I don't think that they've got too many horses among them. They'll be on foot. Of course there'll be about *two hundred* of 'em on foot so I don't really want to stick around for that neither. Personally, I'd rather fight you and your sausage eatin' Bavarians that those colored boys anyway. They don't shoot any better than the rest of you Yanks but they seem to have no qualms about runnin' a man through with a bayonet though, unlike a white man. They rather seem to enjoy it, actually. They don't like to surrender much either and usually fight to the death. I once saw one of 'em pick a man up and bash him against a rock about 4 or 5 times before we finally put enough lead in him to kill him. They are tough bastards."

Stewart reached into the Lieutenant's jacket and felt around for his pocket book. He pulled it out and thumbed through it briefly. There was only about twenty dollars in the wallet. He looked at the young man's face and started feeling around his waist for the money belt he knew would be there. He pulled it out and threw it onto the horse without looking in it. Then he finished tying Foster to the tree behind him.

Foster looked disgustedly at him and snarled, "So, you're going to resort to banditry now, eh, Captain? I was just starting to respect you."

"The spoils of war, Mr. Foster. I won this battle so what was yours is now mine. I do not normally condone that sort of thing but it is simple economics at this point. If what you say is true, then my money is now worth much less than your money is. What kind of severance pay do you think the Confederacy is going to give us? We haven't been paid anything in over five months anyway and that was Confederate scrip. Think of this as a charitable donation or in my case, a loan. Look me up in about five or ten years and I'll pay you back with interest. I might even give you this brand new Colt back, if you're real nice to me…empty of course." Stewart looked at the pistol briefly as he swung up into the saddle of the Lieutenant's horse and noted the equally new Henry rifle in the scabbard. He turned to his men and said, "Gather all of the Yanks horses and put our dead onto them. Take whatever you can of value. Leave 'em with all their personal effects. If it's engraved or a picture, personal letter, whatever, they keep it."

"And to whom have I given such a generous loan, Sir?"

"What's his name?"

"Sir?"

"The horse, son. What's his name?"

"Oh, Gabriel, Sir. What's your name?"

"Gabriel? The Arch-Angel? That's a good, solid name, Lieutenant. First Sergeant Danner! We are leaving! Now!" Stewart wheeled the horse around and noted that all the men were prepared as he had commanded. Danner puffed his chest out noticeably as he recognized his promotion. Let him be proud for a while, Stewart thought, he had earned it.

"Sir, what is YOUR name!" The Lieutenant seemed panic stricken. Stewart realized that it may come in handy one day that this man knew who'd spared his life. He rode back up next to Foster, leaned over and quietly said, "Captain Gregory D. Stewart, First Texas Infantry. 'Remember the Alamo!'" He rose up in the saddle and threw a smart salute. With that Stewart rode straight into the brush across the creek, with his men following close behind him. They were gone just as fast as they had appeared. Foster looked over at his bloody and devastated patrol, now tied helplessly along the side of the road. He hung his head down and groaned in humiliation.

Chapter Two

Stewart spotted the sentries before they spotted him. He rode deliberately toward them sitting straight up in the saddle so they would recognize him. They did, but they went through the challenge and password routine anyway. He smiled slightly at their dedication but felt a twinge of pain at the crushing blow he would have to deal to their spirits in the next several hours. He had read through all of Foster's papers on the ride to camp and had been effectively convinced that the young man was telling the truth. It was a lot of information including an article about President Davis' antics that was downright embarrassing for a Rebel. The man always did have a reputation being excessively passionate to the point of being unreasonable. The sentries waved him through and Stewart and his men made their way into the run-down rebel camp. Sergeant Major Williams came running out of his tent over to the returning men.

"What have you brung me now, Captain Stewart?" the old Scotsman exclaimed in his thick accent as he stood wearing his tartan with his hands on his hips. "Every time you leave with a company you only bring half of them back, sir!"

"I do the best that I can under the circumstances, Sergeant Major."

"Aw...that is bullshit, Captain!" He turned his back on Stewart in disgust and began barking orders at other men to take care of the wounded and dead. Stewart smiled slightly; glad to have a sergeant major that genuinely cared for his soldiers. He knew all too well how the man felt.

Stewart rode up to the command post, dismounted and tied Gabriel to a tree outside the tent. He reached into the saddle bag and pulled out a bundle of papers he'd taken from Foster. A young corporal was sitting outside the tent and stood up and saluted as Stewart approached him. Stewart returned the salute and asked, "Is the major inside?"

"No sir. He's in his tent."

"Figures," Stewart muttered under his breath.

"Sir?"

"Nothing. Don not let anyone touch that horse Corporal Johnson, understand?"

"Yes sir."

Stewart walked around the command post tent toward Major Beatty's tent. He wasn't looking forward to this but he had known for some time that he would have to confront the major about his supposed 'orders from the top.' He could hear Major Beatty going on in his tent, seemingly chewing someone out. Stewart knew that the major was delusional and talked to himself frequently so he backtracked a few steps and walked back toward the tent stomping his feet slightly so that the major would hear him coming. The strange conversations the man had with himself made Stewart uncomfortable and he wanted to make sure he didn't interrupt one.

Major Beatty was the acting commander and had assumed command with the death of Lieutenant Colonel MacGregor three and half months ago. He claimed to have graduated at the top of his class from West Point in '58 but Stewart wasn't too sure of the legitimacy of the story. His stories about 'the Point' were often pretty far-fetched and had to have been embellished somewhat if not downright made up. It was hard to imagine such a worm of a man doing the many valiant and heroic things that he claimed.

Stewart coughed slightly just outside the tent flap and knocked on the center post. "Sir, Captain Stewart reporting."

"Stewart! Get in here! Damn it man, you walk like an oaf! I can hear you coming from a mile away boy! Pick your feet up for Pete's sake!" Stewart stepped inside the ragged tent and stood at attention before the major. Beatty briefly looked him up and down as if he were inspecting the captain; he displayed a look of disgust as his eyes rested on the large brass Texas regimental belt buckle.

"Yes sir," Stewart tried hard not to roll his eyes.

Ignoring the offensive accoutrement, Beatty said, "Where are my prisoners, young man? I want to interrogate them immediately!"

"We didn't take any sir."

"What? I specifically gave you orders to capture prisoners, captain! I was very clear on that point! How did you not complete your mission?"

"Well sir…"

"Quiet! Don't interrupt me again, captain! I have had just about enough of your insubordination, young man!" Stewart bit his lip. Beatty was only a few years older than him. "This is why former sergeants shouldn't be officers! This is what I mean when I tell you that field grade officers who are properly trained in the art of war are the backbone of this army. You will never understand that Stewart! You have neither the education nor the breeding to comprehend the big picture! I should have you shot for disobeying a direct order from a superior officer!" He emphasized his point by standing up on his toes trying to match Stewart's height.

"You'll be all out of captains then sir." Stewart was the next highest ranking officer to Beatty.

"Do not get sassy with me! I will have you in front of a court martial for gross insubordination! I am in command here and do not think that you will be my executive officer when I get promoted! I am sending you back to your Texas regiment as soon we make contact with them again. You will be lucky to go back to sergeant! When this war is over I'm going to..."

"The war *is* over sir!" Beatty's eyes grew huge and round as he stared at him angrily. Stewart looked at him with caution. He was convinced that the man simply was not sane.

"That is treason!" he sputtered. "How *dare* you make such an unpatriotic statement! I *will* have you shot!"

"I did not say that we lost the war, sir. I said that the war is over. Is there something that you have been hiding from us?" Stewart cocked one eyebrow and looked down at the small man suspiciously.

"What are you saying? Are you accusing me of something?" The major said defensively, suddenly looking a bit more nervous than usual.

"I am saying that the war has been over for five weeks and you have had us out here playing soldier, patrolling, killing and dying and I think you have known for some time now that Lee surrendered at the courthouse in Appomattox. That 'secret' message you received last month that you said 'didn't concern company grade officers.' That was it, was it not?"

Beatty started a bit at the mention of Appomattox. He quickly recovered. "Just because Lee surrendered doesn't mean that the entire Confederacy has. Why, I have been assured that President Davis is personally re-organizing the war effort and we are preparing a counter-offensive to drive the enemy from our nation. Then we shall achieve total victory and watch that bastard Lincoln hang on the steps of the White House!" Beatty spoke as if he were trying more to reassure himself than Stewart.

"Bull shit sir!" Stewart thrust the bundle of papers at him. "Lincoln has been dead over a month! Richmond and Atlanta have fallen along with the rest of the South! We have achieved total defeat and any further continuance of your fantasy is a senseless waste of the lives of good men!" Stewart was furious. He had had enough of this pompous little jackass. He leaned closely to the major and lowered his voice. "It is getting dark now sir but I strongly suggest that at morning muster you inform and dismiss the men and allow them to return to their homes." He glared at him in that 'you're about to die' look that he had perfected over the last four years.

"Are you giving me an ultimatum?" The major seemed incredulous and visibly gulped. His eyes darted to his pistol on the desk and he saw Stewart's eyes narrow. Stewart's right hand hovered inches from the new Colt on his hip. The major visibly gulped again.

"And what if I do not follow your *suggestion* Captain?" Beatty said with only a hint of defiance.

"Then I will relieve you of command and do it myself."

"And how will you relieve me of my *rightful* command Captain! You do not have the authority to do that!"

"Maybe I do not but what is more important is that you do not have *any* authority at all anymore either and I will relieve you by whatever means is necessary." Major Beatty was already scared of Stewart but he seemed to look even more fearful now. He shook slightly and turned away.

"I will consider your suggestion, captain," he said with his back turned. He did not think Stewart would shoot him in the back. "We will discuss this matter in the morning. That is all."

Stewart gently set the papers on the desk beside the major's pistol and slowly backed out of the tent, keeping his eye on the pistol and the major whose hands which were crossed on his chest. He kept facing the tent until he was several paces away and then turned toward his new horse. He walked Gabriel over to his tent and stripped his gear from the horse and put it in the tent. After leading the horse down to the corral and asking one his men to care for it, he went back up the hill to see what was for supper at the mess wagon. He was starving and hadn't eaten well in months. He hoped that ol' Cecil had created something decent again.

As he walked up to the mess wagon he could hear the muffled voices of men having dinner conversation in low tones. They all knew that if they made too much noise that it could give away the camp's location to Union scouts. One man laughed a little too loudly and was instantly shushed by several others. Cecil was serving the men from a large kettle trying carefully not to spill any of the precious food.

Cecil was a heavyset slave who had been brought to the unit by his owner, Lieutenant Thomas Walters, at the beginning of the war. Walters, a rich kid from Beaumont, Texas, had been killed almost a year ago and since Cecil seemed to be a fair hand at cooking and every other man was needed to fight, he had assumed duties as the head cook for the regiment which was now a mixed bunch of men from Virginia, Louisiana, Tennessee and Texas. They were officially the 3rd Louisiana Infantry now but most of the men when asked still used their original regiment. Cecil's situation was just one of those things that happened in a time of war. Someone just does what he thinks he needs to do and Cecil had received few complaints. Technically he was now a free man but he did not seem to understand the concept when Stewart tried to explain it to him after Walters' death. He said he needed to take care of his master's soldiers and that was that.

Cecil was unarmed and probably knew nothing of firearms operation but he was a fair hand at trapping. He would set small noose traps on tree branches and collect dozens of squirrels each day in his on-going effort to feed the remainder of the regiment. One man stood in front of the cook and complained about the meal of squirrel stew with tubers and greens.

"Come on nigger. Can't you cook nothin' else? I'm sick to death of this slave stew. Bet if I took a whip to ya, you would do better, boy!" He said leaning menacingly toward Cecil. Cecil just looked down at his kettle and avoided the young man's eyes as he had been conditioned to over a lifetime of slavery. Stewart walked up behind the man and tapped him on the shoulder.

21

"That's enough of that soldier. Take your ration and move along. You are holding up the line." Stewart's low deep tone startled the young man.

"But sir, we have had this same backwoods, nigger crap for over two weeks now!" The soldier stammered.

"You're damn lucky to have anything at all. Now move along. That is an order."

"But this damn nig…"

"This man saved my life, soldier. I took a mini ball in my left shoulder at Wilderness and it knocked the hell out of me. I couldn't move. Cecil picked me up and pulled me out of the battle. He was thanked by the Yanks with a mini ball in his ass! No matter what you think of him or his kind, he has still been a vital part of our unit and I will not tolerate anyone complaining about someone who spends every waking moment trying to find food for a bunch of ungrateful children." Stewart's tone was sharp now but still hushed. The young soldier looked at the captain's eyes in the dim firelight and lowered his head.

"I am sorry sir. I am just…"

"No excuses, son. Now I gave you an order and you will follow it, immediately!"

"Yes sir," he said as he turned to walk away. "Never knew the cap'n was nigger lover," He muttered under his breath. Stewart lunged at the young man grabbing his shoulder and turning him around with his left hand while his right fist smashed his face in. The soldier fell backward dropping his musket and his plate all over the ground. Stewart was all over the young man pummeling him with his fists with an intense fury.

Sergeant Major Williams rushed to the scene and pulled the captain off the young soldier. "Sir! That's enough Sir! He has had enough!" Stewart looked down at the boy's bloody face and seemed to come to his senses. "What is wrong with you, sir?" The sergeant major looked at the captain, cautiously prepared to defend himself if need be.

Stewart shook his head and cleared it a little. The attack was completely out of character for him and all the men around stood staring at him in shock at his loss of composure. Stewart looked at the sergeant major and dropped his fists suddenly embarrassed and ashamed.

"Hayes, your supper is over now. Go on back to your tent and get yourself cleaned up," the sergeant major said to the battered soldier.

"Y-yes sergeant major,' Hayes stammered as he tried to get to his feet. He began to walk away from the mess wagon when Stewart yelled at him.

"Soldier!"

"Sir?" The soldier turned back around, fear in his voice.

"Apologize," Stewart said quietly.

"I am sorry sir."

"Not to me, to Cecil. And thank him for what he does for us."

"Sir?" The young man looked incredulous.

"Do it!" Stewart's anger wasn't yet completely dissipated.

The young bloody faced soldier looked at the captain and gulped seeming to swallow his pride at the same time. "I am sorry Mr. Cecil. Thank you for the supper." He looked back at Stewart.

Cecil shifted a little, visibly embarrassed by the attention. "That's awright, suh. I doesn't mind now, OK?" Cecil said nodding even more apologetically.

"You are dismissed soldier." Stewart said as he turned back to Cecil. The soldier picked up his musket and limped away, humiliated.

"You din haf to do that, cap'n suh. It was awright. I'm purty tired of makin' this here stew tha he's so tired eatin' anyway. He gotta right to complain, suh." Cecil was obviously upset by the whole matter.

"We shall discuss this matter later, Captain," the sergeant major said glaring at Stewart. He looked around at the men and they began to go about their business as if nothing had happened. No words were necessary. Stewart nodded at the sergeant major as he stormed away, brushed himself off and walked back over to Cecil.

"No man has the right to complain, Cecil." Stewart said quietly as he snapped back into his controlled officer persona. He tried to ignore the throbbing pain that he was now feeling in his shoulder. "We all just need to be thankful for what the good Lord gives us from day to day. Now what has the good Lord enabled you to give us on this day Cecil?"

23

"Cap'n Stewart suh, you just come on back here and I fix ya up." Cecil handed the ladle to one of the other slaves who helped him and motioned for him to keep the serving line going.

Chapter Three

The next morning Stewart rolled out of his cot at daybreak. The birds always woke him up and he wasn't one to dawdle in bed. He went down to the creek with his shaving kit and went through his morning grooming ritual. It was the one thing that he had been able to keep constant in his life the past few years. As long as he had at least a cup of water he tried to wash his face, trim his beard, shave his neck, and wash his teeth and mouth out each morning. It made him feel just a little bit human and a little bit normal.

It promised to be a rough day again as he reflected on the last day's events. He wasn't quite sure how he was going proceed with things. Stewart looked at the beautiful morning brightening steadily around him and realized that this may well be his last day on earth. It could get very ugly when he confronted Major Beatty and he didn't think that the man would hesitate to assassinate him if he thought he might get away with it. Beatty would surely be killed if the men suspected him of Stewart's murder but he wasn't a rational man anymore and may not realize that though he had the rank, Stewart had the men.

His life was not that important in the grand scheme of things, he thought. The most important thing is to get the men home to their families before any more of them died for nothing. He was willing to die for that he decided. That would be one redeeming thing that he could bring before the Lord to show that he hadn't lost all faith or decency to the war. He knew that it would not matter much to God because a man cannot earn his way into heaven except by faith in Christ, but it would certainly give Stewart some peace to have at least died for *something*. He had placed his life in the hands of God many years ago and had in fact prayed for two weeks before he felt sure that joining the Confederate cause was the path that God wanted him to take. He was not an openly religious man but he had seen the hand of the Lord work in many ways in his life and he trusted that he would live only as long as God desired, not one minute more or one minute less. He was content with that thought.

He finished his ritual and began to walk back up to the camp as the sergeant major was coming down. Stewart saw that he was going to ignore him and walk right past him so he spoke to him.

"Sergeant Major."

"Hmmph," Williams grumbled as he went by.

"Sergeant Major." Stewart was little louder this time as the man walked by him. Williams stopped and looked back at him.

"Yes, Captain?" Stewart knew that when Williams wasn't happy with an officer that he always called him by his rank instead of 'sir.'

"How is Hayes?"

"Hayes?" He began. He stopped and thought momentarily about what he was about to say but he knew that his first thoughts would be unfair to Stewart. Stewart was good man who really cared about the troopers unlike many of the officers he had known before. Besides, the man had a fine Scottish name. He shook his head.

"Not good sir. He will be alright I am sure, but you gave him quite a beating last night. I hope he deserved it. I was tempted to take you on myself after that, I will have you know. I know you would have given me a beating as well but you would have felt some yourself, sir" Williams was only half joking Stewart knew.

"Yes, I know, you would give me a run for my money and I'm not interested in seeing who would come out on top in that scrap. I want to apologize to the man...in private of course. What he said was inappropriate but I over-reacted to it. It is the right thing to do." Stewart looked into Williams eyes to gage his response. The sergeant major looked back and nodded. He felt a new measure of respect for the captain now. Too bad all officers were not this humble, he thought.

"Aye, sir. I believe you would be correct on that one. I will arrange it. Your tent in say...two hours?"

"Sooner. You and I have business to discuss before muster and after muster may be too late for me." Williams raised his eyebrows at that. He nodded gently and pondered the ominous tone of Stewart's last statement.

"Thirty minutes then?"

"That would be fine, Sergeant Major."

"Very good sir, I've need to relieve myself first so that should be enough time for me." The big Scotsman turned away at

26

that and headed for the woods, intent on his mission at hand. Stewart smiled slightly and turned back to his tent to finish dressing.

Twenty nine minutes later a knock came on the center post of his tent. Stewart sat up in his chair behind his small field desk and said, "Come in."

Private Hayes came in and stood at attention before the captain. He snapped a brisk salute, full of ire, and said in a loud voice. "Sir! Private Hayes reports as ordered, Sir!"

"Stand at ease soldier," Stewart said returning the salute. The sergeant major had obviously not informed Hayes as to why he was reporting to Stewart which was as it should be. It was Stewart's duty to apologize, no one else needed to intercede for his mistakes or make his apologies. He stood up and walked over to Hayes to remove the formality of the setting.

"Sergeant Major, I would like you to come in here for this as well." The flap opened and the big Scotsman stepped inside.

"Hayes, the way you behaved last night was wrong," Stewart began. He saw the young man stiffen up as if preparing for the worst. "What you mumbled as you walked away from me was wrong as well. But how I reacted to it was worse." He let that sink in as the soldier stood staring straight ahead. Hayes suddenly seemed to hear what Stewart had said and turned and stared at him. Stewart looked at the young man and extended his hand. "I would like to apologize to you. What you did deserved discipline, not punishment. I am sincerely sorry for my behavior Mr. Hayes."

Hayes took the captain's hand and stammered, "Aw sure Cap'n, I'm sorry for actin' the way I did. I guess I kinda deserved it."

"No Hayes, I let what you said remind me of something that happened long ago and I let my emotions control my actions. Whenever a man allows that to happen he is sure to make a mistake."

"Yes Sir, I will remember that." Hayes looked embarrassed so Stewart let go of his hand and returned to the chair behind his desk.

"There is one more item that we need to clear up Mr. Hayes. In this army it has been a tradition to levy a fine on officers

27

for their misconduct and the proceeds are usually given to the injured party if there is one, or into the unit general fund if there is not. Since I have no one to fine me, I will have to levy the fine against myself." Stewart intentionally made no reference to Major Beatty's authority. "All I have right now is a twenty dollar gold piece I took off that Yankee lieutenant yesterday but I think that a twenty dollar fine is appropriate for the situation."

Stewart handed the large coin to Hayes who cautiously took it and held it in his hand in front of him. He had likely never held one before. The young man had a cautious and confused look on his face.

"This isn't a bribe, Mr. Hayes," Stewart said quietly. "It is simply the only thing and the best thing that I can do for you under the present circumstances."

"I do not understand, Sir..."

"You will soon enough Mr. Hayes. For now, just take the money. You are dismissed unless there is something else you have to say."

"No Sir!" Hayes closed his left hand over the coin, dropped it to his side and saluted smartly, a slight grin on his bruised face. Stewart returned his salute and the young soldier almost ran out of the tent.

"Twenty dollars, Sir?" The sergeant major eyed Stewart suspiciously. "That's quite a lot for a young private, and Union gold at that? What is this all about, Sir"

Stewart sighed and picked up the small stack of papers on his desk that had been hidden under his saddle bag. He had kept about half of them from the major in case he got smart and tried to destroy them.

"It is all right here sergeant major, the truth. You deserve to know and I am going to need your help." He offered them to Williams who took them and began to examine them. Stewart didn't even know if he could read them, many enlisted men were illiterate, but Williams seemed to comprehend the material fairly quickly. He let Williams study them for some time, waiting for the man's response.

"The bloody, lying bastard!" Williams threw the stack down on the desk. "I will slice him from groin to gullet, I will! I am going rip Beatty's balls off and make them his last meal!" He

28

pulled his knife from his belt and waved it around making cutting motions at groin level. Stewart almost smiled at the man's outburst. At least he knew that he now had an ally.

"I do not think that is the way that we should proceed in this matter, Sergeant Major, though I certainly share your sense of justice. I gave Beatty an ultimatum last night. Either he dismisses the men at muster or I will relieve him and do it myself." Stewart's tone was calm and measured trying affect William's mood.

"Six men died yesterday, Captain! SIX! For what! They should have all been home fu…uh… courting each other's sisters, I tell you!" He looked up to see if Stewart had noticed his near use of profanity which, he had. Williams chose to ignore the slip and continued, "Since April, how many men have died to keep this worm of a man in power? Fifty? A hundred? No more, Captain. Not one more!" Williams sat down on Stewart's cot still shaking the knife along with his head. He looked up at Stewart as if awaiting orders to kill Beatty.

"I completely agree with you Mr. Williams. You will have to get used to that title now and I to 'Mr. Stewart' for we are now soldiers in an army that no longer exists." Stewart paused letting that reality sink in. "We must give the man an opportunity to do the right thing. If he chooses to continue his deceptions, I will personally hold him while you disembowel him. But, for the sake of the men, let us try to accomplish this in an orderly and military fashion. I would like to leave them with as much pride in their service to the Confederacy as possible. There will be enough humiliation for them without our surrender becoming a bloody mess as well."

"Surrender? My God, I never thought we would ever *surrender*." The sergeant major shook his head in disbelief.

"I personally will not." Stewart said. "I have already decided on my course of action and surrender seems to me to be a pointless formality. I have no intention of putting myself through some humiliating ceremony and uttering a worthless oath that does not honestly reflect my beliefs. Though I will cease my hostilities toward the Union, I will simply not surrender. However, if others choose to surrender I will certainly not stand in their way." The two men looked at each other. Neither man could hide the look of defeat. Sensing the uncomfortable moment, Stewart got up and walked over to tent flap. "I will expect you to have the men formed at muster as usual, Sergeant Major. But make sure that they are all there, no one on detail and pull in the sentries as well. We shall give Major Beatty one last chance to prove himself to be and honorable man and if he fails, then we shall take the appropriate action."

"Aye, Sir. That, we will." Williams got up, sheathed his knife, and walked out of the tent. "It shall be done, Sir." He threw back over his shoulder on the way out.

Stewart turned back to his belongings and sighed as he began to pack them. He looked at the brand new Colt in his holster and thought for moment. Though the gun was newer it was also harder to reload than his Remington revolvers. He had carried them before and since capturing the matched set of Remingtons from a Union Lieutenant Colonel, he had bet his life on them numerous times and they had never failed him. He had also never fired the weapon which gave him pause to continue carrying it. He pulled it from his holster and replaced it with the rather worn Remington that now carried a scar along the top of the barrel from Foster's blade.

He thought about the battle of the previous day for a moment. The young lieutenant had chosen the only option he really had at the time. He could pull the saber from his side as he fell to the right but it would have taken far too much time to pull the Colt from the regulation flapped holster that he carried. Stewart could have killed Foster five or six times before he cleared leather. He placed the Colt back in the holster it had come from originally and sighed. Twenty nine men had died yesterday for nothing. Stewart shook his head wondering about the distraught families of the poor Bavarian draftees that his men had killed. He decided that he would keep the gun as a back-up. Where he was going he would probably need it. He knew in his heart that his days of killing were far from over.

The men were assembled as ordered on the small field in front of the regimental command post. The sergeant major stood before them and called the men to attention as Stewart approached. He turned and gave Stewart a smart salute. Stewart returned it.

"Has the major shown his face yet?" Stewart said quietly to Williams.

"No sir." The burly sergeant major shook his head.

"Stand at ease, men" Stewart told the formation. He looked at them for moment. It would be their last formation. They looked proud. Determined and battle hardened veterans, all. First Sergeant Danner stood in front of C Company sporting his new stripes on the sleeves of his uniform. One hundred sixty seven soldiers and six slaves, now former slaves, stood before him. Each of them looked proud to serve in their role. He would have to crush that pride in next few minutes if the major refused to do his duty.

"Walk with me," Stewart told Williams. The sergeant major fell in beside him as Stewart headed toward the major's tent. A senior first sergeant from A Company stepped forward to take charge of the formation. With a minute motion of his hands Stewart checked his guns, ensuring that they were loose in the holsters. Fear was rising in the pit of his stomach but he pushed it down, knowing that what he feared most now was failing at his task. Live or die, he must get these men sent home to their families. Williams observed the subtle motion that Stewart had made while checking his guns so he also made similar check of the knife in his belt. He had a .36 caliber Colt in his belt as well but he would take greater pleasure in cutting the major to pieces. The two men stopped just in front of the tent. They could hear Beatty prattling on to some imaginary audience. Stewart coughed slightly and the voice stopped.

"Who is there?" the shaky voice spoke from within.

"Captain Stewart...and Sergeant Major Williams...Sir." Stewart spoke slowly and purposely. This was not a time for weakness or emotion. "May we speak with you, Sir?" Stewart continued, unconsciously checking his guns again.

"Y-yes, come on in." The major's voice was full of fear.

The two men stepped into the tent prepared for combat but the major sat slumped in his chair behind his small desk. The pistol lay on the table inches from his hand.

"You must think that I am stupid, Stewart. I know you kept some of those captured documents from me. You thought I would destroy them and pretend they never existed, did you not?" Anger filled the man's eyes along with the disheveled look of a man who had been drinking all night. A nearly empty whisky bottle sat on the desk near the pistol.

"I thought that I had made it fairly obvious sir, I only gave you half of a newspaper, after all." Stewart spoke evenly in a 'matter of fact' tone. He did not really want to provoke the man to violence if it wasn't necessary. Though he had little personal respect for the major, he *was* a major and that deserved some level of respect.

"Yes, yes it was obvious." Beatty looked down a bit. He was obviously an exceedingly tormented man. "But you still think I am stupid, do you not, Stewart?"

"No sir. I have never thought you were stupid. I think you are demeaning, arrogant, and delusional and that you have far too many secrets for one man to bear. I think that you may be a fraud and that your whole personal history is embellished at best if not downright made up. I think that perhaps you never went to West Point and that you had hoped that in winning the war we could wipe out that little historical difficulty for you. I have not agreed with you about much of anything but I never thought that you were stupid…sir." Stewart sighed slightly letting the truth of his feelings sink in. The major looked at him sharply at first then the look faded.

"I went to West Point," Beatty said quietly. "But I flunked out my second year; too many demerits. I was too embarrassed to go back home to Virginia so I went down to Princeton, New Jersey and finished college there. I came back home and…well; I think you've already figured the rest out." Beatty looked down at the pistol. He seemed to be looking through it.

"Are you going to dismiss the men, Major?" Stewart asked quietly. The sergeant major tensed up a bit. This was it right here.

"They will kill me, Stewart." Beatty's eyes were dark with fear. "When they find out that I have kept them out here for six weeks unnecessarily, they will string me up." His hands shook as he took the bottle and took a small swig.

"You do not have to tell them when the war ended, sir. They will find out later but I think they will be more understanding if you just explain that you could not bring yourself to quit with such great and valiant men who have yet to be truly beaten. They are all good men who would fight to the death if there were any hope left of victory. Appeal to the men's pride, be sincere, and they will probably respect you for your honesty."

"You think so?" He looked up at Stewart with a small glimmer of hope in his eyes and then he saw the look on Williams face. "What do you think, Sergeant Major?"

"I think you're a dead man... Major!" The man's face was red with fury but he maintained his self control. Beatty shrunk back in his chair. Stewart waved Williams off with a slight motion from his left hand.

"You have a choice to make sir. I am giving you every chance I know how to maintain your honor and dignity. I will personally guarantee your safety if you will simply fulfill your proper duty, Major." He shot a sharp glance at Williams who stepped back slightly, an apologetic look on his face.

"Well... I appreciate that Stewart. I really do. Give me a moment to straighten myself up and I will come and... and... dismiss the men." He stood up, waved them off and turned his back to them. Stewart exchanged a look with Williams, shrugged and walked out of the tent.

"Well, that went a bit better than I expected," Williams said as they walked back toward the formation. Stewart nodded slightly.

"Yes, that was not what I expected. Maybe getting drunk sobered him up." Stewart said smiling wryly at the sergeant major. Williams laughed briefly.

"Huh! If I had known that was all it would take I would have helped him out with that long ago!" Williams shook his head. The first sergeant in front of the formation turned around to call the men to attention but Williams waved him off. "Relax men; it will be a few moments."

They all stood quietly waiting for several minutes. Some of the men spoke in hushed tones to each other. Williams ignored the breach of discipline. Stewart pulled out his watch and looked at it. It had been over ten minutes so far. He would give him ten more before he went back up the hill. Both men stood on a low rise slightly above the field the regiment was formed upon. A few of the lieutenants were milling around behind the formation speaking softly to each other. Stewart could not even remember all their names and he wasn't going to make much effort to do so. There

33

were only five left and seemed like decent men but he hadn't wanted to make any more friends that he might have to bury.

BANG! The shot rang out and echoed across the small valley surrounding the rebel camp. A few of the men jumped but most just looked up in the direction of the major's tent. Stewart and Williams looked at each and slowly started back up the hill together. They walked right in without knocking, both of them knowing what they would find in the tent. Beatty's body flopped around on the floor as it adjusted to its newly found condition of being dead.

"Congratulations Captain! You are now the new regimental commander!" Williams said slapping the Stewart's left shoulder. Stewart winced in pain as the mini ball shifted in that shoulder.

"Sure. For about the next fifteen minutes anyway."

"Do you want his stars, sir? He did this one thing right, put the pistol in his mouth and took his whole brain out, he did," Williams said examining the body more closely. "There isn't too much blood on them. I can pull them off right now." He said as he pulled his knife out.

"That won't be necessary Sergeant Major. More effort than it would be worth."

"He could have at least taken care of his business beforehand, smelly bastard," Williams held his nose and pointed at the soiled trousers on the still twitching body.

"I do not think that was the first think in his mind," Stewart said quietly.

"No sir, I believe the first thing in his mind was a .36 caliber slug; the first *and* the last thing." Williams chuckled slightly.

"Let us have a *little* respect for the dead, Sergeant Major."

"Um…yes sir," Williams said suddenly realizing that he was still in the presence of an officer. "I will have some men clean this up later. Now I think we have some explaining to do to those men outside." A few men had gathered around the outside of the tent trying to see inside. Stewart looked down at Beatty and shook his head. His body looked like it was still trying to breathe while his brains were splattered all over the tent wall. His eyes bulged out of his head and were still flickering back and forth. A small hole could be seen high in the middle of the bloody stain where the bullet had passed through the fabric of the tent.

"Okay men. Let's form it back up and get on with our business. You all heard the sergeant major; we can clean this up later." Stewart walked back out to the field leaving any arguments to be addressed by his back.

Chapter Four

Stewart stood quietly in front of the men with his hands clasped behind his back, clutching the papers he'd taken from Major Beatty's tent. He thought carefully about what he should say to them. He had never been comfortable with public speaking and his words in these next few moments would be remembered by these men for decades. He decided that trying to keep it simple would be best for all of them.

"Men, as y'all know I'm not much of a speaker so I will keep this simple. There is no easy way to say this so I'll just say it. The war is over. They won, we lost." Stewart let that sink in for a moment. Some of the men dropped their heads and wept, others muttered oaths under their breath. The noise level began to rise.

The sergeant major stepped up and barked, "At ease men, let the captain finish!"

The men quieted and Stewart went on, "I know that this is the last thing any of us ever thought would happen but it's true. I will now read General Order number nine, from General Robert E. Lee, commander of the Army of Northern Virginia." Stewart held the paper in front of him, cleared his throat slightly and began to read;

"After four years of arduous service, marked by unsurpassed courage and fortitude, the army of Northern Virginia has been compelled to yield to overwhelming numbers and resources. I need not tell the survivors of so many hard fought battles, who have remained steadfast to the last, that I have consented to this result from no distrust of them. But feeling that valor and devotion could accomplish nothing that could compensate for the loss that would have attended the continuance of the contest, I determined to avoid the useless sacrifice of those whose past service have endeared them to their country. By the terms of the agreement officers and men can return to their homes and remain until exchanged. You will take with you the satisfaction that proceeds from the conscientiousness of duty faithfully performed and I earnestly pray that a merciful <u>God</u> will extend to you his blessing and protection. With an unceasing admiration of

your constancy and devotion to your country and a grateful
remembrance of your kind and generous consideration of myself, I
bid you an affectionate farewell.

Signed

R.E. Lee, General"

Stewart looked up at the men. No doubt many of them didn't even understand the words he had just read. It was hard enough for him to comprehend the enormity of General Lee's words. Everything that these men had worked for in the last 4 years was now for nothing. Their faces were hard to look at, varying in range from sadness, to mourning, to anger, to shock, and to downright terror. A very few faces showed relief. He decided that it was not possible for any man to judge them. He tried to keep his own emotions in check. These men needed his strength now, more than ever.

"Men, I know that words just don't exist that can convey our thoughts and emotions at this terrible time in our lives. It would seem that all of our efforts, all of the killing, all of the dying, and all of the blood have been for naught. It would appear that tyranny has triumphed over justice. That freedom has been vanquished by oppression. We went to war to defend our homeland against an unlawful invasion by foreign states. Our enemy was intent on forcing us to accept laws and tariffs against our will in much the same way as the British king did to the original colonies. Though we all fully understand the reasons for our rebellion against the state of tyranny, it appears that this conflict will go down in the history books as a war to 'free the slaves.' The victor writes the history and we will be forever portrayed to future generations as the evil slave owners fighting to keep a people shackled in servitude. This war shall henceforth be referred to by historians as the war against slavery. It will be the easiest way to vilify us and justify the tyranny of our attackers."

Stewart looked at the six black faces in the back of the formation and saw tears rolling down at least two of them. Some of the men glanced back at them briefly as well.

"I know of not a single man in this formation who now owns or has ever owned a slave. These six men who have cooked for us, nursed us when we were sick, and bound our wounds, have done so out of loyalty to us, not because anyone here owns them. They have been free to go for several months now as ownership of them has ceased due to the death of their masters. Personally, I don't feel obligated to enforce ownership by inheritance. I have been far too busy for such trivial legalities. So, to our darker brothers in arms, you have my sincere thanks for your service to us and our nation and my blessings upon your lives and your new-found freedom. You have earned that and the respect of all the men in this regiment."

A few men coughed or groaned slightly at that until they saw the sharp look from the sergeant major. Stewart suppressed his anger and continued.

"Some of you may wish to surrender formally. Lieutenant Swanson from A Company has agreed to lead the official surrender delegation. I personally will not surrender for two reasons. First, I do not believe that I can utter an oath of loyalty to a nation that has so severely trampled our God-given inalienable rights and the intentions of our nation's founding fathers and thus soiling its principals and constitution. The second and more practical reason is that the battle that we fought yesterday will likely result in my hanging if I was to fall into the hands of the enemy, surrender or not. I highly suggest that any of you men who were with me on that mission seriously contemplate foregoing the entire surrender process and simply go home.

"It is extremely important in these times that we all hold fast to our faith in almighty God. We must trust that our Lord has something planned for each of us as well as a plan that will ultimately redeem the disaster of this brutal conflict. I am reminded of the words of Paul the apostle in the book of Romans, chapter eight, verse twenty eight;

'*And we know that all things work together for good to them that love God, to them who are the called according to his purpose.*'

"I encourage each of you to love God and work toward His calling on your lives, for His ways are far higher than ours. We must each trust our own instincts and obey our own conscience as we hear it in our hearts and as we follow the path set before us by our Creator. Never forget the sacrifices that you have made in your service to your nation. And please, for the love of God, never forget our fallen brethren whom we have left all over these 'United States.' I am proud to have served in the company of you all and I believe that I will never again be surrounded by so great a host of human souls as yours. May God richly bless each of you for all the days of your lives."

Stewart looked down as words failed him. He began to feel choked up but he pushed it back down. He looked again out at the small sea of tormented faces and issued his last commands.

"Regiment!"

The men stiffened as the lieutenants snapped to attention in the front of the formation and shouted back, "Company!"

"Attention!" Stewart's voice echoed across the small valley as the men snapped to. He threw the sharpest salute he'd ever given in his life and said, "Everything in the camp that belonged to the Confederacy is now up for grabs since that nation no longer exists. I only ask that you divide all of it peacefully and equitably. Everything on my new horse is mine. Everything that I have left behind is yours to divide. I salute you all…dismissed!" He dropped his salute, turned and began to walk away.

"Sir, what do we do now?" First Sergeant Danner rushed up to him and asked with a bewildered look.

Stewart turned back to him and said, "Go home Mr. Danner. Go home and live your life as though you must live it for every man that you've seen die… and, for every man that you've killed." With that he turned away and headed up the hill. Danner looked as though he'd been slapped. The reality had begun to sink in. Tears filled his eyes as he slowly turned toward his tent to gather his belongings.

Stewart was finishing his packing on Gabriel and listening to the now noisy camp. Lieutenant Swanson was barking orders trying to organize the fifty or so troops who wanted to formally surrender. Pots were clanging and men shouting as they divided the meager remnants of the regiment. Stewart gave a hard look at two men who were getting a little out of hand over a captured rifle and one quietly relinquished the weapon to the other. Hayes walked up to him and saluted. With tears in his eyes he said, "Thank you Captain. I understand now."

Stewart looked at him and said, "The salute is no longer necessary Mr. Hayes. We are now of equal rank, you and I. Good luck to you."

"Thank you sir," Hayes said quietly as he dropped his salute and turned away. Stewart's mind was churning. He was furious now. How does any man do this? How can any one man tell so many noble and valiant men that they have utterly failed? This was never supposed to happen. He should not have been the one to do this. He didn't have the training, the education, the skill, the rank, or the experience to…

"You have done well, sir." Sergeant Major Williams' voice cut through his thoughts.

"Did I?" Stewart leaned against the horse and hung his head down.

"Aye, sir. It was a fine speech that the men will remember for all their days. I have seen to the burial of our recently departed major." He clapped Stewart on the shoulder, sensing the captain's distress.

Stewart nodded, wincing at the slap on his left shoulder. 'Why always the *wounded* shoulder?' he thought briefly. "Well, thank you Mr. Williams, I hope that it was enough for them. What will you be doing now?"

"I may go back to Texas just to see what is left there. I do not really know yet. I believe I may head west and land where the wind takes me, California maybe. And you, sir?"

"I'm heading west as well, but northwest. There's nothing left for me in Texas. I have heard of a place called 'Idaho' in the Oregon Territory which is on the way to the Oregon coast. It's sort of in the middle of the Oregon Territory but I hear that it has tall mountains that are full of opals, placer, silver, and gold. I figure I will go and find out for myself."

"Chasing after gold, sir? Doesn't seem like your cup of tea. Maybe you just like killing so much that you want to try your luck with the Sioux?" Stewart looked at him sharply. "Sorry sir, you just do not seem like the greedy, gold miner type."

"I'm not really, but I do like the idea of a fresh start in a new land. I worked in the lumber business back in Texas, maybe there will be an opportunity for that in Idaho. I just want to move on and forget the last four years, hell the last fifteen years, maybe." He was getting too personal now so he clammed up suddenly. Williams sensed this and bid him farewell.

Stewart started walking the horse through the trees toward the west side of camp. He wanted to make his farewells as short and painless as possible. He hated goodbyes. As he passed by the old chuck wagon, Cecil ran over to him. Stewart had hoped to avoid the old man but had no such luck. He looked at Cecil's tear streaked face and saw that it was full of fear. His mind went back to the first time he'd ever seen a slave.

He had been about four or five on a rare trip to Corpus Christi and sitting in the family wagon while his father took care of business in the feed store. He remembered a couple of well-dressed young ladies walking down the boardwalk toward him. They were young, beautiful and obviously wealthy. He was entranced by their fancy dresses and hats as they swished down the walk, giggling to each other. He froze with fear when he saw him. A huge black beast walking behind them carrying assorted packages for the girls. Behind him was a cocky young man with a whip and a brace of cap lock pistols who was his handler. The slave wore a dirty old brown coat with a tan hat shading his eyes. He looked like a monster as he walked by. The slave saw Stewart looking at him and returned the gaze. His piercing white eyes with dark pupils were a stark contrast to his black skin. As they locked eyes, Stewart saw misery in those eyes; misery and a deep burning hatred. Cecil's voice broke his thoughts.

"What do I do, suh? What do I do?" Cecil pleaded.

"Whatever you wish Cecil."

"Captain suh, all my life somebody tol' me what to do. Who gonna take care of me? I don' know how to do nuthin' on my own. Can I go with ya, suh? Can I?"

"Cecil, I am not going back to Texas. I am heading up to the Oregon Territory."

"I will go with ya suh. I can hep ya 'long the way. It mus be a mighty long trip, suh."

Stewart sighed, "Cecil, you don't want to go with me. It's a long and dangerous journey. It will take months to get there. I am on horseback and you have a wagon, you will never be able to

41

keep up. There are hostile Indians and wild animals. There are storms and rugged mountains. You are a free man now. Go home and start a family or something."

"I'm too old for a family suh. I will keep up. I promise," Cecil pleaded.

"Go home Cecil."

"I gots no home suh! Just like you."

Stewart was getting frustrated now. "Cecil, here is something most men never understand; with freedom comes responsibility. You are now free to succeed as you are able or to destroy yourself as you give in to personal weakness. You are now responsible for your own wellbeing and you are also responsible to make the choice as to how to spend the rest of your days." He began to turn away.

Cecil thought for a moment and said, "OK suh. If I am free to choose then I chooses to go with you. You can try to outrun me but I will keep up. I swear! You too skinny and need someone to feed ya anyways and I can do that!" Stewart turned to try to argue again but Cecil was already mounting the wagon with grim determination. Stewart shook his head and mounted Gabriel. He suddenly let a small smile cross his face as he remembered something. It was May 16th and he was twenty five years old today. He briefly prayed that the next twenty five years would be far better than the last as he drew a bearing mentally and began the long ride west. The old wagon creaked as it followed close behind.

Chapter Five

January 31, 1871; somewhere in the central Idaho territory…

Stewart slowly plodded through the snow. He was in serious trouble now. The snow was falling more heavily than ever now. It wouldn't be long before he would have to stop just because he couldn't see where he was going. What had been a mild winter had become a blizzard at exactly the wrong time. The good news was that the Nez Perce that were hunting him were probably not fairing any better. He felt the cut on his right arm. It wasn't bleeding anymore but it was pretty deep so he would have to take it easy on it. Almost four years had passed since he'd had to kill a man and he'd killed five yesterday.

The last one before had been a claim jumper who called himself Smith and had tried to befriend them and saw him and Cecil as easy marks. Cecil had known that the man was up to no good and actually shot him first with the old Colt that Stewart had taken from Foster, saving Stewart's life. Stewart had spun at the shot and finished Smith with a slug to forehead, the would-be murderer's gun falling to the hard ground with a thud, as his body followed close behind it. He had tried to shoot Stewart in the back and had wrongly assumed that being a Negro, Cecil would be unarmed. The old former slave wasn't much of a shot for all of Stewart's attempts to teach him but he had wounded the man seriously enough to keep him from shooting. Cecil had saved his life with a poor shot into the Smith's shoulder. Now Cecil was in a cold grave some thirty miles away, not a hundred yards from where they had buried the claim jumper. He thought back to his last awful day at their small creek side camp high in the mountains.

Cecil had stayed behind to watch the camp and cook as Stewart went out to hunt for game as he did two or three times a week. He was returning to camp with a spike buck tied to the back of his saddle when he heard the shots. He rode up to the top of the ridge that overlooked the camp, dismounted, pulled out the Henry, and crawled up to see Cecil trying to defend the camp from behind some rocks with the old Colt in his hand. Two Nez Perce warriors lay dead in the creek and Cecil looked to be in bad shape with at least four arrows in him. Stewart laid the Henry across a fallen tree. Several of the Indians were trying to surround Cecil. He saw at least five of them as they moved between the trees. All but one of them was in range of the Henry.

He quickly picked off two before they could react to his presence. He missed the next one as the man spotted him and took cover. The furthest one took this opportunity to rush Cecil and took a slug in the stomach from the Colt as a result. He flopped around several yards from Cecil who, satisfied that he was no longer a danger, ignored the seriously wounded man. He was wisely saving his ammunition for the others. Cecil took a shot at the one Stewart had just missed. The shot was close but only motivated the man to move away from Cecil and back into Stewart's line of fire. He was dead two seconds later as Stewart fired the Henry again.

The last Nez Perce saw that he was now outnumbered and did what so many of these fatalist warriors do; he began launching a barrage of arrows as he rushed at Cecil in a desperate attempt to win the battle by sheer guts. Cecil fired at him but missed three times and clicked on an empty chamber. Stewart fired and hit the man in the leg but he was on Cecil with a tomahawk too quickly for either man to stop him. Cecil took two blows from the weapon before he picked the man up on the third swing and smashed him down against the rock that he'd been hiding behind. Stewart vaguely recalled seeing similar scene years ago but it was a friend of his in gray being smashed and a Negro in blue doing the smashing. Cecil looked down at the broken warrior now twisting and screaming in pain with a very sad look. He then swayed and fell to the ground.

Stewart had tried to get down the hill as quickly as possible but it was all over by the time he got there. The broken Nez Perce warrior looked up with wild eyes shaking his tomahawk and screaming in defiance at Stewart as he raised his pistol and shot the man in the head. He turned to the wounded Indian a short distance away who was crawling toward him, knife drawn. He repeated the procedure with this one as well as the brave tried one last effort to charge him. The warrior didn't make it to Stewart and dropped in a heap as his brain functions were interrupted by the sudden presence of lead. Stewart looked down at Cecil and helped him sit up against the rock. The big black man was in really bad shape.

There were actually six arrows in him, one in each leg, one in his left arm, and three in his mid-section. Blood pooled all around the old black man. The tomahawk had also left serious wounds on Cecil's head both of which were spewing large amounts of blood. Breathing heavily, Cecil looked up at Stewart with a sad, tired look. He was dying and both men knew it.

"Just relax Cecil. I'll be right back," Stewart said quietly.

Cecil nodded and lay back as Stewart searched out and ensured that all of the other Nez Perce were dead. As he shot the last one, he caught a glimpse of movement out of the corner of his eye and ducked as an arrow soared out of the trees at him, barely hitting his upper right arm. He looked up as a very young brave on a pony screamed at him with his bow raised. The arrow had left a deep wound on his arm and it throbbed when he raised his pistol. The Indian boy kicked the horse and was gone before Stewart could get a shot off. Stewart went back to Cecil and tried to make him comfortable. Using his Bowie knife, he cut the arrows off and rolled him onto his side to keep the blood from collecting in his wounded lung and then he took out a kerchief and started wiping the blood from Cecil's face. The old man's breathing was hard to listen to.

"Read ta me, suh. Please?" Cecil asked quietly.

"What? What do you want me to read, Cecil?"

"Just anythin' from your ol' bible, suh. Anythin' at all. Your words comfort me and I'm afraid I'm in need of some comfort just now, suh." His voice was strained as he gasped the words out.

"Of course Cecil." Stewart finished covering him with a blanket and then reached into his saddlebag, pulled out the old bible and began to read Psalms 119. He knew that the clock was ticking now and it was only a matter of time before more Nez Perce showed up. He would have to leave as soon as possible. He quietly vowed that he would not leave until Cecil was dead and buried. It was the least he could do for the faithful old man who had been his only friend these last five years.

He didn't have to wait long. About twenty minutes later Cecil looked up at him one last time and said, "Thanks for teachin' me how to be free Captain Stewart, suh."

He then coughed blood and died. Stewart reached down and closing Cecil's eyes with his hand said, "I think that you taught me far more about freedom than I ever could have taught you, my friend." He quietly said a short prayer, wiped the tears from his eyes and then rose to take care of the many chores he now had before him.

In the end, he had just made it. The Nez Perce war party showed up just as Stewart was clearing the ridgeline south of camp. He saw them as they came into the camp but they didn't see him which he knew mattered little as they would easily find his tracks and hunt him down. He had only one real chance; get as far away from them as possible and hope they give up.

Now all he could see was snow. He was trying to make it down to the little mining town of Warren which should only be a few miles further south in a small valley near the hot springs. It was now getting dark and he knew he would have to stop for the night. He began looking for a place to give him shelter from the storm. He found a large fir tree with good solid cover over it and placed some of his gear under it. He then staked Gabriel and Cecil's old mare out about ten yards from the tree. He then checked to see that the horses were still visible from his hiding spot and thenthought for a moment.

He could leave the strong boxes full of gold dust on the mare for a possible quick escape or he could put them under the tree, giving the mare a rest from the three hundred plus pounds of the boxes and gold combined.He contemplated the pros and cons of each action and decided to put it all under the tree. He still had four bags tied inside his shirt and one in each boot. He figured that including the pound and half or so of gold on his person, he had two hundred fifty or more pounds of it. He was a very rich man now if he could only survive long enough to spend it.

He and Cecil had worked their claim hard for the last several years and he had tried to keep himself from catching the fever. Greed does bad things to a man and he fervently tried to avoid that pitfall. He had honestly intended to split the haul equally with Cecil but his death made that just a good intention. Stewart sighed as he thought of his old friend with whom he had shared so much with as he began to make a small snow cave under the tree.

He may freeze to death himself by morning but at least the horses wouldn't have to bear the burden of his gear, he thought as he stripped the animals down. He settled into the small snow cave under the tree with the two strong boxes. He then covered himself with a wool blanket and closed his eyes. 'What could God possibly have in store for me next?' he thought as he dozed off to a cold, fitful sleep.

He awoke suddenly. Something was wrong. He felt a tremor of fear run through him that made him shudder even more than the shaking he was already experiencing from the cold. He did what he normally did when he was afraid and mentally took a step back from himself and analyzed it. There was something strange about this fear. He had felt fear many times in his life but this was different. It had an artificial feel to it, like someone or something was trying to *make* him afraid. He then shoved it to the back of his mind and began to force himself to action.

He slowly lifted the blanket until he could see out of his small lair. He tried to ignore his body's shivering as he stared out at the landscape. It was still dark but it had stopped snowing. The horses stood stock still in the small snow covered clearing ahead of him illuminated by bright moonlight. He looked past the horses at his surroundings. He was on the bank of a small creek that was about thirty yards away. Across the creek was a sharp cliff rising up from the creek about fifty feet. He noticed a rock formation that looked for all the world like the face of an Indian right in the center of it. He tucked that away as a landmark.

Something was still very wrong. He then realized that the horses hadn't moved at all. The seemed frozen with their eyes open. He tried to focus his thoughts. Had the Nez Perce caught up to him? He struggled to pick through his confusion. It was probably about three o'clock in the morning. He could rise and begin loading the horses. He could probably be ready to leave in about ten minutes…

A bright light appeared suddenly just down downstream. He felt his heart jump into his throat. It was a strange, unnatural light which was moving up the creek. It was blue in color and emanated from above, finally settling on the two horses. The beam of light began to tighten around the animals and changed to a yellow-orangecolor. Looking up at the source of the light, Stewart could just make out a silhouette of what appeared to be a triangular ship of some kind behind the blinding light.Stewart felt his jaw drop as he saw the horses begin to float up into the air.

It took Stewart less than a second to consider all of the implications of what was now occurring before his eyes. For him, it came down to a choice between the gold and his horses. He quickly chose the horses as he would probably die without them. The gold was just money and he may be able to return to it at a later time if things went bad. He took a deep breath and sprinted from his cover for the horses. He was struck by the cold as he emerged but made for Gabriel's reigns which were hanging down right in front of him. As he reached the beam of light he was stopped suddenly. He felt as though he had hit a warm, wet blanket. His skin tingled strangely as he tried to move. He quickly realized that he was stuck on the outside halfway into the light beam like a bug on fly paper.

He could just barely move his head as he looked up to where he was now goingalong with his horses. It was definitely a ship of some kind but God only knew who or what was controlling it. It was triangular in shape with rounded sides and one side shorter than the other two. That side was presumably the stern while the point on the opposite end was probably the bow. The strange craft twinkled with multi-colored lights all over its surface. He would have some words to speak to the occupants when he got to the top of this light elevator or whatever it was. He noticed that the strange fear was completely gone and he was now quite warm, at least on the front side.

Stewart looked back to the ground and saw it shrinking away. He was about a hundred feet off the ground and rising. He then looked back up the creek and saw a sight that amazed him. About thirty Nez Perce warriors were stopped dead in their tracks about 200 yards upstream. In the light of the full moon he could see them very clearly as they were staring open mouthed at him and the horses rising up into the strange ship. Stewart had to smile at the irony. He tried to wave at them but his hands wouldn't move. He ended up kind of shaking his left elbow at them which probably just looked silly. Oh well. He had more pressing matters to concern himself with.

He looked up again and suddenly realized the serious implications of the fact that only part of him was in the beam. He didn't know the physics of this thing but he began praying as he realized that he may not make it into the ship with the horses. He could be stripped from the beam as he hit the top and fall to his death or worse, it may only bring the part of him that was in the beam up into the ship. He nervously contemplated the idea of the front half of his body being ripped up into the ship as the back half fell back to the earth. He smiled again at the thought of the Nez Perce being left there staring at his ass and heels lying in a heap on the ground. That would certainly leave a lasting impression on them.

The ship was now just a few feet away and he began trying to squirm his way farther into the beam of light with a little success. As the bulkhead brushed the top of his head, he felt himself being sucked into the beamed with a strange noise. 'A safety measure?' he thought briefly.

He kept rising until his feet were clear of the opening in the ship whereupon it solidified and he felt himself standing on a firm surface. The beam of light shrank further in diameter until it was just around the horses. As he looked at the poor creatures he saw that their eyes were still full of fear.

Stewart was freed as the beam shrank. He stumbled slightly when he was released and discovered he was in a large, round, featureless room. There was some sort of array of tubes and lights above the horses but other than that it was void of any detail. The room glowed with the yellow-orange light from the beam. Staying close to the outer wall, he drew his pistols and began looking around the room.

He spotted a slight discoloration on the floor on the other side of the horses. It was a perfectly round circle about two and half feet in diameter. It looked just like the rest of the floor except that it was a darker shade of the yellow-orange that everything in room appeared to be. He suspected that the room was really white and the color was just the reflection from the lift-beam thing. Gingerly, Stewart touched the circle with his toe. The circle glowed brightly as the touch and he quickly pulled his foot away. He looked up and saw an identical circle above in the ceiling. 'This could be a smaller version of the "light elevator",' he thought.

Cautiously he stepped onto the circle which glowed brighter as he put more of his weight on it. He was surrounded by light as he began to rise toward to the other circle which was also glowing now. He stopped suddenly. He looked down and noticed that his right pistol wasn't all the way in the beam. He pulled it in slightly and began to rise again; another safety measure, no doubt. The circle above disappeared as he approached it.

Stewart found himself facing the center of a smaller room as he came up through the circle. Once again, the floor solidified beneath him. He saw a figure across the room with its back to him. The figure was tall, thin and gray in color and had distinctly male buttocks above skinny legs. Stewart stifled a laugh as he looked at the back of the creature's large head and noticed that it almost perfectly matched its buttocks with a well-defined crease running down the center of it.

The creature heard the noise and turned suddenly to face him. What happened next, Stewart would remember for the rest of his life. It was one of those events that happens in just a few seconds but seemed to take an eternity. The creature was a demon. The face he now saw was horrible. It had large, slanted black eyes like a snake. The nose was just a small bump with no discernible air holes and its mouth was just a small slit with no lips. The thing was also sexless with only a small bump where its genitals should be. It was a weird, small face on a large head and Stewart's reaction was instant.

He began firing at the creature with both pistols. The evil apparition began to fall back under the hail of bullets. It quickly reached back and then pointed a small metal tube at Stewart. Stewart felt the strange tingling sensation again only much stronger and suddenly he couldn't move or breathe. He fell back against a bulkhead unable to move anything but his eyes.

He was filled with horror as the creature approached him stiffly making strange noises. Stewart could see marks where at least seven of his bullets had hit the creature but with no apparent serious damage. It seemed to be choking as it fell to it knees a few feet in front of him. It was desperately clawing at the back of its head. Stewart's horror peaked as the creature pulled its head apart from the back and the small, disproportioned face collapsed in eerie folds of gray flesh. The creature pulled its head in a downward motion as a slimy yellow liquid spurted out all around it. Stewart stared in fascination as the creature's head fell away revealing a smaller head beneath it covered with the strange, pale yellow ooze coughing and struggling to catch its breath. The features were unmistakable even through the flow of gook coming from its nose and mouth.

For the first time since the war, Stewart swore, "I'll be damned…a nigra."One of the thin, gray hands reached toward him as everything went black.

Chapter Six

Stewart slowly became conscious. He felt very strange, like he was floating in water. He couldn't focus his eyes either. Was he dead? If so, he was looking forward to a detailed conversation with the Lord Jesus about the events just prior to his death. He had a lot of questions about that. He saw a blurry movement ahead of him. He reached his right hand out to feel out his surroundings but it stopped short after a few inches. It was a smooth curved surface in front of him. He pushed his face closer to it and suddenly could see better. The creature, no *man*, which he had fought with earlier, was sitting with his back to him at some kind of control console.

Stewart suddenly realized that he was immersed in what appeared to be the same pale yellow ooze that had come out of the strange man's suit. He began to choke as he tried to stop breathing the liquid.

"Just breathe normally, it's easier if you don't think about it," Stewart heard the voice as if it were in his own head. "The gel you are in is identical to the fluid in my suit and is keeping you alive at the moment." The man remained at his console not bothering to look at Stewart. Stewart tried to breathe again. It wasn't comfortable but he was doing it. It became a little easier as he relaxed but the unnatural feeling of the fluid was unnerving to him. He looked around and saw that he was in the same room he'd been in before but was now in some kind of clear tube filled with the strange liquid. There were two other empty tubes on his left side.

"Why are you holding me prisoner?" Stewart tried to ask. The words didn't come out right due to the liquid and he doubted that the man understood him.

"Don't try too hard to speak. The electronics will process your words so that I may understand you. You're not a prisoner. In fact if you reach down with your left hand you'll find a latch which will drain and open the travel tube." Stewart reached down and felt the latch.

"But wait! Before you do that you need to know that as soon as you open it you will die a very gruesome and presumably painful death. Although you snuck aboard my ship and tried to kill me, I have no personal desire to see your body smeared all over the bulkheads. Plus, I would have to clean up the subsequent mess."

"Smeared? Why would I be 'smeared?'" Stewart asked as he quickly removed his hand from the latch.

"We are currently traveling at an extremely high velocity, beyond your comprehension. The suspension gel that you are immersed in allows your body to survive the stresses placed upon it by external forces. If you step out of that travel tube you will be suddenly subjected to extreme gravitational forces which would propel you toward that bulkhead at several billion feet per second." The man pointed at the wall Stewart had collapsed against earlier. "You are very lucky that I didn't initiate the drive earlier. A few more minutes and you would have been crushed instantly. Consider it a consequence of stowing away on my spacecraft."

"You were stealing my horses!"

"Ah. A 'hanging offense' in the old west wasn't it? Well I apologize for the theft but my information states that the horses in question were abandoned; an unfortunate error that I will have to address later. I am almost done with them anyway."

"Then you will return them to me?"

"If you wish, although they won't be of much use to you now."

"Why?" Stewart was getting angry at this pompous man.

"Well, I've just completed harvesting the DNA from the mare and the stallion was completed about two hours ago. It takes quite some time to isolate all of the strains after I remove their fluids. Both animals are now dead and their remains are not far from where I picked you up. You may find them there when you are returned."

"You bastard!" Stewart gurgled angrily.

"I'm simply doing my job. It is most unfortunate that you have been caught up in the course of my duties. I'm afraid you will have to be patient and endure some discomfort until we can repair the damage." The man now turned to face him. The suit had apparently been repaired as the scars from the bullets were still present.

"You almost killed me, you know. This suit is fairly durable but it is not really meant to stand up to repeated, kinetic attacks such as your primitive weapons provide. Horrible devices,

53

firearms, they do so much damage to things." The man shook his head slowly and looked over at the console he had been standing in front of when Stewart opened fire.

"Well, that is the general idea…" Stewart retorted.

"Yes, I suppose it is." The man walked in front of Stewart. "It took me quite some time to repair the damage both to this suit and the ship's systems. I should be angry with you but it is actually my own inattention which has resulted in this mishap. Had I been properly monitoring the lift-beam, you wouldn't be here now and I wouldn't have this dilemma. Of course if I hadn't been alone on this trip…" His voice trailed off.

"Look, I am Captain Gre…"

"No!" The man interrupted holding up one hand. "Do not tell me your name! I cannot know it. For the sake of simplicity, I will call you Captain and you may call me Doctor. Fair enough?" The 'doctor' turned the raised hand like he was shaking hands as if to signify some sort of deal.

"You are a doctor? That's quite an All Hallows Eve costume for a physician." Stewart said sarcastically.

"Well, yes, I am a PhD. I'm more of a researcher or scientist as the people of your time called us."

"So, you are from the future." It was more of a statement than a question.

"Yes, or more accurately, *a* future; not necessarily your own."

"There's more than one future?" Stewart was incredulous not just at the implication but at the fact that the man didn't seem to even notice his sarcasm.

"Theoretically. More than likely we are from the same time line as the theories of parallel time streams are vague and suggests that crossing streams is unlikely if not impossible. However, the possibilities of transformational time-line errors do exist and therefore I must do what I can to mitigate the impact of that possibility in this instance. "

Stewart thought about that for a moment. "So when are you going to put me back where you found me. I have some ideas about how and where I would like you to do that." He thought of the thirty-odd Nez Perce back at the creek.

"That's my dilemma. I can't be in two places at one time. I have to take you forward to my time and a special re-insertion team will have to return you." The doctor let that sink in.

"So we are traveling through time *right now*?" Stewart tried to think about how that would work.

"Yes. Technically you are always traveling through time at a much slower rate but currently we are traveling forward rather quickly toward my own time period and we will arrive just a few days after I originally left. That's sort of a safety measure that we use to prevent accidental co-existence problems.

"What happens if you are in the same place at the same time?" Stewart asked curiously.

"No one really knows. It's never been done and there are a lot of people trying very hard to keep it that way. None of the theoretical outcomes are pleasant and the worst of them would doom the entire universe." He shook his head as if to emphasize the seriousness of the matter. He turned toward the wall in front of his console. "If you look over at this monitor you can actually see our travel as it occurs"

Stewart looked up and saw a screen portraying a multi-colored ball that he assumed must be the Earth. Nearby was the moon. The image was rapidly getting smaller until it disappeared on the left side of the screen. Then it reappeared on the right growing larger until it was in the center and then it repeated the process. Each time the moon was in a different place in relation to the Earth.

"I assume that that is the Earth. Why are we going around it in circles?"

"You assume correctly…and incorrectly. Now I don't expect someone from your time to grasp this but we are actually moving in a straight line or a mild curve really, relative to the universe. The Earth is never in the same place twice. It is in constant motion due to its rotation, orbit, solar orbit, galactic orbit, and etcetera. In actuality, all calculations combined place the mean velocity of someone or something on the Earth, or any other planetary body for that matter, at several times the speed of light. Sort of like a rather sophisticated carnival ride actually."

"The speed of light? I didn't know that light had a speed." Stewart tried to think about how light could actually travel over distance. He had always thought of light as either being present or not. Not traveling from place to place.

"Yes, of course you wouldn't know that. Light travels in excess of 186,000 miles per second. For a man who has never traveled faster that a horse can run, that would be inconceivable." Stewart rolled his eyes at the man's arrogance. He was still mad about the horses.

"I've been on a train. Some of them go over a mile a minute," Stewart replied defensively.

"Of course, I didn't mean to insult you. Your time period is simply far less advanced than my own," Doc replied turning back to face Stewart.

"Why does the planet keep growing and shrinking on the monitor?" Stewart asked.

"Good question!" Stewart's eyes narrowed a bit as Doc held up a finger in excitement. This man was treating him like a five-year-old. "Actually the Earth you're seeing isn't the same Earth each time. We are traveling along the tangent of its orbital locations through time, effectively skipping along the edge of the planet's path about a million and a half miles away, plus or minus twenty thousand. The people of your time, and even later periods, think of time as a straight line with a beginning and an end. As far as we can tell there is no actual beginning or end but it is definitely not linear, that is, not a line."

Stewart rolled his eyes. "I know what 'linear' means, Doc. You speak strangely as well. Combining words like, 'is not' and 'I am.' Why is that?"

"Oh, again, I'm sorry. I've just never spoken to a primitive before and I'm not really sure of how to do so. You are speaking of modern contractions. I believe you had some of your own from your time such as 'twas' or 'shant.' It's a lingual device that I believe became widely accepted in the twentieth century. It became proper English sometime in mid-century, I think. Every English speaker uses them now. Are you having difficulty understanding me?"

"No, it just sounds strange. I will get used to it. A primitive, huh?" Stewart raised his eyebrows. 'Doc' was talking fighting words and seemed completely unaware of it.

"Yes." Doc went on. "There are events in your future that will drastically change the human race and bring them out of their primitive state of existence. It doesn't really concern you as you will be long dead when that happens. Anyway, as I was saying, the Earth is in constant motion and never in the same place twice, therefore, in order to travel through time one must also travel through space. We are not going to where the Earth is now rather, we are going to where it will be in my time. Do you understand?"

"Yes, actually, it makes perfect sense when you put it that way."

"Oh! Well, that's good then." Doc seemed pleased with himself.

"What is it that drastically changes the human race?"

"Now that you won't understand even if I did explain it."

Stewart was blunt. "Try me. Is it the return of Christ?"

"Hah! That's a primitive for you! You couldn't understand because you have neither frame of reference nor the mental ability. That isn't an insult it is simply a fact." Doc turned his back again as if to emphasize his superiority,

"So you don't believe in God then?"

"God? You know nothing of God. You know only riddles and allusions that keep you begging for more information that if given you would not comprehend."

"I have been a Christian since I was a small child and I have read the bible cover to cover at least a dozen times. I *know* God! Don't tell me what I know." Stewart was offended by the attack on his faith and he was losing his patience with Doc.

"If you say so. We will speak on this matter no further. It has no amicable conclusion." He turned away as if to dismiss the conversation.

Stewart decided to change the subject. He still wanted to know more about this event but he had other questions as well. "How long before we reach your time, Doc?"

"We are only about twenty percent there right now." Doc said as he turned back toward the travel tube. "We still have several hours of conversation left if you choose. Of course, it will only matter to me so perhaps I should ask my own questions of you. Tell me, have you ever killed anyone?"

"Why won't it matter to me?"

57

"You'll be mind wiped before re-insertion. You won't remember any of this. You didn't answer my question." Doc stared at him through those big slanted eyes on the suit with his head cocked to one side.

"Mind wiped? That does not sound pleasant at all!" Stewart suddenly found his spirit of adventure waning.

"It's not. It's also not as bad as it sounds. The upside is that it erases the memory of the procedure as well though your subconscious mind remembers everything. Still didn't answer my question. You seemed to be well accustomed to shooting people the way you reacted to me. I'm very curious."

"Yes. I've killed men. I'm a war veteran Doc."

"The American Civil War?" Doc's voice sounded excited. "I'm something of an expert on the subject. I studied it intensely as an undergraduate. Which side were you on?"

Great, Stewart thought, an academic. "I proudly fought for the Confederate States of America against unlawful Northern aggression. I don't want to be 'mind wiped' Doc."

"It can't be avoided, Captain. A fierce defender of the rights of property, were you? Keeping the colored man in his place? So how many men have you killed for so noble a cause as slavery?"

Stewart stared back at the lifeless eyes and reminded himself that there was a man of flesh and blood behind that mask. His anger burned as he felt like he was being interrogated by Satan himself. He decided to ignore the debate for the moment and answer this "civil war" expert's question. "I honestly don't know. I lost count a long time ago."

Doc visibly jumped back, apparently shocked by this answer. "You don't know? How can you not know? It would seem that ending the life of another human being would be a significant enough event that you could remember it."

"Well, sometimes you shoot at someone and they go down but you never find out if they died. That's just part of war." Stewart shrugged. "How about you? Ever have to kill a man?"

Again Doc seemed shocked. "No! Um, we don't kill others in my time. It's...uh... not necessary anymore."

"Good. It is not any fun. I wish that I had never had to kill anyone."

"'Had, have to?' You make it sound like an obligation. Surely you had a choice in the matter. It would seem that picking up a weapon and slaying another man is a wholly conscious decision. Especially in a conflict as clearly defined in ideology as the Civil War.'"

"Cowardice isn't much of a choice; certainly not one that requires any backbone or integrity. As long as mankind is fallen, we will have to defend ourselves against the desires of evil, selfish men. It is an obligation to humanity and a God-given duty for a man to defend himself and his family. Your understanding of The War Between the States may not be as clearly defined as you suppose, Doc."

"I see," Doc nodded. Stewart doubted that he really did.

"It is the obligation of all good Christian men to rise up against evil and strike it down with courage and honor. We men of the Confederacy had no desire to defend slavery anymore than we would defend murder." Stewart said emphatically.

"I'm not judging you Captain, I only want to understand. Honor isn't a foreign concept to my people but courage probably has a far different meaning in my time than yours. And to my point of view, defending war is defending murder." Doc turned back to watch the Earth grow on the monitor again.

"War and murder are entirely different enterprises, Doc."

"How so?" Doc turned back to Stewart to re-engage the conversation.

"War is fought in defense of land or liberty. Murder is the pre-meditated killing of another for selfish gain. I see quite a difference between the two."

"But you fought to keep blacks in slavery, how is that fighting for liberty? As you may have seen earlier, I myself am descended from those you intended to keep in slavery. How does persecuting people who look like me fit into your justification?" Doc cocked his head to one side again as if examining a curiosity. The habit was beginning to grate on Stewart's nerves.

"I have nothing against people of your color. I have no love of slavery in any form either. You could never begin to understand how I feel about these things. I have experiences that you could not fathom. If you were an 'expert' on the Civil War, then you would know that slavery didn't become a central issue to the conflict until

59

Lincoln made it one in 1863 with the Emancipation Proclamation. I assume that you believe that that act freed the slaves and brought some resolution to the issue."

"Well that is the accepted version of history…"

"*Accepted* version! Hah! If you read the language of the statement, it simply frees the slaves in the Confederacy while those who remained in the northern slave states were still bound to their masters. It was a poor attempt to incite an insurgency in the south and cause an uprising of the Negros. It actually caused quite the opposite. Lincoln almost lost his entire army over that. He ended up with the uprisings and riots. Northerners had no desire to free the slaves either, Doc. Although I have learned hard lessons in this regard, all men are afraid of that which is different." Stewart paused to see if his words were sinking in. It was so hard to talk to that expressionless mask. Doc tapped his fingers on his arm for a moment.

"Very well, let's see if your right." He turned back to the console and began punching buttons. The picture of Earth disappeared and was replaced by multiple pictures and text.

"You can research history from here?" Stewart was incredulous.

"Yes, I have a fairly large hard drive in the system and it's updated automatically each time I re-enter my own time period. I can research almost anything." He began scanning screen after screen. Stewart tried to read some of it but the type was small and distorted through the liquid from this distance and the man only seemed to scan each page for a moment.

"What's a hard drive?" Stewart asked.

"Memory storage. It's how we store information on computers. These are kind of old and outdated but they still work very well." He continued scanning pages.

"Computers? You mean you are calculating this information?" Stewart tried to comprehend how information could be calculated.

"No, well yes, well, sort of. All information can be stored in bits of numerical data which can be calculated for storage. In effect, all data can be stored in the form of mathematical values of ones and zeros and converted back into data with the right processors."

"Huh?" Stewart still didn't quite get it.

"I can't be expected to succinctly explain 400 plus years of technological advancements in a few minutes can I?" Doc seemed to be getting frustrated.

"400 years, huh? So you are from the twenty-fourth century?"

"Close enough. Well, I have found some interesting articles that would support your theories." Doc said as he turned around.

"Theories? You are the academic, Doc. I am the one who actually experienced it."

"Yes, but I have a much higher education. I am able to view the events from a more objective and analytical perspective. That is what academia enables one to do." Doc smugly folded his arms.

"I have known a few academics, Doc. It seems to me that they deal far too much in theories and not enough in the real world. Your experience is based on countless hours spent in a classroom reading what others have written and reading what others have written about others writings, effectively being educated in third, fourth, and fifth-hand knowledge. My experience is based on the fact that I saw the war with my own eyes. I lived it. I tasted it. I saw thousands of men die, some for what they believed in and others because they were told to. The North invaded the South, Doc. They lied, stole, and violated the Constitution and admittedly some men did so in order to 'free the slaves' but most did it for money and power. Sherman's scorched earth march to the sea is a prime example of the greed and brutality of Yankee aggression. That wasn't an act of war, it was wholesale murder and destruction. Regardless of their motives the ends never justifies the means. That kind of moral relativity never leads to anything good. I will go to my grave believing that I fought for that which is right. Slavery would probably have been abolished eventually anyway. No one wanted to fight a war over it. The North fought to keep us in line, the South fought for their own freedom. It's that simple."

"Interesting perspective, Captain. I will definitely review my studies on the subject." He turned back toward the monitor which once again showed the Earth appearing and disappearing. Both men were silent for a moment when Doc turned back to Stewart.

"You know…" suddenly the ship lurched and the panel where Doc had been standing during the shootout erupted in sparks. The growing Earth on the monitor stopped growing and lights began to flash all over the room.

"What is that?" Stewart asked.

"Your handiwork, Captain. The repairs I made to the drive system you destroyed earlier have apparently failed. We have ceased to travel through time and have dropped out some-when along the stream." Doc was audibly alarmed by the problem. Although the face on the suit did move some during conversation the suit currently showed no expression. He went about extinguishing the fire and sparks with a small, red, tubular device.

"Some-when?"

"Yes. I'll have to calculate when we are but we are somewhere along the tangent between my time and yours." He began taking the console apart and looking at the various components. "I can't work on this while we are under way. I'll have to set us down. This won't be easy; I have to make sure that we are undetected."

"Undetected by whom?"

"Primitives. Uh, people from this time."

"What time is it?" Stewart asked nervously.

Doc looked back at the monitor. "It looks like we are in the early part of the twenty-first century. Some-when around 2007 or 2008, I think. This computer isn't that accurate. It wasn't meant for exact time displacement calculations."

"What *was* it meant for?"

The emotionless face looked up at Stewart but the stress showed in his voice. "It was meant for…look, I'm just a low-level researcher trying to restore the earth's equine population. I don't get all of the really high-tech equipment that some of the high-level time jumpers do. I'm sure to you I appear to be a sophisticated superman from the future but this ship is over thirty years old and wasn't top of the line when it was built. I assure you I am only a simple errand boy trying earn a living with the meager tools I am given, despite my over-education. My training hasn't really prepared me for this sort of event which is very unusual to say the least. I have to send a distress call."

Doc turned back to the console and began to frantically punch buttons on the console. Stewart tried to suppress a smile. The man's attempt at humility was almost touching except for his apparent contempt for his station in life. He tried a little sympathy; "I too am familiar with being given a task greater than what I felt able to endure. You will do as you must and I'm sure it will turn out just fine. When will we be landing?"

"We're going down now," Doc replied curtly.

Stewart watched as the Earth began to increase in size on the monitor. There was no perception of motion but he braced himself for the landing.

Chapter Seven

There was no need to brace for anything after all. Stewart felt only a slight bump as the ship landed. He began to earnestly think about the situation he was in. This had been a very unusual day after all. 'Early twenty first century,' Stewart thought about that. Could he escape from this 'doctor' and possibly make a life for himself in this time? He wondered how much things had changed in the last 130-odd years. Of course it had been less than twenty four hours for him but they had had 130 years of advancement and human beings were still considered 'primitives' by the people of Doc's time. Questions poured through his mind so fast that he could scarcely keep track of some of them.

His biggest concern right now was being mind-wiped. That was something he was willing to avoid at almost any cost. Regardless of Doc's assertion, he knew he was in effect a prisoner. He either went along with the scientist, submitting to all of his demands or he would pay some kind of consequence which was as yet unclear; presumably death. Most likely the future man was counting on using his technology to incapacitate Stewart and thus fulfill whatever protocols he was required to regardless of Stewart's objections.

Stewart watched as the man worked on the damaged console with his strange looking tools. How was he to get out of the ship? Presumably Doc would have disabled any portals or lifts he might use to escape or he may just be counting on his ignorance of their operation. He would have to try to outsmart this intellectual as best he could. For all of his superior education and advanced intelligence, Stewart wasn't too impressed with Doc. He seemed to be just another arrogant academic with opinions on everything but little knowledge of practical matters. His arrogance might be the key to Stewart's escape.

He took a quiet assessment of his stores while he patiently watched as the man worked on the ship. He still had everything he'd been wearing when he came on the ship except the two Remingtons. He did, however, still have the Colt tucked in the back of his belt though he was sure that it was useless now that the powder was wet from the chamber's fluid. He had his overcoat; his saddlebags were still tied over his shoulder with all their contents, his uniform (which his still wore just because he liked it), his twice re-cobbled army boots and his trusty kepi hat. He could also feel the six bags of gold dust still in their various hiding places. He felt certain that the people of this time would surely still value gold since they were still considered 'primitives.' What he had on him in the way of gold dust was probably worth several hundred, if not a thousand dollars in his time. He was assuming that people still used dollars though it occurred to him that even that may have changed.

"Can I come out of here now?" Stewart asked.

"Um, yes. Just give me a moment." Doc wriggled and shrugged himself away from under the console. He carefully wiped off and replaced some tools before facing the travel tube containing Stewart. "OK, we have to get some things straight here first." Doc said nervously.

"Like what?" Stewart pretended not to know his concerns.

"Well, like you not trying to kill me again. We just can't have that sort of thing. I realize that my appearance frightened you, the suit is designed specifically to do that in primitives but I assure you if you simply cooperate with me then you shall not be harmed. You will be re-inserted in your time, as protocols dictate and you will simply have a 'missing time' feeling about what has occurred. You will remember none of this."

"Can I be re-inserted somewhere other than the location where you picked me up?"

"Again, there are protocols for this sort of thing. It is up to the re-insertion team but they generally place you as close to the point of disruption as possible as I understand it. Your missing time will probably be longer now as a result of this delay. Normally it's only a few hours or so."

"Look Doc, I'm not excited about being mind-wiped but if your people put me back where they found me, I'll be dead within a few minutes. There are a couple of dozen Nez Perce warriors just a few hundred yards from there. They were hunting me for killing some of their people."

"I can't help that. Perhaps you shouldn't go around trying to kill every person you meet. Have you ever thought of adopting such a strategy?" Doc said, cocking his head to one side.

65

"It was self defense, and I was trying to save my friend from them."

"White men trespassing on Native American land sounds like it might be good reason for them to attack you. Have you thought that maybe they were acting in *their* own self defense? Or maybe you just can't see it that way" Doc crossed his arms and cocked his head to one side again. Stewart was annoyed with his lecturing.

"We had been mining peacefully there for nearly five years, Doc. We had even traded with the Nez Perce a few times. I was out hunting and when I returned they had all but killed my friend and he wasn't a white man. He was a Negro; a former slave that served with me in the war."

"Oh really, you mean 'served you' don't you?" Doc shifted his arms and cocked his head the other way.

"I meant what I said." Stewart said through gritted teeth. This fellow was really beginning to irk him. "Cecil was the best friend I have ever had. He saved my life…twice! I just wish I could have saved his…"

"Well, the racist southerner had an African-American for his best friend. Now I've heard it all. I may just have to keep you in there for a while, Captain."

Stewart fumed. "You could at least get me something to eat. I haven't eaten in two days."

"Nice try. I know that you're not hungry, the nanos wouldn't let you be hungry."

"What are 'nanos'?" Stewart asked surprised, realizing for the first time that he actually wasn't hungry.

"Nanobots." Doc said as he turned back to the console again. "Tiny robots that are in the fluid you're breathing. They are necessary for the fluid to work properly. They not only provide you oxygen but they automatically feed you as well, using nutrients in the suspension fluid and your own fat stores if you have enough. They also help prevent and repair injuries due to the acceleration forces on your body. Oh, and you won't need to use the restroom while you're in there either, so don't even try that routine."

Stewart suddenly felt ill and had an intense crawling sensation all over his body. "Machines? There are machines in my lungs?" He started choking again and felt like he was going to pass out.

"Yes, they are very tiny though, microscopic actually." Doc seemed amused at his reaction and went on. "There are actually about a million or more of them all through your body right now flowing through your bloodstream. It is the only way that we can ensure the survival of a human body through time-space travel."

"A million?" Again, Stewart was incredulous.

"About that. It's a lower quality fluid than what I have in my suit so there are fewer nanos and they aren't as quite as good as my own but they still work pretty well. No one puts the high quality stuff in their emergency tanks because of the cost involved but you are still alive after all so it does work."

"How do I get them out of me?" Stewart worried.

"Oh, don't worry. The re-insertion team will de-activate them prior to your release and they will simply quit working. After a year or so, your body will have completely eliminated most if not all of them. It's no big deal really. Everyone in the future has nanos. It's just like having a cell phone, only better."

"What is a cell phone?"

"A cell phone is an ancient communication device from around this time period. They were actually part of the technology that produced nanos. Nanobots are so far advanced now that it's difficult to tell the better ones apart from a white blood cell. Again, it's no big deal."

Stewart wasn't convinced. Machines were inside of his body! It was disgusting and just too unnatural. This whole experience was just getting worse by the minute. He tried to calm down by assuring himself repeatedly that God must have a purpose in all of this madness.

"So, they will heal my injuries as well?" He began to think of the wound on his arm and the bullet in his left shoulder.

"Yes, it still takes time but they repair physical damage much faster than the ordinary human healing process." Doc was working on the console again.

Stewart felt the wound on his arm and look down at it. He couldn't see it through the fluid but he could feel that it had already healed significantly. There was a scab over it that was as thick as what he would expect in four days from a wound that deep. At this rate it would only be a scar by tomorrow. He wondered what, if anything, the tiny machines were doing to the bullet in his shoulder.

"Ok Doc, can I just get out of here and breathe some air? I don't like confined spaces very well." Stewart was being honest with that. He really didn't like being confined in any way for any reason.

"Well, can I trust you not to attack me?" Doc asked from under the console.

"Sure, Doc. I know that you're not a demon now, why would I attack you?" Stewart was trying to be as non-committal as he could without actually lying. He hated lying.

"The question was really more for me than you, Captain. I was just wondering aloud if I could trust you." He kept working on the console.

"Oh. Well, you could just shoot me with that fancy, silver pencil thing you shot me with earlier if I get out of hand." Stewart tried to reassure him.

"Yes I could, although repeated exposure causes…uh, ill effects upon the nanobots in your system so I would like to avoid that if possible." Doc suddenly jerked his head up with a start and looked over at the console.

"What is it? Stewart asked.

"A response to my distress call," Doc replied as he went over to examine a smaller screen on the console.

"What is the response?"

"It doesn't make any sense. This whole mission hasn't made any sense."

"How so?" Stewart wanted to keep him talking. He didn't seem to be the kind of man who was careful with his words and Stewart had a lot of questions that Doc might answer without actually being asked a question.

"Um, they are telling me to self repair in place."

"Who are they?"

"I.T.M.S., the Inter-Time Management Service. They regulate the time travel industry. Basically they are my bosses while I am traveling. I have to do whatever they tell me to."

"Oh, like policemen."

"Sort-of," Doc nodded.

"So what's wrong with that?"

Doc sat back on the forward control console and his masked face stared off seemingly lost in deep thought. "A few things; I've never done it before and shouldn't be expected to at my travel level; I'm not trained in how to do that, and that response was way too quick. It usually takes at least an hour for any response, let alone one this detailed. I'm not trained to interact with prims of this or any other period. I could really cause a lot of damage if I commit any errors."

"Oh? Like accidentally picking up someone from the past?"Stewart ribbed.

Doc looked over at him. "Yes. They are aware of you, it was in my message. I'm to leave you on the ship and forage for the parts and tools I need among the population. This never happens, ever. They even sent me instructions on how to make the repair. I will have to restrain you somehow." Doc looked over at Stewart.

"Maybe I could help you, Doc. What do you need?"

"Hmmph!" Doc snorted." I doubt that you could help me with much of anything. It will be hard enough for me to find the things that I need here in this time period as it is. The technology is better than in your time but nothing like my own."

"What exactly do you need?" Stewart repeated.

Doc looked down at the list he printed out from the response. "For starters about two pounds of pure gold 18 gauge wire, two 3 carat rubies cut into the shape of equilateral pyramids, one pound of titanium, one pound of billet aluminum, three quartz tubes, some Plexi-glass, a foundry, a four axis CNC machining center with a Fanuc controller and about three weeks of food." Doc sighed, crossed his arms again and looked down at his feet. "They know that I don't have the technical skill to do these things. Why can't they send a repair ship?"

"Things always happen for a reason Doc. Why am I here on your ship instead of sitting in a hot tub of water at the Wong cabin in Warren? Why are my best friend and horses all dead? Why have I survived so many horrific things that have caused others to perish? All are valid questions but not useful for the moment. I am here. I will deal with it as I must. A man has to do the things he knows to do the best that he can and leave the rest in the hands of the almighty."

"I suppose you're right Captain. This just isn't the kind of thing I ever imagined I would have to do." He turned back to face Stewart. "Alright, release the pressure in the tank by turning the handle under your left hand one quarter turn to your right."

Stewart complied and felt his ears pop gently as the fluid began to drain from the cylinder.

"Now, you're going to probably cough quite a bit as the fluid clears. That's perfectly normal so just go with it until you can breathe normally," Doc went on. His voice sounded deadpan; defeated.

Stewart felt the fluid pour out of his mouth and nose as the level dropped below his face. Sure enough, he began coughing violently for almost a minute. Doc just watched as he leaned against the console with his arms crossed. Stewart was almost doubled over in the cramped space when the coughing finally subsided. He stood up straight in the tiny chamber and felt warm, clean air blowing down on his head.

"Now when the level is below the metal grate on the bottom, turn the same handle one full turn to your left and the door will open. Sit over there on the seat in the far wall and stay out of my way for a while. If you so much as approach me, I'll stun you again."

Stewart looked at the far wall that Doc had indicated and saw a small chair suddenly grow from out of it. 'Yeah, this old tub is a real junk heap,' Stewart thought in amazement. He turned the latch as instructed and opened the door. He slowly stepped out of the tube and looked over at Doc. Doc produced the small metal tube from under his folded arms and slowly shook his head at him.

"Not gonna try nothin' Doc. Just gonna go over here and sit down," Stewart said as he slowly walked over to the wall chair. It didn't look all that comfortable but it stretched out to fit him as he sat in it. He leaned back slightly and the chair reclined. It molded itself to his body and he suddenly felt the urge to just put up his feet. The chair complied with the thought and stretched out a gray appendage to support his legs and feet. He stretched back and thought that he had never been more comfortable in his life. Doc went back to work on his console.

"So, where are we Doc?" Stewart asked from his relaxed position.

"Central Nevada, why do you ask?"

"Just curious is all. Is that still an American Territory or is there even such a thing as America in this era?"

"In this period it would be one of the fifty United States of America which at this point in history is the most powerful and most advanced nation in the world."

"Fifty states huh? There were only 37 in my time and a bunch of them were very new. Most powerful and advanced too? What happened to Britain, France, Spain, Portugal, all those world powers of my time?

"If I have the time right they are all members of what is now the European Union which is a weakly linked economic community with a common currency, except Britain which kept the Pound Sterling. After the devastation of World War Two Europe thought that they could escape further mass violence by unifying this way."

"World War Two? And did they?"

"I shouldn't even be having this conversation with you." Doc looked up at Stewart.

"Why? As you said, I won't remember any of it. I am just making conversation. So how many of these 'world wars' were there?"

"At this time just the two."

"No. How many total? How many times is the entire world at war?" Stewart tried to imagine the magnitude of the chaos that must describe a world war.

"Um, three. Each one more than twice as bad as the one before." Doc sighed again as if he were bearing the grief of each war all on his own.

"Three huh? How bad was the first one?" Stewart was genuinely curious now.

"More than 20 million people were killed in the first one. More than 70 million people died in the second world war."

Stewart sat up. "Million!? Seventy million?" It was inconceivable. Stewart couldn't believe that that many people could have died fighting a war.

"Where did they get armies that big? They must have drafted half of the human population! Those numbers are huge!"

Doc shook his head. "In the First World War the nations of Europe actually fielded armies in the millions and the dead were primarily military but even though armies were even bigger in the second war, most of the casualties were civilians. That's why it was so much higher."

"Why did so many civilians die?"

"They were targeted. It was called Total War. Nation destroys nation until one side is destroyed completely and only one remains. Plus 10 million or more were simply executed by the Axis powers."

"Who fought these wars?" Stewart had to know every detail now. He was feeling obsessed.

"Essentially both began with Germany and France fighting. Britain came in with the French both times. America came in later in both wars and ultimately won the victory. There were many other nations involved like Canada, Imperial Japan, Italy, Turkey, Russia, and Hungary but those were the main forces involved."

"These must have been long wars to have killed so many. They must have lasted decades."

"Oh no, Captain. You underestimate the advancement of technology. The science of mass murder was perfected in the twentieth century. Both wars only lasted about five years."

Stewart shook his head in amazement. He couldn't fathom the weapons that could create so much destruction.

"Did these wars actually solve anything?" he asked.

"Solve anything?" Doc replied.

"Yes. The whole point of armed conflict is to resolve disputes. The War Between the States resolved that the South was no longer free to conduct its affairs as it saw fit. Obviously there was a serious dispute to lead to so much violence. Surely something was resolved?" Stewart stared at him waiting for the 'academic' answer.

"Well in many respects the first war led to the second. Very little was really resolved from the first. The German Empire originally sought to increase its land ownership and was so devastated by the war that it destroyed its entire culture. That led to the rise of socialist fascism, a form of totalitarian government which controls basically everything in a society. Under the National Socialist Workers Party or Nazis as they were called, the

Germans conquered all of Europe and some of Africa. Only the British remained until the Americans joined them in 1941. Look, I'd love to stay here and play history teacher to you but I have much to do so I will allow you limited access to the database to amuse yourself with." Doc punched some buttons on a portable key pad and brought it over to Stewart.

"Here, now just type in what you want to know and the search engine will show you all the information it has on the subject. This flat area on the right side is called a mouse pad. Use your finger to guide the cursor and tap it twice quickly to select something." He touched a wall next to Stewart and a screen appeared and swung out from the wall. "You can use this monitor. I've blocked everything past the twentieth century so don't even bother looking. Enjoy." Doc briefly moved the cursor to demonstrate its operation.

Doc turned and walked to the other end of the cabin. The wall glowed brightly at his touch as he stepped through it and then went solid again. Stewart stared at the keyboard and sighed. He was almost afraid to start looking. His faith in God was truly being tested by what he had already learned. The fall of humanity had apparently become far more horrific than he had ever imagined.

Chapter Eight

Stewart sat back in the gray wall chair and thought. He looked around the cabin in fascination. The room was mostly an off-white color with gray metal looking devices throughout. Light filled the room from an unknown source. The room was an oval shape with a large console in the center of the floor and other control consoles around the front of the cabin. The curved bulkhead he was sitting against appeared to be less important to the function of the ship and seemed more like a seating or rest area to him. Maybe it was the galley, he thought. There were cabinet doors with shiny latches on them lining the wall one either side of him. The travel tubes were on his right side and the large screen was on his left. A night view of the Nevada desert appeared on it now. There was what appeared to be an oval window above the central console in the ceiling but it was dark now and filled with stars. He wasn't sure if it was another screen display or an actual window. It was high enough above the room that he hadn't noticed it before.

He was relaxed now and the strangeness of the situation was beginning to wear off. He could kill Doc but he felt in his soul that that was the wrong thing to do. He had killed many men but he had always felt at peace with every instance, except for one; the first one. He thought back to that painful day so many years ago when he was just fifteen.

His father had always been against his reading and schooling while his mother had encouraged him to read since he was a toddler. She had read the bible to him by candle light for as long as he could remember every night before bed. His father had argued many times with his mother over his reading and was always insisting that it was a waste of time and that Stewart should spend his time in more useful and productive pursuits. She passed away from the consumption when he was only twelve and his father, who was illiterate, forbade his reading except at school, which he allowed only to honor the deathbed wishes of his mother. To circumvent this rule, Stewart took up fishing on Sundays after attending church (another deathbed request from his mother) and always took a book to the fishing hole on a slow moving part of the

Nueces River, a few miles from the family farm. He always made sure that he brought home a few catfish or crappies just to show his father that he had been 'productive'.

A few months after he began his fishing trips he met her. Pain welled up inside Stewart as he recalled how he had heard her screaming when he got to the river. He ran to see what the fuss was all about and saw a young slave girl, about his age, being chased by a large Cotton Mouth snake. At first he laughed but then the snake struck and she screamed even louder as its fangs pierced the dark skin on her bare leg. He ran over and clubbed it with the butt of his squirrel rifle. When it was sufficiently dead, he turned toward the girl and reached down to help her up. She screamed again.

"Stop that!" Stewart told her sternly. "There aint no need for anymore of your hollerin' girl. Let me help you."

Gingerly, she took his hand and tried to stand up. She screamed again, this time in pain.

"Alright, alright. Just sit down on this log here and let me look at the bite." Stewart helped her over to a nearby fallen tree. He checked it for more snakes before she sat down, just in case.

"You took some poison there. It's going to have to be drained." Stewart looked up at her face and for the first time noticed her incredible green eyes. He'd seen colored people before but never with such piercing green eyes. Her face was also very pretty and he suddenly felt very strange. He had never seen anyone like this little slave girl before.

"Wh-what's your name?" he stammered. Now he felt really stupid. He tried to get his confidence back but she was just so darn pretty. Then she smiled; a big bright smile with amazing white teeth inside those full red lips.

"Julie," she said with a voice so sweet that it ran shivers down his spine. With that he now realized that he was stupid in love with a slave girl. He felt like he had gotten just about as dumb as a boy could get right now. He shook his head a little to try to get his mind right. If he didn't work fast Julie, the Pretty, Green-eyed Slave Girl was going to be Julie, the Dead, Green-eyed Slave Girl, or at least the One-Legged, Slave Girl which amounted to pretty much the same thing in the world of slaves.

"Um, okay. If I don't drain some of that poison, you'll either die or your owner will cut your leg off. If they don't put you down, that is." He hated being this blunt to her but the swelling was getting bad and the snake had given her a pretty good shot. She looked scared. He looked down at her perfect, dark-skinned thigh where the bite was swelling. "I can help but you'll still be sick for a while. If you were running away, you're through now. You won't make a mile on that leg."

"What you gonna do?" She asked in a light, sweet voice that sought to melt his heart. It was working.

"I need to cut it open and squeeze as much out as I can." He pulled his small knife from his pocket and began to clean it on his trouser leg. She shrunk back from him.

"Is it gonna hurt?" She asked. Her voice and the look on her face broke his heart.

"Yes, a lot. But living hurts sometimes. You have got to die for all your pain to go away. I would like to try to keep you around a little bit longer if I can."

"Aw right, if'n ya hafta do it." She looked at him in a way that he swore was going to melt him or cause him to burst in flames.

"All right, let me fix you up and then maybe we can work on your grammar a little bit. Here, bite down on this." Stewart handed her his deer skin belt. She placed it in her teeth and bit down as he quickly made an 'X' on top of the bite, just like his father had taught him just a few months before when he himself had been bitten by a Copperhead. She screamed into the belt but he could see on her face that she was trying to be tough about it. He felt bad but tried to disassociate himself from what he was doing.

When he had pressed the wound sufficiently, he rinsed it with his water flask and tied his handkerchief over it. If she hadn't been so skinny it wouldn't have made it all the way around. He took the belt back from her and looked at the deep teeth marks in it.

"Sorry," he said. "But that's the only way to do that. See?" He lifted his pants leg to show her his own, similar scar on his left shin. She smiled again.

"Thas awright. It weren't so bad, I guess. Thank ya fo' yo' hep, suh."

76

"Well stand up and see if your dress hides the wound." It wasn't much of a dress; more of a long, gray, sleeveless shirt really. It did cover the bandage but just barely.

"I know that you want to be free," he told her. "God has placed that desire in the hearts of all mankind. But right now you need to return to your master and heal up. Maybe try again when you are older and healthier."

"I not runnin 'way," Julie smiled. "I just out playin' is all. Massa's go ta church on Sundees and I gets away for a few hours. I caint run 'way, don' know wheres ta go. My family is heah." She shrugged.

"Well you'd best get back home then. I come here every Sunday, except when it is raining. If you ever come back, I will be here and we can work on that grammar."

"What be grammar, suh?"

"Never mind that now. Go home and get better, okay? And watch out for snakes." She nodded and walked back into the woods. He watched her small, lean frame as she went. She seemed to sense his gaze and turned and waved to him as she limped her way home.

He saw her every Sunday after that. He would fish and read aloud to her for hours until she had to go home. His stays at the fishing hole grew longer each Sunday. His father would grunt at him when he came in close to dark but nod when he saw the string of cleaned fish he brought home. Fishing was an excellent way to get some reading done and though he never let on, he was sure that his father suspected that reading was why he really went fishing. As long as he was being 'productive' and bringing home fish, it would probably be tolerated by the old Texas Revolution veteran.

His father had fought at San Jacinto and a few other places as well, Stewart thought, but he never spoke of it. He was just a private in Sam Houston's army but he had the respect of his fellow Texans everywhere he went. He was a proud man and he had evidently killed many Mexicans in the war. He was so headstrong that folks said that he should have died from all of his wounds but he simply refused and made a full recovery against all expectations.

Stewart respected his father and even admired him. The only disagreements he ever had with the man had been over his

77

education and church attendance, and one other thing; slaves. His father hated slavery but he seemed to hate slaves even more. He often spoke of them as if they were animals, less than human. He believed that they were vermin and that they should be exterminated. Stewart could never let him find out about Julie.

They became best friends, he and Julie. They talked for hours and he did help her with her grammar but warned her never to use it in front of her masters. She was very smart and she even started to understand the written words in his books though he made no serious efforts to teach her. The law was the law and he didn't want to go to prison just for teaching someone to read. Eventually, after a couple of years, they discovered what all boys and girls do and became lovers. He was very careful not get her pregnant using the best techniques he knew. It was sin, he knew, and he felt very guilty about it but he couldn't help himself when she was around. It felt right, but he knew that in this world it was horribly wrong. He also knew that it would end one day but he didn't know how. He hoped for it to be easy. He couldn't have been more wrong.

He and Julie went swimming after he had caught a sufficient number of fish and since they were young, healthy and naked, one thing led to another and when they had finished; they lay in each other's arms on the grass by the river. They were sharing their own private heaven. He gently stroked the smooth dark skin of her gorgeous young body as they lay basking in the summer sun. It was time for her to go and they started to get up and get dressed. He was pulling on his pants when it hit him. It felt like a large tree branch and as he went down his eyes confirmed that it was indeed a tree branch when it began to pummel Julie mercilessly as it was wielded by his father. What followed was the most horrific event of his life.

Julie began screaming, his father was screaming, and Stewart's head was throbbing and bleeding. Julie tried with little success to ward off the blows as his father yelled obscenities at her. He called her a whore and an animal, among many other vulgarities. Stewart struggled to his feet and tried to stop his father from beating Julie. He turned and struck Stewart again, knocking him to ground. Then Julie made a break for it; her dark naked body running as fast she could make it go. She had gotten about thirty yards away when his father shot her with one of his pistols. It seemed like slow motion to Stewart. He could still see that perfect little body shudder as the bullet entered her back and destroyed her heart. He could see the spray of blood as the bullet made its exit and her lifeblood spewed out of her. She convulsed grotesquely and fell into the slow-moving river. He stared at her quivering, ruined body floating face down as it gently drifted down stream. Her perfect little bottom stuck out of water as he stared helplessly at the gaping hole in her back, still gushing blood.

His father turned around to face him, his second pistol in his hand. Stewart just reacted. He didn't think. He didn't reason. He just reached down, picked up his squirrel rifle, and shot his father in the chest with it as the pistol was coming up. He father fell back, a stunned look on his face. He was only about seven yards away and the small bullet went straight through him. He dropped the pistol and fell backward to the ground.

"I was not gonna shoot ya, son. Though ya lay with animals and defile yourself, I could not kill my own flesh and blood." His father croaked the words out. Stewart's ears were ringing from the two shots so he barely heard him. He went over to his father's side and knelt down beside him. The full weight of what had just transpired hit him like a train. He broke down and began to sob uncontrollably.

"I forgive you, son. I forgive you." His father reached up, gently touched Stewart's face with his hand and then breathed his last.

He had often wondered what it was like to kill a man. He'd wondered many times if he would ever have to kill or if he would be one of those men to whom violence was a stranger in life. Now he knew. It was the most awful thing he'd ever felt. All those boyhood fantasies of being the hero in a huge, glorious battle against evil foes disintegrated instantly. He was a murderer now. He, Gregory Dean Stewart, son of David Patrick Stewart, was now the murderer of his own father, a white man, over the life of a slave girl. If caught he would surely hang. He could spend all the rest of his days trying to be a godly man and do right by others but he would still probably burn in hell for this.

Now that he was a murderer he did what murderers do. He covered his tracks and ran away. He took his father's pistols, powder kit, and his Arkansas toothpick and dragged the body into the river. He then went home and packed a few things and left. As he was walking out the door of the little farm house he stopped and went over to the mantle. He pulled down his father's old Springfield musket that he had used in the war and replaced it with his squirrel rifle, the murder weapon. He then walked out the door and began walking toward Austin.

It was a long way and he may not have made it if he hadn't hitched a ride on a small wagon train headed that way. They had to fight off a small Indian attack just north of the town of Seguin and Stewart killed again. Two Apache braves lay dead by his hand that day when he fired the old musket in the short battle. Though he felt no remorse over the lives he had taken in self defense, he felt sick about being a killer, even though others in the train were full of handshakes and backslaps over his performance under fire.

He felt now that he was cursed; born to be a killer. He finally made it to Austin two weeks after he had left home and found a job working for a lumber company. It was June of 1855 and he worked there peacefully, never killing another man until 1861 when he began killing more men than he could count over the next four years.

Stewart wiped his eyes as he sat in the wall chair. He didn't quite know why he was thinking about that horrible day. He had tried so many times to put it out of his mind but it always came back, often in dreams. In some dreams he was the one who had shot Julie. In others, Julie shoots his father while laughing in that playful laugh of hers as she pulls the trigger on that old cap-lock pistol. He could never determine which emotion was the more powerful one; the loss of the only love in his life or the guilt over killing his father. They seemed to fight with each other, wrestling for dominance of his soul. In the rare moments when he lost his temper, the two emotions would combine to create an almost super-natural rage within him. He thought back to the beating he had given to Private Hayes. It was a rare loss of control for him but he knew that it was horribly dangerous to anyone near him when it happened, including himself.

Stewart shook his head and tried to focus on the here and now. Since that day by the river he had grown accustomed to dealing with unusual circumstances. This was now the most unusual situation in his life, by far. He thought about the apparently horrendous wars fought on Earth since his time. He had so many questions and right now Doc seemed to have all the answers. He couldn't even conceive of not remembering this entire event or what kind of machines could exist to 'wipe' his mind.

This was certainly not the first time he'd had only poor options to choose from but it certainly seemed to be the worst. If he were to return to his own time period in the same place and mind wiped, it would be certain death. With his horses dead he would only last a few minutes at best against the Nez Perce warriors that awaited him. That was only if he could somehow reload his pistols and somehow get his hands on the Henry. It would take a miracle to save him. In a sense, a miracle had already saved him. He would surely have been discovered by the Indians had it not been for this 'Doc' and his ship. Either way he would be dead for certain. He could only conclude that God's purpose for his life had not yet been fulfilled.

Stewart sat in wonder of his circumstances and was so lost in his thoughts that the bright glow of the room portal startled him when Doc returned. The man stepping through the glowing doorway in no way resembled the creature that had left earlier. Though he had seen his face earlier, before he had blacked out, Stewart scarcely recognized Doc's face without the horrible gasping expression accompanied by the yellow-green fluid pouring from his various orifices. What appeared before him now was a tall, young looking man with short cropped hair in a strange style of clothing. The outfit was tight fitting with what appeared to be a short undershirt with a strange picture of a big-haired black man on it and pants that appeared to be made of faded blue canvas.

"What on earth are you wearing?" Stewart asked.

"Period clothing. This is the type of clothing common to this era. The pants are called 'jeans' although I don't know why and this is called a 'Jimi Hendrix T-shirt'. I understand that he was a drug addict and that he died at a young age but he was arguably one of the best guitar players who ever lived. Even though he is dead in this time he is still very popular." Doc's voice sounded strange now. The ominous tone was gone and he was speaking as though he hadn't used his voice for quite some time. Stewart was familiar with this as he personally had spent weeks without speaking a word and had found it difficult to do so when the time came.

"You sound different now." Stewart probed the man.

"I haven't actually used my voice to communicate in several months. The nanobots translate the thoughts that I push out into a voice that you 'hear' in your head. It's time saving and eliminates some level of miscommunication." Doc wasn't looking at him but was busily tapping buttons on his machine.

Stewart looked him over. His skin was light for a Negro but he had the distinct wide nose and facial features of one. He briefly glanced up at him and Stewart froze with a chill. Doc had green eyes. Not the same as Julie's but they were similar in color. There was something eerie about that. He wondered if there was some distant relation between the two. He pushed the thought aside and decided to try to keep the strange man from the future talking.

"So, what are you doing now?"

"Working." Doc answered curtly.

"On what?" Stewart asked, careful to avoid any sudden moves that might startle the man. He didn't want to be locked up or zapped with that silver tube again.

"I am manufacturing a surface transportation device. I don't want to have to walk everywhere to get the things I need so I'm programming the ship to make me a car; something suitable for the time period but not too extravagant." He continued punching buttons.

"A car?"

"Yes, an automobile to be technical; something that Americans invented late in your own century. I believe they were referred to as 'horseless carriages' for a time. I'm trying to determine what model I should make it. I'm thinking of a Lexus or Mercedes but they may be a bit flashy, let's see, German or Japanese? Hmmm…." Doc seemed lost in thought.

"Why not an American car? Didn't you say that the Germans and Japanese fought against us? Why would you choose something made by our enemies?" Stewart was shocked by the blatant disloyalty of a man he had assumed was an American from the future. He began to wonder about the man's home nation and whether there even was an America in his time.

"Well first of all, they are not, and never have been *my* enemies. Secondly, they did make some of the best vehicles of this era although there were some exceptional American…wait a minute!" Doc looked up at Stewart now with a grin on his face. "I *will* choose an American car, one that will really irritate you, Captain!" He said triumphantly.

"How so?" Stewart eyed him cautiously. It was strange seeing the expressions on his face for the first time. He was far more animated that Stewart had expected.

"I'm going to build a car named after the president that you fought against; a Lincoln!" Doc looked back down at his machine and punched the buttons like an excited kid. Stewart rolled his eyes. A car named after President Lincoln. He doubted that anyone had named a car after President Davis or General Lee. Not that it really surprised or even bothered him. It was just slightly annoying that this jackass took so much pleasure in this childish decision.

"That's just silly, Doc. What kind of car did they name after President Lincoln anyway?" Keep him talking, Stewart thought.

"Really nice ones, actually. Some of the best ever made. I think I'll build a 1997 Mark VIII. It's new enough that it won't catch too much attention but old enough not to stand out as a new car. They quit making them around this time but it was really sexy for its time. Fast too."

"Sexy?" Stewart tried to think of how a vehicle could be 'sexy'. Doc ignored him and went on.

"Of course it won't be a real Lincoln but it will look like one from the outside. The base for the vehicle already exists in the ship's hold, I'm just modifying the exterior" He tapped some buttons a few more times, slapped one last button with a flourish and then stepped away from the console.

"There, all done. The Lincoln will be complete in about twenty minutes and then I can get on my way to get what I need. It's black by the way, like me." He smiled at Stewart who rolled his eyes again.

"You're not all that black, mister. You're more of a light brown color, not that I really give a damn what color you are. You can be purple with red and pink stripes and it would all be the same to me, Doc." Stewart was amazed at the man's lack of maturity. Doc pointed to the screen on the wall where an image appeared.

"Isn't it pretty, Captain? I think that you helped me pick the perfect vehicle for this venture, don't you?" Doc had silly grin on his face. Stewart actually felt a little relieved that the man was showing a little human character, even if it was annoyingly childish. He looked at the sleek image on the screen. It actually was a pretty amazing looking vehicle.

"Well Doc, I have to admit, it is quite a sight to behold. Do I get to go for a ride in it?" Doc's smile instantly faded.

"Absolutely not! You will remain here until I return. You will not leave this ship under any circumstances, is that clear?" Stewart eyed Doc carefully. His demeanor had gone from childish excitement to lecturing arrogance so fast it was crazy. This man had some mental frailties, Stewart was sure.

"So I'll just stay here and play with your machine for three weeks, huh?" Stewart said sarcastically, wagging the keyboard at him.

"I'll be back in less than twenty four hours. There is enough food in the pantry chamber to sustain you for several days if need be. I will be retrieving more while I am away. It may be difficult to find any pure enough but I can purify the food mass when I return to the ship. Just tap the armrest twice and the computer will ask you what you want. It's pretty versatile but if it doesn't recognize the request, don't repeat it. Too many failed attempts will lock up the program and you'll go hungry. Keep your orders simple like, 'chicken soup' or 'turkey sandwich,' okay?"

"Okay Doc." Stewart tried to think what exactly the term 'okay' was and what it really meant other than the obvious affirmative. It must be similar to 'alright.'

Doc stepped over toward him and stood on the circle that Stewart had used to enter the cabin earlier. As he began to began to descend, he shook a finger and said once more, "Remember, stay here in this room. I've locked all the exits."

"Okay Doc." Stewart smiled and waved from his comfortable chair as the strange man from future disappeared into the floor.

Chapter Nine

Stewart sifted through the information on the screen slowly at first. It took him a little time to figure out how to use the device but it became easier over time. It was very fast and efficient, moving from one subject to another in the blink of an eye. He tried putting a couple of dates past 1999 but they all came up 'access denied' on the screen. So Doc wasn't a liar anyway, that was a little comforting. He struggled to understand the profound events that played out before his eyes. He studied the world wars first and came away feeling drained by the sheer violence of it all. He thought that he had seen all the brutality that man had to offer but was finding out that he was sadly mistaken. He had one small comfort that came from it all. The loss of his own war was ordained by God. Not because it was an unjust cause but he saw glaring evidence that without the United States being whole and united, the entire world would have fallen into utter darkness under Imperialism, Communism, or Fascism. America had stood against it all although they had apparently dabbled in all of these things themselves. It actually made some sense now although he still felt that he had been on the right side morally.

He took a break and rested his eyes. The glare from the screen seemed to wear on his vision, especially during the moving pictures that he saw. He ordered from the computer as Doc had instructed though he didn't really feel all that hungry.

"Turkey Sandwich, please" He said to the machine. The screen displayed options for him and he looked through them. Mayonnaise, mustard, pickles, lettuce, tomato, avocado... He looked through the myriad of choices and deciding to keep it simple, selected 'all.' There, he should get a sandwich from somewhere in this contraption in a few minutes he thought. He was looking at the screen trying to figure out where it would come from when he felt something under his left hand. It was his sandwich. It had appeared out of the arm of the chair in less than fifteen seconds. He was amazed. He sat up and the arm of the chair moved in front of him creating a small table to eat on with the turkey sandwich on a plate right in the center. A napkin popped up next to the plate as the word 'drink?' flashed on the screen. He saw the choices and only recognized four, coffee, tea, milk, and water. He wasn't much of a milk drinker and again keeping it simple, he said 'water' to the screen. He pulled his hands back to keep from spilling the drink in case it popped up somewhere unexpected. A clear cylinder of water gently rose from the table just to left of the sandwich plate.

Stewart was impressed. He was more impressed when he began eating the sandwich. It was delicious in every way. He had never had such a great tasting sandwich. Even the water was more refreshing than any he had ever drunk. He thoroughly enjoyed every bite and sip of the entire meal and he was completely satisfied when he finished. This ship may be strange, he thought, but it can cook!

Stewart looked back to the screen and thought for a moment. Doc had been gone for a couple of hours now and should be quite a ways away. He had no idea how fast the Lincoln could go but he figured it would be safe to bet he was probably a good 80 or 100 miles away, if the car moved as quickly as Doc had suggested. At the very least he was two hours away which would give Stewart time to get at least eight miles from the ship. He didn't like walking but he liked being a prisoner even less. So he needed to think this through.

He would need food and water. He ordered three more turkey sandwiches choosing the 'wrapped' option and observing them coming out with a tight clear coating on them that he was sure he could peel off when necessary. He then perused the drink menu and chose 'water, bottled' and 3 nice little bottles of water appeared. That would hold him for a couple of days. Next he started searching for 'spaceship' information. Doc hadn't locked him out of that part of the data-base. Arrogance rears its ugly head once again. Within a few minutes Stewart had located the type of spacecraft he was on and began looking into its workings. It was a Time Master 17B, built by Ford Space Industries. He wondered if it was the same Ford that he read about that revolutionized the automobile industry in the early twentieth century. The doors were indeed locked by a voice code that only Doc could unlock (again, not a liar) but there was an emergency manual override that anyone could operate so that they weren't trapped inside! Hah! Another excellent safety feature! Stewart was beginning to like Ford Industries even if they did make the Lincoln. He thought about seeing if he could make some kind of vehicle for himself but he couldn't figure that one out so he resigned himself to being on foot.

He asked the computer where his guns were but it just showed him a locked cabinet over by the control console. It wouldn't tell him how to open it. Oh well, they were empty anyway. He still had the Colt which he took out and checked carefully. The goo that he had been immersed in dried pretty thoroughly when exposed to air but left a light powder residue that he hoped hadn't affected the powder in the cylinders. Maybe he wouldn't need the gun. He put it in his empty right holster just in case.

He triggered the manual exit as the computer had told him to and an actual door opened beside the big screen on the wall. It was dimly lit but he could see metal stairs going down. He followed them down to the next level where it opened into a short hall lined with clear tubes filled with various colored liquids. He briefly inspected them and decided that this was what remained of his horses. He shook his head sadly and moved toward the exit that was actually lit up with a sign that said 'Emergency Exit.' Pretty difficult, he thought sarcastically. He looked at the door and followed the picture instructions to open the hatch. The hatch fell away and a metal ladder dropped to the ground from beneath it. He adjusted the saddlebags on his shoulder, looked back into the ship briefly and then stepped down to the surface.

It was cold and windy. It was strange being outside again. He had gotten too comfortable in his prison. Doc had relied on Stewart's ignorance to keep him trapped in luxury. Stewart wasn't that kind of creature. He liked nice things and appreciated all of the refinement placed into the miracle machine that brought him here but he wasn't going to let himself be lulled into complacency and end up mind-wiped. He still didn't like the sound of that. He looked up at the ship and noticed it had an odd shimmering look to it. He stepped away from it and it disappeared. He stepped back under it and there it was again. He walked about a hundred feet from it and looked back at it. It was gone. He picked up a rock and threw it at where the ship should be and watched it bounce off thin air.

"Huh. Neat trick." He muttered to himself. He took a bearing off the setting sun and began to head north. Just maybe, his gold was still there, several hundred miles and 130 years away.

He walked all night. He felt very good. He felt well rested and it seemed effortless to move across the country side. He was in high desert with rolling hills and sparse vegetation. His night vision seemed extremely keen. He wondered if that was the 'nanobots' doing. He spotted a small sidewinder gliding across the desert before it spotted him. It stopped and coiled in surprise just a few feet away from him but Stewart simply stepped away and gave the deadly snake his room. He had no love of snakes but he wasn't in a snake killing mood. He was enjoying the cool night air, the light from an almost full moon, and the smell of sage brush hanging on the breeze. He felt alive as he hadn't felt in years.

He moved soundlessly in dark. All of his old aches and pains seemed to have gone and he felt like a cat stalking his prey in the night. He actually almost stepped on a coyote that hadn't sensed him moving. The creature yelped and ran screaming into the night. He felt as if he owned this desert on this night. He was master of all he surveyed…except those lights over there. He hadn't really noticed before but there were lights on the horizon. He looked back toward where the ship was and saw an enormous glow on that horizon. He walked to the top of a hill to see better what it could be. He was shocked to see what had to be a city; an enormous city of thousands, maybe millions of lights. He would like to see that someday but there were two problems; one, it was in the wrong direction. Two, that's probably where Doc went and he had no interest in ever seeing that man again.

He turned back to his path and looked at the lights in the distance. They were moving east and west. Must be some of those 'cars' Doc was talking about on a road of some kind. They seemed to be moving pretty fast though. He couldn't tell how far away they were but they seemed to travel along at a good clip. It would be daylight before he got there, he thought. He pushed on.

Several hours later he found himself just a few hundred yards from the road. It was still dark as he watched the vehicles go by at a seemingly breakneck speed. He sat and watched them for a while. Some were small and some where huge. Some were very quiet whiles others made a lot of noise. He saw many big box vehicles passing by and smaller vehicles of all shapes, colors and sizes. The big boxes were almost as big as a train car. He decided that they must be some kind of freight haulers. Like huge land-borne ships on giant metal wheels. It was fascinating. He contemplated whether he should try to hitch a ride with someone but then thought better. He should stay low and inconspicuous until he understood better how things worked in this time period. He would keep moving and the Lord would show him the way. He carefully crossed the giant, divided road when the traffic was clear and proceeded north once again.

Daybreak came and he found himself hungry so he sat down on a rock and ate one of his sandwiches. The clear coating pealed of easily as he had suspected and this sandwich was just as good as the last. He drank about a half bottle of water and started moving again. He was in an area of rocky canyons now. He would have to be careful not get lost in a blind canyon. If it had been his own time, he would be concerned about Indians and bandits in this area but his reading had led him to believe that those days were long gone. So it was with some surprise that he saw the dirt kicked up in front of him by several bullets.

He ducked down behind a nearby rock as the sound of the shots reached his ears. Either it was a whole bunch of fellows shooting at him or it was one gun that shot lots of bullets. He heard a shout and saw an ugly looking bastard running toward him with a strange looking firearm. He drew the Colt, prayed briefly for the powder to be dry enough and fired. It was a long shot of about a hundred yards but he seemed to instinctively know where to point the pistol and the man dropped to the ground.

"Dale! Are you okay! Dale! Alright cop! You're a dead man!" Someone out there apparently thought he was a lawman. Stewart idly wondered if his Confederate uniform resembled that of modern police officers. Poorly aimed bullets kicked up dust all around Stewart's hiding spot. He looked over the rock as his assailant and saw a young kid. He was brown-skinned, maybe Mexican or even Indian carrying a box-shaped handgun that sprayed lots of bullets, mostly up into the air. The kid fired again, screaming expletives and insults to the perceived law enforcement threat. He thought about talking it over with the kid but his gun was so loud he was probably deaf from firing it. He saw him drop down to re-load the weapon and Stewart carefully maneuvered for a clear shot. When the kid stood back up Stewart shot him in the head. The weapon discharged again spraying bullets all over the canyon and hitting just about everything but Stewart.

He went back over to where 'Dale' was laying and looked him over. The man was older but still young and still alive. Dale clutched his stomach as blood poured from the wound Stewart had given him.

"Where's my brother, Pig?" the small man screamed at him.

"He's dead. Why are you idiots shooting at me? I am a man who shoots back." Stewart genuinely wanted to know. He was confused as hell right now and wanted some answers to this nonsense.

"You killed my brother! You fu..." The man never finished the sentence as he raised his weapon; Stewart's bullet shattered his skull. Now he was really confused.

Stewart started searching the smelly man. He removed the weapon which was like a rifle, only shorter and had a long protrusion sticking out from under it. He also had two pistols in his belt, a large billfold full of money, and what looked like perfectly manufactured cigarettes. These guys were obviously look-outs for some type of bandit operation so Stewart carefully took stock of the situation. They will be missed and either the bad guys will be here in force soon or they aren't far away and will be waiting. He gathered all the weapons and money from both men (he would probably need both) and looked at the bills. They were smaller now, about six inches long by two and half wide. The newest bills bore the date of 2006 so he knew that it was at least that year.

The younger brother had two pistols also but they were large revolvers instead of the flat newer type guns the other carried. He holstered the two revolvers and set aside the others not really knowing how to use them. He began walking slowly toward where the men came from and discovered that the awful smell on the men seemed to be coming from that direction. He saw a small wisp of smoke coming up over some rocks not far away so he cautiously approached. He stopped short as he looked around a rock at the camp. There was a strange wagon that looked like a small house with wheels. Two other vehicles were there, one large and one smaller. A couple of two-wheeled machines also sat just outside of the wagon. A bigger brown-skinned man with a dirty apron on stepped out of the wagon and yelled out at the rocks.

"Dale! Ronnie! Quit wasting ammo and get in here and help me, dammit!"

Stewart could see that he was also armed. This was some kind of illegal family business it looked like and he had just walked right into it. The big man stopped suddenly and spun toward him with the speed of a skilled gun fighter. The big gun came up and fired. Stewart was very familiar with the heightened state one experiences in battle but he felt differently now. He could actually see the bullet as it traveled, it seemed. He stepped out of its path slightly as it just missed his left arm. Stewart's shot was better but not by much, hitting the man in his shooting arm. He ran over to the man and saw that his bullet had destroyed his arm, entering at the wrist and exiting above the elbow.

The big man rolled on the ground and screamed in pain and grabbed for the pistol with his other hand and shouted, "I'm not going back to jail! I'm not going back to jail!" The gun came up and Stewart pulled his trigger but the old Colt finally misfired. Instead of shooting Stewart the man continued bringing the gun up and shot himself in the head. The man's body went limp and a large pool of blood began to form under him.

Stewart was dumbfounded. "What the hell?" he muttered to himself. He thought that things had been weird before but now it was downright crazy. These guys were all nuts! Well, dead nuts now. And that awful smell! He looked inside the little wagon. It was disgusting. He pulled his shirt up over his nose to choke off the smell. He stepped inside and saw something cooking on the stove in a large pot. It was the source of the smell. He turned the knob under the burner and shut the flame off then took the pot outside and dumped it. It was a foul pot and smelled evil. It had to be some kind of narcotic or opiate that they were making because they were all out of their minds!

"What the hell is this stuff?" he muttered to himself. '*Meth-amphetamine, an illegal narcotic made from common pharmaceuticals and household chemicals*' came the response. He

91

almost jumped out of his skin. The Nanobots? Were they talking to him now? '*Yes, we can provide you with any information you require as long as we are connected to the ship*, he heard in his head.

"You are connected to the ship right now?" Stewart asked worriedly.

"*Yes*." The Nano-bots replied.

"So the ship can tell where I am right now?"

"*Yes*."

"So Doc can find out where I am from the ship?"

"*Yes. He is already aware of your location*."

"Is he on his way here now?" Stewart looked around nervously for the approach of the ship.

"No. He is currently being detained in a facility called the Clark County Jail. Apparently there is a limit on how fast one may drive a motor vehicle on Nevada highways in this time period. He was detained for traveling at more than 140 miles per hour when he was only allowed to travel at 70 miles per hour. He was unaware of the legal requirements."

Stewart laughed. Doc was in jail for speeding. Well he would make sure that he didn't make the same mistake if he could figure out how to operate one of these vehicles.

"Can you disconnect from the ship completely so that I can't be tracked?" He asked the Nanobots.

"Yes, if that is your request."

"It is my request that you disconnect from the ship so that I may not be tracked." He wanted to be very specific about that.

"It is done. Sir, we will not be able to provide you with as much information now unless we re-connect."

"That is fine." Stewart replied. "I'm sure we will do fine without it." Stewart was certain that somewhere far away in a small cell, Doc was groaning in frustration. The thought brought a smile to his face.

He took stock of everything at the camp. Lots of guns, bullets, cash, booze, beer, trash. There were books and journals of naked women doing sexual things with men sometimes several men, some with other women. Some were too disgusting to look at. Twice he almost vomited. There was an evil spirit about this place. He would take what was useful and destroy everything else.

First he looked through everything to find all of the cash. There were several stashes of it in and around the many heaps of bags with the white crystals that must have been their illegal product plus there were healthy amounts of cash on each of the men. He stacked it all on a small table inside the wagon and began rounding up guns and ammunition. There were 18 guns in all of various calibers and types. The two big silver revolvers he now had in his holsters were made by Smith and Wesson and called model 29s. They were serial numbered in sequence being only one digit off and both in caliber .44 Magnum, whatever that was. He tried shooting them and although they were reasonably accurate they were also painfully loud and very powerful. He decided that that must be what 'magnum' meant.

He worked each weapon individually until he felt he had a good understanding of how they all worked and what type of ammunition they fired. The small box-pistol that Ronnie shot at him with was kind of a piece of junk. It was stamped with 'Ingram,' 'M-10' and '9mm' on the side. It fired a lot of it too, emptying one magazine in just a few seconds. The problem was it just sprayed bullets everywhere with no real ability to control the shots. He decided that that gun would only be used for emergencies. He didn't like a weapon that wasn't accurate. It was too easy to hit an innocent bystander and not hit your intended target. The gun that Dale was carrying was a little more useful, an AK 47, according to the 'Bots. It also was capable of spraying bullets but it could be fired one round at a time as well up to thirty times before reloading. It hit generally where Stewart shot it.

The 'Bots retained some information but insisted that they were limited to only 30 terra-bytes of information now, whatever that meant. Dale had also carried a pair of Kimber .45 caliber pistols. Once he figured out how to use them (the 'Bots helped), he instantly fell in love with them. They were the finest firearms he had ever used. They were easy to handle, held nine rounds each, were accurate and extremely powerful, and yet not so loud that he couldn't hear after shooting them. These were keepers.

He turned to the vehicles. He thought two wheels might be easier to operate than four so he tried getting on one that was about his size. It was a Kawasaki KLX 250, according to the 'Bots and they began to instruct him how to ride it. He started it up, revved the throttle, and released the clutch as instructed and watched the vehicle fly away from him at extreme speed and fall over about thirty yards away. He was pretty sure that he didn't do that right. He turned to look at the two larger vehicles now. The smaller one was a blue 1979 Chevrolet Camaro Z28 and, according to the 'Bots, it was highly modified and very fast. Although the vehicle appealed to him it looked too complicated to drive and again had a clutch which he had already had difficulties with.

The big vehicle looked as though it was designed to pull the wagon. It was a 1999 Ford F-250 crew-cab pick-up truck XLT with a 5.4 liter V8 gas engine and automatic transmission. The 'Bots were really good at giving him much more information that he needed. It was a dirty brown color and kind of beat-up looking but he saw that it only had two pedals on the floor instead of three like the Camaro. He hoped this would be easier to drive.

Stewart retrieved the keys to the pick-up from the big man's pocket and opened the vehicle up. He rummaged through the various compartments and found the owner's manual for the truck. As he began to read the 'Bots started explaining the operation of the truck.

"Shut up. I can read."

"Sir, we can quickly explain..."

"Shut up."

"Yes Sir."

It took him about ten minutes to feel confident that he understood the operation of the truck so he started it up.

"Okay 'Bots. You guys keep quiet unless I'm about to do something really stupid, okay?"

"Yes Sir," was the tinny response.

He put his foot on the brake and moved the gear selector to 'R' and promptly backed into the trailer. Then he put it down into 'D' and stepped on the right pedal. The truck lurched forward and he stomped the left pedal just in time to keep from crushing the Camaro.

"Okay guys, that was two stupid things I just did. Where's the help?" Stewart complained to his tiny helpers.

"You said <u>really</u> stupid. To us, that means endangering your life or the lives of others."

"Oh, okay. I feel much better now." Stewart gingerly tried the controls again and before long he was driving around pretty smoothly. He pulled up next to the trailer and began loading the guns and money into the cab. He would count it all later. Right now he needed to get away from here as quickly as possible. He didn't want to have to explain any of this to the authorities and he was sure that Doc would head here looking for him as soon as he got out of jail. He suddenly had a thought.

"Hey 'Bots, when do you think Doc will be getting out of jail?" Stewart inquired.

"He was attempting escape when we disconnected earlier."

"Dang! So he'll be headed this way soon."

"Presumably."

Stewart started moving in haste. He moved the bodies of the men, who he decided were all Indians though they didn't look like any Indian he had ever seen. He placed them all inside the travel-trailer (that's what the 'Bots called it) along with all the drugs and trash from the pick-up and the pot he had dumped outside. Using the 'Bots information he rigged the propane stove to fill the trailer with gas and made a simple ignition switch from a device called a 'butane lighter' which he rigged to the door. As a last thought he loaded the Kawasaki into the back of the truck and headed down the road out of the canyon.

The fuel gauge on the truck read about three fourths of a tank so he should be able to drive for a ways before he needed fuel. The ever helpful 'Bots informed him that he would need to get another vehicle soon as the truck that he was now driving would be linked to the men at the drug camp. They also were helpful with directions helping find his way to the main road, US 95 which he took straight north. He was getting an ear full of driving lessons from the 'Bots and it was nerve racking at first but he eventually got the hang of it and he was able to drive the truck smoothly down the road obeying all traffic signs and signals. Most of it was really common sense stuff anyway.

He saw a sign that said Tonopah, 74 miles. That seemed like such a long way to him but the gauge on the truck said that he was traveling at 70 miles an hour which was faster than he'd ever been in his life (except for a certain space voyage he once took). He figured that he should be at the town in a little over an hour. He would stop for fuel there and find a map to help him navigate this strange land. The 'Bots offered to guide him but he felt better looking at a map. He was amazed at how quickly he traversed the distance and soon pulled into a filling station.

After paying the cashier and filling up the truck he used the station's restroom and simply stared at the makeup and contents of the small store. Even the restroom was amazing though it was also dirty and smelled of urine. Some things never change. It took him a while to figure out the hand dryer and was somewhat displeased with the noise it made. The young man behind the counter sold him two maps for six dollars each, which he thought was outrageous. He held his tongue as he realized that a dollar just wasn't worth what it once was.

After looking at the map he decided that his next stop should be Winnemucca. It was a fairly good size town and he felt certain that he could probably find a place to rest and plot the remainder of his course there. He would also have to buy another vehicle if he could. He climbed back into the cab of the truck and started north on Highway 95 again. As he left the Tonopah city limits he said a quiet prayer that the drug maker's dirty brown vehicle would make it as far as he needed without trouble.

Doc was furious. He hated these ignorant primitives. He'd had to bite his own flesh to release a sufficient number of Nanobots to affect his escape from the silly jail. He felt that he was failing miserably at every turn. He had to use his Nanobots to release the lock on his cell, disconnect the alarm system, open the lock on the outer door, and disrupt the close-circuit television that monitored the prison. Then he had them infiltrate the weapon systems of the guards and disable them. Then he had to use his faster Nanobot enhanced reflexes to get to his own stun weapon and immobilize the guards to finally get out of there and get to his car. He removed the simple restraining block from the car and opened it with his voice command.

As he hopped into the vehicle he heard warning shouts. He ignored them and started the vehicle up in disgust with the whole situation. Shots began bouncing off the car as he started driving away. He looked at the grim faces of the law officers attempting to end his life with their stupid guns and decided that he was through playing their game. He flicked a switch and the bullets suddenly began ricocheting wildly back at the officers from the Lincoln with just as much energy, hitting one of the officers. They stopped firing and stared dumbfounded as they watched a black 1997 Lincoln Mk VIII slowly rise into the air and then streak away like a jet into the northern sky.

Chapter Ten

Doc landed just beside the old trailer. This was the last location the Captain had been according to his Nanobots. He looked over the scene carefully looking for some sign of the troublesome old warrior. He noticed the large blood stain on the ground in front of the trailer door and groaned audibly. He had let loose a killer on the populace of this era and someone had paid the price, he was sure. The smell of the place was horrendous. He wondered what crime the Captain could possibly have committed here and what he was trying to accomplish. The thought of self-defense never even crossed his mind. The Captain was a brutal killer and who could know a murderers motives, he thought.

He walked up to the door and tried to prepare himself for what may be inside. He wasn't wearing his suit so he must be careful lest the man be waiting to ambush him. He cautiously opened the door and saw a spark in the darkness of the interior. He jumped away from the door and sprinted away with fright. The explosion just caught him and sent him into the dirt. He picked himself up slowly and surveyed the scene. His ears were ringing badly. Once more the Captain had tried to kill him and he had barely escaped serious harm. He screamed aloud more out of frustration than from the pain caused by the minor cuts and scrapes he now had.

He looked over the wreckage of the camp sight and saw the burning bodies through the flames of the destroyed trailer; three victims of this madman. He had to stop him whatever it took. He would need all of his intellect to help him find the fugitive. Protocols were protocols and must be followed regardless of the personal danger. He could hear sirens in the distance and he could see flashing lights far down the road. He wanted no more contact with the local authorities so he climbed back inside the Lincoln and turned the craft toward his ship. He needed to rest and re-think the situation.

Stewart arrived in Winnemucca in the early afternoon. He'd never been there but he'd heard of the town on the Oregon Trail and while in Boise years ago. It had been the home of a large population of Chinamen who worked on the railroads during his time but it had obviously changed much since his time. He was shocked at all of the lights and sounds. He was so distracted by it all he nearly crashed a couple of times. Even in the daytime the lights from the casinos were impressive. He knew that he needed to get rid of the truck and find other transportation. He pulled into a gas station and parked.

"What do I need to buy a new truck, Bots?" Stewart asked.

"A valid driver's license, proof of insurance, and a sufficient amount of money," was the response.

"Okay, how do I get those?" The 'Bots went on to explain the proper licensing procedures and insurance laws of the state of Nevada as of 1999. Again, his access to anything beyond 2000 was denied.

"I don't have time to do all that and I don't have a birth certificate. Even if I did no one would accept it being 160 years old. Is there another way?"

"We can modify the driver's license of one of the men from the camp."

Stewart looked around and found the billfold of the big man which he had thrown in the truck after retrieving the truck keys. He found the license and pulled it out. Johnny Ray Redbear it read. He looked at the ugly man's picture.

"I don't look anything like this man." He told the 'Bots.

"We can change that. Prepare to spit please." The 'Bots instructed.

"Spit?" He asked.

"Yes, just a small amount of saliva onto the license should be sufficient. And remove your hat please." Stewart complied and watched the license. The picture slowly began to change. Within a minute or so it began to look like him. He was amazed at these little critters. They were proving to be very valuable. He was beginning to like having them around.

"Birthday?" the 'Bots asked.

"May 16th, I'm about thirty now." Stewart volunteered.

May 16th, 1977 appeared in the DOB section of the card.

"Address?" the 'Bots inquired again. Stewart thought for a moment. It had to be very different from the one on the card which listed Las Vegas as the city of residence. He didn't want anything to tie him to the dead drug makers.

99

"Just a minute" he told them. He put the truck in gear and drove onto a side street next to the gas station. He proceeded through the residential area and began looking at the house numbers. The address already on the card listed a number, 5242, and a street, Brook Drive. He assumed that all addresses would be similar. He drove around and saw that each house had a small box in front of it by the street. Most had a number on them. He drove up to an open one and look inside. He pulled a small piece of mail from the box, showed it to the 'Bots on the license and returned it to the box.

"Make the address look like this, okay 'Bots?" Stewart instructed.

"Yes Sir." was the expected response.

9299 Lone Star Lane, Winnemucca, NV 89445 suddenly appeared in the address portion of the card.

"Name?" the 'Bots inquired.

Stewart thought again. Well it sure as hell couldn't be Johnny Ray Redbear. He smiled suddenly and said, "Foster. Gregory D. Foster."

He knew that he couldn't go by Brian as he would eventually fail to respond to it at some point. A first name is harder to fake than a last name. He figured Foster wouldn't mind much. He already took much from the man; he may as well take his name too. Besides, Foster was long dead anyway. He felt a twinge of guilt at having not repaid the man. He surely would have had the opportunity presented itself. He felt sad knowing that the young man had probably died more than a hundred years ago. He looked down and noticed that the name on the card had changed to reflect his request.

"We are finished now sir. If you wish to retain the Nanobots you've excreted, you will have to lick the driver's license. Otherwise you will lose their capacity permanently." the 'Bots informed him.

"How many are on there?" He asked.

"Over seven thousand."

That was a lot. What the hell, they've been useful so far he thought. He felt stupid as he licked the driver's license. He drove back out to the main road and started looking at the businesses that obviously sold cars. He saw several pick-ups of the same model he was driving but in various different colors. He saw a nice silver truck with black trim that was in much better shape and looked newer than the one he was driving. A sign on the front showed $22,500. He was shocked by the amount. That was a fortune in his time but with the number of trucks he had seen that were just like the one he was driving it must be affordable somehow. He stopped again behind a small hotel down the street. For the first time he started counting the cash that he'd picked up from the drug makers.

He counted $134,312.00. He should be rich with that but if a pick-up cost $22,500 then he probably couldn't even buy a house with the full amount. It seemed crazy that so much would buy so little. He took $25,000 in $100 bills and stuffed them into the saddle bags. He locked the truck and walked over to the car lot where the silver truck was. He walked up and began looking at the inside. It was a very nice pick-up.

"Civil War re-enactor?" a voice spoke behind him. He'd heard the man approach and turned to see what he was sure was a fat lazy-looking salesman. He was right. There was that gleam in his eye that all salesmen seemed to have when they sensed a mark. He would have to watch this one.

"Yup." He replied not really sure what a're-enactor' was.

"We don't get much of that around here. Doin' shows in Vegas are ya?"

"Tell me about the truck, sir" Stewart said changing the subject.

"Well you picked a good one; it's a 2006 Lariat, low miles, one owner, guy who owned it was a rodeo man who lost his butt in a casino one night and really needed some cash. It's loaded with all the bells and whistles; leather seats, lift kit, big tires and shiny rims. One nice truck and a steal at twenty-two five, I'll tell ya." The fat man stopped for a breath. He was definitely a salesman.

"Anything wrong with it" Stewart asked looking the man in the eye.

"Not a thing, sir. Just has that big V-10 in it that uses a lot of gas that folks don't like much. Lots of power though. You'll pass anything but a gas station. It does have dual tanks though. I think it holds about 60 gallons total. Here let me start it up for you." The fat man climbed up and opened the truck door, reached in and turned the key. A powerful roar came from the truck and then dropped to a low rumble.

Stewart had seen no deception in the man and decided that he was telling the truth about the fuel consumption. He liked the power and wasn't worried about the money for fuel as gasoline was about $1.40 per gallon. He could buy a lot of fuel for what he had left. He let the man show him around the big rig and he insisted on showing Stewart the mileage on the odometer. 16,318. Very low, he said, for a two-year-old truck. It seemed like a lot of miles to Stewart but the 'bots assured him it was very low.

"So what can I do for you today to get you to sign the papers on this baby, Mr…uh…" the salesman pitched.

"Foster. Greg Foster. You can fill it with gas and sell it to me for twenty thousand, even" Stewart replied.

"Mr. Foster, Bill Wilson." He said as he shook hands with Stewart. "Now look, I can't go down that much Greg. Let's go in the office and see what we can work out…"

"Let's settle right here or I'll go down the street and buy that blue one I saw. Twenty thousand, cash." Stewart eyed the old man.

"Cash?"

"Cash."

"You hit it big on the slots or somethin'?" Wilson asked.

"Something like that."

"How 'bout twenty one, five?" Wilson pressed.

"Twenty one, not a penny more." Stewart haggled.

"Done! Let's do the paperwork!" Wilson seemed pleased and shook Stewart's hand once again.

Stewart was pleased as well because he would have paid the full amount if need be and it wasn't really his money anyway. He knew that it was best not to be too eager with a horse trader from any era. They walked inside and Stewart enjoyed a very good cup of coffee while the chubby car man did all the paperwork. Stewart wanted to be as legal a possible so he asked Wilson for a good insurance firm. Of course his brother, David just happened to own a local Farmer's Insurance agency. Wilson made a call to his brother and after a few minutes and a check of his driver's license number (which went through clean. He would have to ask the

'Bots how they did that later) he had a liability policy required by the state of Nevada.

He paid for the truck and drove it over to the small insurance agency and paid Bill's equally chubby brother the $893.00 for the first six months premiums. He took the rather expensive papers and placed them in the glove box of his new truck. He then filled the truck with gas as Bill had not included that in the deal. Bill had simply handed him back $100 rather than actually fill the truck up for him. Stewart came out ahead on that one spending only $78 on gas. He then drove back to the hotel and cleaned out the other truck, transferring the contents to the new one. There he left it with the key on the floor and unlocked. Maybe someone else would borrow it and move it further away from where he'd left it. The more the vehicle was separated from him, the better. He pointed the shiny new (well, almost new) truck once again north on US 95 and headed once again for Idaho. He liked the new truck and he really was beginning to like this modern America he had found himself in.

Doc was beside himself. All of his computer simulations had failed to produce a reasonable approximation of the whereabouts of the Captain. Maybe he should have asked his name. No, that was against protocols. He racked his brain in his broken ship. The police officers had laughed at the money he'd tried to bribe them with. The paper he'd manufactured was apparently very wrong and was an obvious forgery to anyone in this time period. He couldn't even buy the things he needed for repairs. So much for his brilliant research. He looked again at the map of the area and the track left by the Captain as he'd made his escape. He was heading north, away from the populated areas. It made no sense to him. Why, if he were trying to escape from him, would he not go to the city and try to blend in with the masses. That would be what any criminal would do.

He was missing something that must be obvious here, he was sure of it. What would I do if I were a crazed lunatic killer from the past in a future that I had no concept of and no frame of reference for? The culture shock alone should be enough to drive such a primitive man insane. Maybe this is why he killed those men in the trailer. He thought about the gruesome scene and wondered what the authorities must be thinking of the grisly murder. He suddenly realized that he could monitor local transmissions for that sort of information.

"Computer! Scan all frequencies for transmissions of criminal events in the past 10 hours in the immediate area. Use a radius of 150 miles," he ordered.

Several broadcasts came up including one about an African American suspect who shot his way out of jail in Clark County and was last seen heading north in a black Lincoln Mk VIII. He groaned and rolled his eyes. Finally a small story came up about a local family of drug dealers murdered, presumably by a rival drug gang, in a trailer found in the desert. Drug Dealers? Doc looked back at the map. The Captain had wandered straight into their camp and was probably unaware of what he'd stumbled upon. No wonder he'd killed all of them, he probably hadn't had a choice or they would surely have killed him.

Doc stared now with new understanding. He looked again at the Captain's path through the desert. It was amazingly straight for a man on foot with no navigation equipment. He took the centerline of the path and drew it out further. The line passed very close to Boise, Idaho. It seemed that he was heading right back to where Doc had found him in the first place. Why? Who could know? But it seemed obvious now. And that was what he'd been missing, wasn't it?

Stewart was tired. He could feel the 'Bots working to keep him alert but it was becoming very clear that he needed some rest. He had pressed on but decided to stop when he saw a nice looking hotel in Caldwell, Idaho and checked into a room. They wanted something called a 'credit card' to rent him a room but he came up with enough cash to get them to drop the issue. He decided after more of the 'Civil War re-enactor' comments that he needed a new change of clothing. He would find something first thing in the morning. He walked up to his room and dropped his gear on the floor after figuring out the card lock mechanism. All those guns were heavy but he hated to leave them in the truck. He needed a better bag for them as well. He was still using an old blanket that he'd found in the trailer.

He was very impressed with the room. It was clean with nice furniture and even some nice artwork on the wall. Various cowboy pictures were spaced all around the room. He walked into the toilet room and was shocked. After working all of the devices in the small room and deciding that he knew what each was for, he also decided that he liked modern indoor plumbing. He'd heard of it before of course but had never actually seen it. It had become common in the big cities on the East Coast in his day but he was sure that this was much better. He spent over an hour washing the grime off of his body and out of his hair. There was even some pretty smelling stuff to wash his hair with. It wasn't all that manly but he decided that he wouldn't be meeting anyone who mattered anyway.

He felt incredibly refreshed after bathing in the running shower and the sheets on the bed felt so crisp and clean that he just jumped into bed buck naked. He fell instantly asleep and stayed that way until sun-up.

He woke in the morning and realized that he'd slept late. It must be after nine o'clock he thought. He looked around the room and saw the red numbered clock that read 8:32. Well, that was still pretty late for him. He looked around the room and suddenly decided that he wasn't really in hurry. He would stay one more night and spend the day here in Caldwell, just for the hell of it. He would have to find a way to get a credit card though. He wasn't sure how to do that yet. He suddenly had a thought.

"Hey 'Bots."

"Yes sir."

"How did you fix my driver's license number yesterday?"

"We had data on all driver registrations in Nevada in 1999. There was a Greg D. Foster in Las Vegas. We simply used his license number. He is not a known criminal or currently sought by any law-enforcement agency... as of 1999 of course." the 'Bots efficiently replied.

"You guys are clever. I'll need to be more careful in the future, I was sweating bullets for a few minutes." Stewart sounded relieved. He rolled out of bed and looked at his shabby clothing lying in the chair nearby. They didn't smell very good and had numerous stains on them, only some of which he could even remember what they were. He was also hungry but he would have to find some clothing soon. He stopped at the front desk and asked directions from the young lady to a nearby clothing store. She smiled and suggested a western apparel store just down the street. He thanked her and went ahead and paid for the next night's rent. He then climbed into the truck and drove down the street to the store. He could clearly see the store from the hotel and it was an easy walk but he was feeling self-conscious about his clothing now. He didn't want to attract too much more attention.

The store was closed until nine but a nearby restaurant wasn't. A little place called Denny's was located just a few hundred feet from the store. He went inside and waited to be seated as the little sign said in the foyer. A short, plump, middle-aged woman with a friendly smile greeted him and led him over to a small table. She set the menu on the place closest to the door but old habit made him pick it up and seat himself facing the door. He didn't like unpleasant surprises. He looked around and suddenly felt uncomfortable when he realized that he was the only one carrying guns. Not too common anymore, he thought.

He ordered a big breakfast with chicken-fried steak, eggs, hash browns and pancakes with coffee and orange juice. It was one the best meals he'd ever had and he finished every last bite. A couple of local law men came in and sat down across the room. Stewart knew that he stood out in his outfit so he tried to act casual. He saw them look him over several times. He finished his meal, paid the check and left the nice lady a five for the tip. That was a lot of money in his time but it didn't seem like so much now.

He walked by the officers on the way out when one of them spoke up.

"Where you from, mister?" the officer asked.

"Sir?" Stewart replied.

"Well, I'm more concerned where you're going dressed like that with all that hardware on your hips." The officer was smiling and didn't have his hand on his gun. It was obvious that he was trying to be inquisitive but non-threatening.

"Well, I sort of left my luggage in my friend's vehicle and I almost forgot I was wearing them." Stewart said, not quite lying. "I guess I should have left them in the truck. Is there a law against it here, sir?"

106

"No sir. This is Idaho; open-carry law. It's just that most folks don't bring them into restaurants around here. What state are you from?" The officer still kept it friendly but was obviously trying to sort out something that he wasn't accustomed to.

"Texas originally, sir. I live in Winnemucca now. I know about the open-carry law I just thought maybe Caldwell had passed a city ordinance or something." He was really juggling the truth now so he decided to cut it short. "I'll be sure to be more socially sensitive in the future officer, good day gentlemen."

Stewart calmly walked out of the restaurant and casually climbed into the truck. He felt the stare of the officers without even looking at them. He made a little show of removing his pistol belt and placing it in the center console of the truck before starting it up and slowly driving out of the parking lot. He made a complete stop and turned down the street and just as slowly turned back into the clothing store parking lot. He pulled his worn Confederate Jacket off and placed it in the back seat. For the first time in his life he was embarrassed to be wearing it. The store was open now so he sauntered inside to shop for some new duds.

He came out about an hour later with two new pairs of boots, one on his feet, six pairs of pants, six shirts, a couple of new belts, three new luggage bags, a bunch of socks, boxer shorts and undershirts. The pants were all jeans except half were blue and half were black. The shirts were all different colors but his favorite was a gray, double breasted shirt that reminded him of his uniform. The young lady in the store was very helpful (another salesman) and seemed to like everything he did a little too much but he could tell when she was laying it on and when she was actually impressed. He was wearing a pair of black jeans with black boots and the gray shirt now. He also bought a small brimmed cowboy hat made out of gray rabbit's felt. He felt like he looked pretty good. He only needed a shave and a hair cut to complete the package, which he made his next stop.

Doc flew his ship to a small valley north of Boise where he hid it in a small clearing in the forest. He had the ship re-configure his vehicle to look like a 2000 GMC Yukon, which would fit into the local area well, he thought. It would also enable him to drive out of the woods without looking like an idiot who might take a

Lincoln Mark VIII off-road. It proved to be a good choice as the drive out was pretty rough. The Captain had probably left something of value near the spot he'd been picked up but he was sure that the man would stop in Boise first before heading into the back country. He had learned from other broadcasts that a pick-up belonging to one of the dead drug dealers had been found in Winnemucca so it appeared that the Captain had somehow figured out how to drive. He was becoming a surprising adversary for someone from such a primitive era. He would have to be more careful in the future and not risk under-estimating the Captain again.

He still needed a way to purchase or, if necessary, steal the items to repair his ship. He wasn't certain how he was going to do that but for now his main mission was to find his lost charge. Without the Captain in his custody, it would be best for him to never return to his own time, though the ITMS would search for him and would eventually find him. He didn't want to imagine what they would do to him then. This was all a huge mess. He remembered his father's strange speech to him the night before he left on this nightmare mission.

"You need to learn to have faith," he had said. "You will find true understanding, beyond simple knowledge if you just learn to have faith."

Faith in what? He thought. He was only feeling intense frustration and futility. He didn't know how to feel faith. That had always been his problem as everyone had told him throughout his life. He had no faith. He studied all the wisdom and knowledge of the ages and he was a failure because he had no faith. It seemed obvious to everyone else but ridiculous to him. The overwhelming sense of inadequacy and failure poured over him as his drove down the winding road to the Treasure Valley. He had one small hope left. He could detect Nanobots from several miles away with some of his equipment.

It would be hard to find the Captain out there to be sure but the signal from his Nanobots would give him away eventually. Without them being shut down and being disconnected from the mainframe, the Nanobots in the Captain would go into preservation mode and begin reproducing. Each generation would be more powerful and greater in number until they reached the saturation point of his system. The resulting signal would also be much stronger but if he learned how to use them properly, the Captain could become an even deadlier adversary than he already was.

Chapter Eleven

Stewart was enjoying shopping though he felt a little guilty at benefitting from the drug maker's ill-gotten gains. He found a big store that carried guns and accessories where he bought proper cases for all of the guns and ammunition he'd collected. He also found a really nice wrist-watch that was gold-plated. The idea of a bracelet watch would have been effeminate in his own time period but all the men of this period seemed to wear them. He still stood out a bit in his new clothes but not as much. He soon realized that the standard wear of the day was a T-shirt, jeans and sneakers. He bought a couple of T-shirts at the store as well as some very comfortable and light-weight sneakers which didn't look too dumb. They were white and blue and pretty bright for his tastes but he wanted to at least try to fit in.

He'd also found a nice black, leather jacket which would help on the chilly northwest nights he remembered. It also helped to hide the Kimbers that he decided to keep close by in the fancy hidden shoulder holsters that he'd bought as well. The only thing he was missing was a decent knife which he didn't buy simply because he didn't like what he saw of the mainly folding knives the store had. He just wanted a good solid knife with a good blade. He didn't trust a folding knife to hold up under the rugged abuse he was used to putting a blade through. He went by a large electronics store and bought a rather expensive laptop computer recommended by the 'bots so that he could 'surf the net' and actually see things that he couldn't find out from the 'bots due to the limitations that Doc had placed on them.

He felt great. Better than he'd ever remembered feeling in his whole life. He had to keep reminding himself that it was artificially induced by the nanobots but he chose to enjoy it while it lasted. He knew that they'd be taken away or shut down eventually and he really didn't want to live the rest of his life with machines in him anyway. He put off thoughts of what-ifs and decided to focus on the right now. He needed some social time and he'd seen a small bar near the hotel that he could drink at and walk back from if necessary. Since the 'Bots had greatly cautioned him during their extensive driving lecture on the dangers of drinking and driving, he wanted to avoid it at all costs. Mostly he just didn't want to run afoul of the law. The police officers he'd met at Denny's had seemed friendly enough but they looked as if they could be all business when necessary.

He treated himself to a large steak dinner at a local steak house and then he strolled over to the bar after freshening up with some new-found hygiene products like deodorant and aftershave. His beard was now a much neater and more stylish goatee thanks a nice young blond lady at the Supercuts. His hair he wasn't so sure about though. She assured him that it was very much in style now. She said it made him look like Keith Urban, whoever the hell that was. It still looked kind of wild and strange to him though.

He walked into the bar and was instantly disappointed. It was all men except for two fat women with dates in the corner. Well, he could at least get a drink and celebrate being alive and not being mind-wiped yet. He stepped up to a vacant spot at the bar and waited for the bartender to come by. He suddenly realized that he really didn't know what to order. He looked over the back of the bar and saw numerous bottles of alcohol and beer and he suddenly felt like a greenhorn in a saloon for the first time. It wasn't something he'd done much of in the past but he wasn't a stranger to it either. He was lost in thought when the bartender, a humorless old man, finally walked up and asked, "What'll it be buddy?"

"What would you recommend, sir?"

"Well, um, what are you doing? Celebrating or forgetting?" he replied.

"Celebrating, I don't want to forget anything," Stewart said, thinking of being mind-wiped.

"Okay, got a special going on Mai Tais; five dollars until ten. It'll make you think you're naked on a beach in Hawaii. That's celebrating, isn't it?" the bartender said flatly.

"Yeah, I guess it would be. How much are they normally?" Stewart inquired.

"Seven fifty."

"Okay, let me try one."

The bartender rolled his eyes and turned to make the drink. Stewart looked around. It wasn't a very exciting place and most people just sat quietly and drank while a few had quiet conversations. Some kind of music was playing in the background but Stewart obviously didn't know it. It was a strange song that kept saying something about a hotel in California. One guy in the corner by the pool table was singing with it and apparently pretending to play an instrument of some kind on a pool cue. The whole recorded music thing had fascinated Stewart at first especially while driving in the truck but he was getting used to it. He decided it wasn't a bad song though he didn't understand the words much and couldn't figure out what instruments could possibly create those sounds. It was a strange and haunting tune with intricate strings and powerful rhythms in parts.

He drank his Mai Tai and indeed it did taste like a celebratory drink, full of fruity flavors and just a mild kick. It went down very smoothly and since he felt no ill effects he decided that it must a mild alcoholic beverage. He ordered another. He realized vaguely after the third that they were much stronger than they appeared but he had ceased to care somehow. He imagined himself on a beach in Hawaii, wherever that was, sipping these with his beautiful Julie, naked on the beach, just the two of them with no stupid world with wars and slavery and human ignorance or insecurity to screw it all up.

An old black man was sitting at the bar and moved to the stool next to him.

"You seem to be celebrating tonight, my friend." He spoke in a deep, cultured voice.

"I am." Stewart replied, a little slurred.

"What might you be celebrating? Maybe I could join you."

"Being alive and not being mind-wiped!" Stewart said emphatically.

"Well then, that certainly is something to celebrate. Here's to being alive and not being mind-wiped." The old man raised his glass and Stewart obligingly clinked it with his own.

"Living I understand, my friend. Mind-wiped I don't but it doesn't sound pleasant and I'm sure that would be something to be avoided, if possible."

"It's a horrible thing," Stewart explained in a slurred voice. "They make you forget all the stuff they put you through and then send you back where they got you from."

"Maybe If I get as drunk as you are, it will begin to make sense to me. My name is John. John Fonseca. Whom might I have the privilege of conversing with?" Fonseca's voice was low and calming as he offered his hand.

"Um, St-Foster, Greg Foster," he said as he shook Fonseca's hand.

"So who wants to wipe your mind, Greg?"

"The Doc from the future; he wants to take me back to the future where he's from to mind-wipe me and then take me back to past where I'm from where I'll then be killed by a bunch of Nez Perce Indians!"

"Wow, this is getting good. Bartender! Another round over here on my tab, he's got a great story going and I'm in the mood to get drunk enough to believe it!"

"Right away Doctor Fonseca," the bartender replied in monotone.

"Okay, now tell me the whole story, Greg," Fonseca calmly persuaded Stewart.

Stewart began to tell him his whole incredible story. Fonseca cross-examined him and checked his facts and timeline throughout. He continued asking probing questions and nodded continuously to keep him going. After about two hours the bar was closing and the two men were the only patrons left in the establishment. Fonseca stood and paid his tab at the bartender's prodding and stumbled outside with Stewart into the cool night air. They continued talking for a while and Stewart began to sober up quickly with some help from the 'Bots. Turning to Fonseca he said suddenly,

"You think I'm crazy, don't you?"

"Let me explain something, Greg. I have a PhD in psychology, a PhD in archaeology, and a PhD in Anthropology and a Master's degree in Electrical Engineering. People think I'm crazy for the things I believe which some might lump into the same category as your story. I may be an old washed-up drunk but I can still tell when a man is sincere. Your story is one that you firmly believe and is incredible mostly in its consistency. It would make a fantastic movie, I would think. Whether it's all true, only you know for sure. I am simply grateful to you for your honest delivery of an amazing story that has kept me entertained all evening and spared me from another dull night of drunken boredom and stupidity. You have honestly made me think about some things

113

with this story of yours. I find your theory of time travel particular intriguing as it is the only one I have ever heard that makes any sense. I applaud you sir, whether you are delusional or not." Fonseca swayed as he finished with a slight clap that was at least a little genuine.

"Well, those nanobots I told you about? They've cleaned out the alcohol in my system now and I'm actually quite sober. I feel like a blithering idiot now. How could I possibly expect anyone to believe me?" Stewart slumped against the wall of the hotel.

"Well I'm still drunk so maybe you can convince me. Show me what these nanobots of yours can do, Greg." Fonseca's eyes were glazed over but they were brightly lit in wonder. Stewart suddenly realized that he *wanted* to believe him. He thought for a moment.

"Do you have a piece of paper handy, something fairly clean preferably," Stewart didn't relish the idea of licking something filthy to get his 'Bots back. Fonseca dug around in a pocket and pulled out a small silver tin. He opened it and offered Stewart a small card.

"How about one of my business cards, Greg? Will that do?" Fonseca offered.

"Yes, that will be fine. Bots! Get enough into my saliva to draw a picture on the card."

"Yes sir," the 'Bots replied. Stewart was sure only he could hear them. He spit lightly on the card and said, "Now draw a picture of Mr. Fonseca here."

He held the card back to Fonseca and let him watch as a perfect image of Fonseca's face appeared on the back of the card. When they were finished Stewart licked the card to recover them and handed it back Fonseca.

"Sorry for the spit, John but I don't know how else to do that," he said.

Fonseca stood in amazement. He teetered back and forth staring in fascination at his own image now indelibly burned into the card. He could even smell smoke faintly.

"Incredible! If I hadn't seen it with my own eyes I wouldn't believe it." He looked up at Stewart and said, "My friend, you have got to tell me more about yourself."

"I think I have said too much already, maybe you should tell me about *your*self now." Stewart replied.

"Well here, first take another card," he said handing Stewart another. "I want to keep this one if you don't mind and I want you to be able to contact me if you ever need any help. Anything, just name it, like how to dial a phone or how to flush a toilet or how to build rockets to the moon, anything at all!"

"Why would you do that for me, John? I'm a complete stranger to you."

"No, no, no, you are *much* more than that, my friend. You sir, are proof! Living proof that all is not what it seems and that this mad old scientist may be one of the few sane people left on the planet! None of my discoveries or theories really point to your situation but it ties many of them together; Lost civilizations, ancient 'alien' visitations, evidence of human sophistication that pre-dates all of history. There are so many holes in our past and modern science has chosen to plug them with oddball half-theories and superstitious nonsense instead of truly investigating the evidence objectively without bias and pre-suppositions! I'm not sober and I'm drunk enough to believe you even if you do turn out to simply be the best Las Vegas magician I have ever seen. What the hell Greg, it sure beats being alone in the world labeled a crackpot! As one crackpot to another, and believe me I know a crackpot when I see one, welcome to my very tiny club, Greg!" he finished with a slap on the back which was once again, Stewart's wounded shoulder. Stewart flinched as the old familiar pain stung him; the 'Bots had obviously not made any progress on that yet.

Stewart woke up in his hotel room late that morning. He was refreshed despite the large amounts of alcohol and late hour to which he and Fonseca had spoken. He agreed to meet him again today at his office at the local community college. Fonseca was eager to ask him more questions and show him some of his own discoveries. Stewart was eager to get on the road to Boise where he intended to set up a base of operations for the search for his lost gold. He had mentioned none of the gold or even the incident with the drug makers to Fonseca. He felt that that would be going too far and was surprised he managed to keep it all in despite the fact that he even bared his soul about Julie. His heart ached again at the thought of her. He really needed to heal and move past that in his life. There was nothing he could do could to save her or bring her back and everything happens for a reason, he thought.

He ate a lighter breakfast this morning again at Denny's and drove to the address on the card Fonseca gave him. It wasn't far as Caldwell was a small town but it was a nice and very modern looking campus. He found the old man's office and knocked on the door.

"Just a moment please," was the response in the familiar deep voice. He could hear hushed talking inside with a young female voice. He couldn't make it out very well but suddenly the 'Bots turned up the sound for him and he heard a sweet young voice making very sexual suggestions to Fonseca if he would help her with her grade. He could hear the old man politely and gently rejecting her to the young ladies apparent disgust. She became more furious with each exchange as the old man patronized her in that smooth, deep voice.

"Enough!" he whispered. "Turn my hearing back to normal!"

Instantly he was unable to hear the words within the room but he secretly chuckled at the conversation. Within a few minutes the door flew open and a very attractive, although tastelessly dressed, young lady came out the office in a rage. He saw Fonseca standing behind his desk waving and smiling at her back.

"Feel free to come and talk to me at anytime Miss Titus. Anytime," He said as she stormed off muttering obscenities.

"Come on in, Greg! Glad you could make it." Stewart walked in smiling and shook the old man's hand.

"I couldn't help but overhear some your conversation..." he began as he closed the door.

"The nanobots help you hear through walls too?" Fonseca asked.

"Well, yes but it wasn't intentional. They sometimes do things that they think I want them to do without me actually having to ask them. It's kind of scary at times but they've generally been very well behaved for me."

"Good. Nothing worse than machines behaving badly in your own body, I'm sure." He pulled out the card again and looked at. "It's like a photograph the quality is so good. Tell me, can you sacrifice a few for my observation?"

"Bots? Can I?" He inquired.

"Yes," the tinny reply came.

"They say 'yes'"

"Excellent. See this glass slide? I just want a small sample on it so I can view them through my microscope. The glass is clean, I assure you." Fonseca smiled as Stewart sheepishly put his tongue to the small glass plate.

"There," Fonseca said as he turned toward the small microscope on the counter behind him. He placed the plate on the device and began focusing knobs. It was small but it looked very complicated and expensive.

"One of the best in the world this little baby," Fonseca spoke as if he had read Stewart's thoughts, "I had it imported from Switzerland many years ago. There we are now. Oh my!" His mouth dropped open as he stared at the tiny mechanical creatures. "These are incredible! So intricate and complicated in design yet very efficient looking. And you say these are low-grade devices?"

"Yes sir. That's according the other black doctor I've met recently. I much prefer your company though. You're more likable." Stewart added.

"Experience versus education, Greg. I got the former before the latter which usually makes one a little wiser." He stood up from the microscope and looked at Stewart. "I was once a soldier too, Greg. Vietnam. I was a combat medic in the Twenty Fifth Infantry Division in the Mekong Delta. I did more than bandage wounds though. I killed a lot of those gook bastards because they would have killed me if I hadn't. I know a man who's been under fire when I see one and you've seen more that I have. At least I got medals for my service even if I didn't have the appreciation of my country. You got even less. I can't help but feel your pain in that."

"I'm not one that's much for sympathy, John..." Stewart started.

"I know that and I'm not offering any because that would insult you as it would me. I only offer understanding from a fellow brother in arms. Enough said." He turned briskly back to the microscope and began taking down the slide sample. "Can I keep these?" He asked as he put the sample away.

"Bots?" Stewart checked.

"Yes, but they will deactivate in time without a host."

"They say it's okay but they'll quit working after a time."

"I assumed that," Fonseca said nodding. "No problem. I just want to study their function and compare them to other devices I know of. I'm sure that I could not possibly reproduce them."

The two sat down and talked again for hours, this time as if they were old friends. Stewart felt that he was talking to a combination of Julie, Cecil, Sergeant Major Williams, and a whole new-found friend at once. They spoke of religion extensively and Stewart was a little surprised that Fonseca was a man of faith in God although he had many questions. Fonseca explained simply that one cannot survive mortal combat with other human beings and not recognize the miracles that God does in the midst of the chaos of war. Stewart had to agree. Fonseca filled him in on many aspects of modern America while Stewart explained modern fallacies about the Civil War and other aspects of the nineteenth century. Fonseca explained how Stewart could get established and gain a credit card by opening a bank account.

"I already have a bank account," Stewart said.

"You do? When did you open it?" Fonseca asked curiously.

"1866."

Fonseca's eyebrows went up. "With how much money?"

"A little over four hundred dollars."

Fonseca leaned over and began working the keys on his computer. He stopped after a moment and stared. "My god, you're rich!"

"I am?"

"I'm not really good at compound interest equations but you should be worth over five million dollars, if I'm not mistaken. That's assuming that the account is still open, the bank didn't fail during the Great Depression and providing that you can somehow prove that you have a legal right to it. All very big 'ifs' if you ask me. It's certainly enough to look into it though. Tell me something, you didn't by any chance buy any stocks over a hundred years ago, did you?" Fonseca was getting very interested in this now. Wealth was exciting to him regardless of whose wealth it was.

"Well, now that you mention it, I do have a couple of certificates that I bought from guy in Boise once in sixty-nine while I was on a supply run. Something called New York Gas Light Company. I felt funny about it at the time but he cornered me saying it would be really valuable some day and he really needed the money. I bought some just to get rid of him," Stewart reflected back.

"New York Gas Light Company? I think that's Con-Edison! Please tell me you bought a lot of it!" Fonseca's eyes were popping out of his skull with excitement.

"Well I was feeling kind of rich at the time having just cashed in some gold dust so I guess I bought about two hundred dollars worth. It was about twenty cents a share, if I remember right and I just bought the stack in his hand because he was pestering me something awful. I felt like a greenhorn sap afterward."

"If you still have those in your possession, you are a multi-millionaire and I like having rich friends!" He reached across and looked into his eyes. "Tell me you still have those certificates!"

Stewart was getting a little spooked by all this excitement and said, "Do you need money John? Is that why you like rich friends?"

"Nooo! I have my own millions from books, patents, and mineral rights. I've been rich since I was about thirty years old. Constantly working on building a fortune was a great distraction from remembering Vietnam. I really just teach now for fun. No, I just hate poor friends that always leave me paying the check!" He began to laugh. Stewart had to join him with that.

"They're in the truck. Tell me what I need to do with them."

"Let's start with your real name and go from there."

John Fonseca watched through his window as the tall Civil Warrior left in his pick-up. When Stewart had driven out of the parking lot he reached back to the shelf and retrieved the slide with Stewart's saliva and stared at it for a moment. It was dry now but he knew that they were still there. He made his decision and after he had licked the slide thoroughly, he returned it to its place on the shelf and calmly went back to work on his computer, feeling just a little ashamed.

Doc was really beside himself now. He had scoured the entire valley for the past two days and couldn't find a trace of the Captain. He did surprise one old time traveler who he discovered was working in the area. The man recognized his own nanobot's signature and ran him out of the small automotive repair shop that he was working in, warning Doc to mind his own mission and never return. He resorted to walking the streets at night to see if maybe he could stumble upon the Captain. He thought of the ways he may have been able to shut down the nanobots completely. The only method he knew to be effective was electrocution, which would require a suicidal jolt of Alternating Current. The Captain seemed crazy to him but he certainly didn't appear suicidal. He had a small stroke of luck in finding a one dollar bill on the ground and he was able to accurately reproduce over a hundred copies. This time though, he made sure that all of the serial numbers were different from each other. People took them from him for payment without issue except for one waiter at a restaurant who commented on him 'just coming from the strip club.' He had no idea what that meant and ignored the comment. The waiter apparently thought it was funny though. He had to run constant body cleanses with the Nanobots from all the pollution he was eating and breathing. This made him have several stressful moments looking for a public toilet facility which were surprisingly hard to find as most businesses had signs stating, 'restrooms for customers only' or something to that effect.

Doc would frequently go up into the hills and try scanning for the Captain until the cranky old mechanic finally sent a nano-blast at him telling him to stop scanning him. He went back to his ship and sent out a small, hidden drone that began searching the valley for him while he rested in the ship. He was careful not to include the area around the mechanic's shop in the pattern. He didn't need any more grief from that guy. He woke up the next day so depressed that he resorted to something he had deemed pointless long ago. He began to pray.

Stewart was beaming he was so pleased. Fonseca had helped him set up accounts under his own name, had helped him find a good unused Idaho Driver's license number without conflicting with any real Stewarts and had further helped him get a

Social Security Number, which was apparently necessary for all sorts of identity issues. He also helped him rent a nice apartment in Caldwell, which gave him a real address and a place to store some of the guns and clothing he had accumulated. They ordered nice furniture for the place and the company came and set it all up complete with video and stereo equipment. Stewart had spent tens of thousands of dollars now, counting the truck. The best part was that he now had over eighteen million dollars available in various accounts including one in the Cayman Islands, wherever that was.

The disappointing part was that he had paid about two million dollars in 'capital gains tax' when he sold his very valuable stocks. Fonseca assured him that the capital gains tax was much better than the personal income tax which would have been almost half. It turned out that with all the splits in stocks and growth over that last 135 years, his stock was ultimately valued at just over twenty million dollars. Con-Edison itself bought the stock from him presumably because they were the oldest known stock certificates in existence. The whole transaction took six long days but he was now independently wealthy and lacked nothing that he could ever really need. He told Fonseca that he wanted to personally track down the old bank account in Boise and so he drove to Boise in the pick-up he'd become so fond of.

He had made a reservation at the Red Lion Downtowner with an expensive penthouse suite for his stay but that was his limit on frivolities. It was much nicer than he'd imagined and the room was so high up that he felt a little giddy standing next to the windows. After settling into the room, he then he went down to the Ada County Clerk's office and tried to find someone to help him with his search for the bank. He paid a twenty five dollar fee and was told that they would send him a response by mail in within sixty days. A very frustrated Stewart then went to the Boise Public Library and began trying to find any information on the bank which held his lost account. He was having trouble understanding where to start so he went up to the help counter and stood in line to speak one of the librarians. When it came his turn he stepped up to counter holding the old bank book and said, "Yes ma'am, I…"

His draw dropped as he looked at the young woman behind the counter.

"Yes sir, how may I help you?" she asked in the sweetest voice he had ever heard.

He was dumbstruck. The woman was small, about five feet three inches tall with a slender build in a very flattering hunter green dress suit. She was obviously mixed African American, had long wavy black hair with red highlights, smooth dark skin, and the most amazing *green eyes* he had ever seen!

Chapter Twelve

"Sir! May I help you?" the young woman asked again as she crossed her arms and stared back at him with an irritated look.

Stewart quickly regained his composure and apologized. "I'm very sorry miss, it's just that you are possibly the most beautiful woman I have ever seen in my life and I honestly wasn't expecting that when I walked up here just now."

She actually smiled and blushed! "Oh stop please! Just tell me what you need sir, I'm here to help and flattery will just get you just about anywhere." Stewart shot a glance at her left hand and made a quick note of the vacant ring finger. She caught the glance and looked back in genuine surprise.

"Well young lady, what I *need* is for you to have dinner with me tonight when you get off work but what I came up here for was some help tracking down this old bank record." Stewart just decided he was not going to be shy with this one. She was something special, maybe even that special one. Too early to tell yet but it wasn't looking bad so far.

"Sir, I can't just go to dinner with any stranger who walks into the library. I would never have any time for my fifteen cats then, would I?" She was teasing him and she was enjoying the little game. He looked around and noticed that no one was waiting behind him.

"My name's Greg, and if you have fifteen cats I will kiss each and every one of them, on the lips if you like." He held out the booklet to her.

"A man who calls my bluff; I'm impressed Greg. My name is Cynthia and I don't have any cats, as you already know. You may call me Cindi and I get off work in an hour and a half which I'm sure is about how long it is going to take me to personally help you find your little lost bank record." She gently took the book from his hand giving him a little rub in the process and then gave him a nice little strut to follow as she led him back into the research stacks.

What are you doin', girl? She scolded herself. She didn't even know this guy and she had let him charm her into a dinner date. She didn't even like white guys and here she was playing cat

123

and mouse with one of the most dangerous looking men she'd ever laid eyes on. There was something in his eyes. She was generally unimpressed with him except for those pale gray eyes that looked right through her and seemed to read her soul. She saw pain, heartache, danger and a depth of love and passion that she had never seen in a man's eyes before. It was as if she *knew* him. The look she saw in his eyes when he first looked at her was the look that she wanted her man to look at her with everyday for the rest of her life!

She'd quit looking for a man months ago and had decided that they were all insecure pansies looking for someone to be their momma. This man? This man was no pansy at all. He looked, acted, smelled like, and breathed like pure man, and she liked it! She worked hard to maintain a professional demeanor while she helped him find a record of the old bank and its accounts. She also made it take over an hour as well which was difficult for her because she was very hot and bothered by this man's presence.

It was taking longer than it should but Stewart didn't mind. Every moment with Cindi was sweet ecstasy. He could feel his heart pounding in his chest. He felt the longing to reach out and take her in his arms. He pushed it all back down and focused on the task at hand. In due time, he thought; all in due time. Cindi was finally able to find records that tracked down the old bank. It had closed during the Great Depression and never re-opened. The account was long gone.

"Too bad," she said. "It could have been worth a lot of money by now."

"Yes. Too bad," Stewart repeated. He really could care less about the account right now so in keeping with his direct approach he asked her the thing that was most concerning him now.

"So, what are you hungry for?"

She looked up and him and smiled with her brilliant smile and his heart melted.

"Chinese?" She asked timidly.

"Oh, a cheap date! I can do that too, sweetie." Stewart gently brushed her cheek with his hand as she blushed yet again.

He met her outside after she helped close up the library. The big silver pick-up waited behind his large frame. She wore a light pink jacket with matching knit mittens which she waved at him when she saw him. She rolled her eyes as she walked down the steps to the behemoth vehicle and hid her face in her mittens and said, "I can't believe I'm doing this, I can't *believe* I'm doing this."

"Doing what?" he asked.

"Going out with a cowboy I don't even know in his big, huge red-neck mobile!" She smiled nervously at him in the dimming light. He understood.

"You know me. I'm Greg, remember? From the library this evening? Little lost bank account? That guy." He smiled back and she hit him in the chest with her mittens.

"Oh come on, silly. Let's go." She giggled. He opened the big door for her and held her hand as she climbed up into the cab. He made sure she was all inside and he closed the door. As he climbed up into his side he asked, "So what exactly is a 'red-neck mobile, Cindi?" She loved the way he said her name.

"Oh you know, one of these big ol' trucks with the big tires that you white country boys like to drive."

"Sorry sweetie, but the limo was in the shop. A man's got to use the tools he has readily available." He began driving toward the Chinese restaurant that the 'Bots directed him to.

"Don't call me 'sweetie' I'm not your sweetie..." she murmured.

"Yet. You mean yet, right? So you don't like sweetie?" He teased.

"I didn't say that," she said batting her eyes at him and blushing again.

"I have never seen a black woman blush before and you do it so well."

"Okay now just stop," she pointed a pink mitten at him threateningly as she blushed even more. "That's not funny. Okay so you're a real sweet talking guy with a high-dollar truck that treats me nice, so far, what's the catch?" She asked him

"Catch?"

"You heard me, catch. What's wrong with a handsome, sweet talking guy like you that you don't already have some pretty little white girl all wrapped around you yet. Been in prison? Got a bad disease? Married? Five kids at home with seven legs between them? Child raper? What?"

"Child raper?" Stewart almost retched. Cindi looked at the shocked look on his face and realized this was a very ugly thought in very clean mind.

"I'm sorry," she said. "It just seems that every man I ever date has some major issue and you come traipsing into my library and sweep me off my feet. That only happens in movies and fairy tales. Hell, I didn't even know I liked white men 'til you showed up. So back to the question, what have you been doing that no other woman has snagged you yet? You must be at least thirty. Are you divorced?" She prodded.

"No, never married actually."

"Were you ever engaged?" she continued.

"No Cindi, I was never engaged. In fact I have only met one woman in my life that I ever really considered marrying." He countered.

"Oh really now. What happened to her?" she asked jealously. The very thought of this man with another woman just infuriated her for some reason. Oh dear God, she thought, I *am* his sweetie. She was *already* in love with him.

"I'll let you know how it works out in a couple of years." He smiled over at her. She blushed again and turned toward the window to hide it. She looked back at him and said, "You just have all the right answers don't you, cowboy?"

"Yes ma'am," he replied with that crooked little smile and slight tip of the hat. The cute little bastard! She thought, Lord help me I really am in love with him. Please dear God don't let him break my heart. She felt a warm feeling through her insides suddenly and felt as though a soft voice whispered in her ear, *'he won't.'* She breathed a sigh of relief and felt at peace now as she looked back over at that strong, rugged face lit up by the dash lights and passing cars.

"Can we relax and enjoy each other's company now sweetie?" He asked quietly.

"Yes, Greg. I'm sorry. I'm just a little nervous."

"I understand, I am too. Can we have fun now?" He said gently.

"Yes," she smiled back at him.

"Good. 'Cause we're here." He winked at her as he parked the truck, got out and went over to open her door for her. She saw that look in his eyes that she loved so much as he looked at her through the glass of the door. She smiled and forgot all of her concerns in that moment as he took her hand and helped her out of the truck.

They talked all through dinner. They talked of everything under the sun. Well, mostly Cindi talked.

"I can't believe that I like you so much," she said.

"Why is that?" Stewart replied.

"Well, it's just that... Well..."

"I'm a white man."

"Yes." She replied, obviously embarrassed. "You know we'd be breaking a law if we were having dinner together a hundred years ago."

"I imagine we would. I'm glad that the world has learned to treat all people with respect." Stewart added.

"Well, maybe for the most part, at least here in America. It's still pretty bad in most parts of the world. You're not one of those guys who supports gay marriage are you?" Cindi inquired.

"What's wrong with a gay marriage? Shouldn't all marriages be happy?" Stewart responded.

"No, silly. I mean gay people. Homosexuals?"

"Homo... what?"

"Oh come on, you know men who like men and women who like women. Don't play dumb with me." Cindi admonished.

"Men who like... how can a man, marry another man?" Stewart started getting queasy as he thought about the mechanics of a male on male sexual relationship. "That... that's disgusting."

"Shhhh," Cindi said quietly. "Not so loud, people will hear you and think you're a bigot. I don't like it either, it goes against God's Word but it's becoming a popular idea."

"Why? Marriage is meant to produce a family. How can two men, or two women for that matter, produce a family?" Stewart was dumfounded.

"I know. It's crazy." Cindi replied.

"If a man can marry another man then he could marry two men, or seven, or a horse. Where would it end? It would destroy what it means to be a family. The family is the foundation of any society. Society would die." Stewart seemed mournful as he spoke.

"I've been trying to explain that to my friends at college and they all say *I'm* the one who's ignorant. I'm glad you can think for yourself." Cindi said, obviously relieved.

They talked more about social issues, politics, religion, and all of the things people say you shouldn't talk about in polite company. They agreed on virtually everything though at times Stewart was lost on some of what was 'acceptable' in the modern world. It was as if they had been life-long friends. He was careful to leave out details that would expose his true past. He didn't want to deceive her but he didn't want her to think that he was insane either. They sat in the back of the tiny Chinese restaurant and laughed and simply enjoyed each other's company until it was late. Stewart was just thinking of leaving when a dark figure entered the restaurant and yelled into his mind.

"You almost killed me again you barbarian!" came the cruel thought. Stewart managed to keep his smile but his eyes narrowed visibly.

"Sit down, behave, and order something Doc or I will kill you right now." He pushed back. Doc took a seat on the opposite side and looked straight ahead.

"At least pretend to read the menu, you idiot. The Mandarin Chicken is quite good. I highly recommend it." Just then Cindi's cell phone rang and she looked up at him with sad eyes.

"Do you mind if I take this? It's my mom and I told her I'd call her a while ago but I lost track of time." She asked pleading.

"Please do." He said with a smile secretly thanking God for Cindi's Mom's timing. He continued staring at her beautiful face and smiling while he mentally dueled with Doc.

"Now then, where were we, Doc?"

"You were going to try to kill me again, Captain. You are making the inevitable far too difficult. If I fail to return with you they will send others that are not as forgiving as I am." Doc calmly gave his order to the waitress.

"If you hadn't tried to follow me, you would have never even known of any danger much less been directly exposed to it.

128

Besides, it appears your superior education and intellect saved you from my primitive trap. You look well, Doc." He didn't really. Cindi prattled on with her mother. Stewart smiled and nodded concentrating on the other conversation.

"You will come with me at once and leave here before my food arrives or I will be forced to..." He stopped suddenly as he noticed Stewart's companion. *"Who is she?"* he asked vaguely.

"My fiancé."

"What? She's..."

"Black? Yes, I'd noticed Doc. She's also the most beautiful woman I have ever known and I will marry her one day. You will not interfere."

"I can disable you from here very swiftly, Captain."

"And I am now carrying two of the most accurate firearms I have ever fired under this jacket and I will not miss from this range. If you choose to ruin my life, I will end yours." He saw Doc visibly shudder out of the corner of his eye.

"You must come with me!"

"No. You will do exactly as I say because I have what you need more desperately than my war-torn carcass, Doc."

"What might that be?"

"First, you have no money. Not only to buy the things to repair your ship but not even enough to pay for your meal." Doc shuddered again. *"You've already been to jail once; I don't think you want to return. Second, I have the gold you need as well and if you want it in the form that you need it, then you will stay out of my affairs entirely."*

"How do you propose to give me these things, Captain?"

"Shortly I will excuse myself from the table and go to the men's room. Wait a full minute and I will hand you some money on my way out. It will be enough to get you started and I will contact you next week to deliver more. If you try anything, you die."

"How did you come by all of this sudden wealth, Captain?"

"It was a primitive method, Doc, you wouldn't understand." With that he rose, excused himself to Cindi and walked to the restroom.

Once inside he sorted some money into a small stack of $100 bills, stuffed them in his coat pocket and turned to wash his hands. He was drying them when Doc walked in. The anger was intense on the man's face.

Stewart handed him the money and whispered, "Here's two thousand dollars. It's only because I care about you…no really, you're like the bastard stepson I never had, and I mean that. Seriously though, I am trying very hard not to kill you because I think God wants me to keep you alive and I have no peace with ending your life. I also have no qualms about it if you cross me. If I see you again before next week, I am a concerned boyfriend that killed an attacking rapist in defense of the love of my life."

"That would be murder."

"Check your statutes, Doc. This is Idaho. They're even more lenient here on self-defense than in Texas." With that he walked out the door leaving Doc to begin his scavenger hunt.

"Who was that?" Cindi asked she stepped out of the ladies room and met him.

"Oh, just some guy with a Jimi Hendrix T-shirt on. I was just commenting on what an amazing musician he was and how it was too bad that he'd died so young." Damn it! He was lying to his true love. He was really beginning to despise Doc. He may have to kill him after all, just on principle.

"You just talk to any ol' stranger that you meet?"

"I'm from Texas sweetie, there aint no such thing."

"I guess not for you. Yes Jimi was good. I always wondered why more blacks didn't go after his type of music rather than that soul-train, hip-hop stuff. He was truly amazing though his music is so dated now it's hard to listen to…" Cindi rambled on all the way to the truck. He smiled. `

He looked over at her after they got in the truck and asked, "So am I taking you home now or to another, safer place where your mom and brothers are waiting?"

She giggled and said, "Where do you want to take me?"

"I want to take you up to my hotel room, drink some wine and get the clothes off that incredible little body of yours." He didn't know where this was all coming from. He would normally never speak to a lady in this manner but his passions were running very high right now. "I honestly don't think that's what we should do though and it's not exactly Christian is it?"

"No, you dirty minded boy but I'd be lying if I said I wasn't feeling the same way. Damn you do things to me, cowboy!" She was breathing hard now. He saw the moment and gently reached over and took her cheek in one hand and brought her face to his. It started as a slow gentle kiss, but began increasing in intensity until they were wrapped up all over each other. Their hands groped and squeezed, pulling emotion from every muscle in their bodies. Stewart slowed it down just a bit and ended with softly kissing her full red lips. She pulled back from his grasp and looked into his eyes briefly and collapsed against his chest breathing very heavily. "Oh Lord, take me home Greg or I will rape you in this truck, cowboy." He patted and rubbed her shoulders and she lay on him the whole way back to her car at the library. She awoke when he parked the truck beside it.

"Oh I forgot I had to get my car home," she said. "Will you call me tomorrow, Baby?" she purred as she kissed his stubbly face.

"Absolutely, give me a number to call." She started rattling the numbers off and kissing him. "Do you got it, Baby?" He checked with the 'Bots

"I sure do Sweetie. Goodnight." He stepped out of the truck and opened her door again. He picked her up off the seat and gently set her feet on the ground beside the small car. She just looked up at him and began kissing him as though there were no tomorrow and then held him tight as if to show herself that he was real. He wished he could assure her that he would never leave her. It was his full intent but he knew how bad things could go eventually. He had the upper hand now on Doc, but that could change very quickly if he wasn't very careful. Like Beatty, Doc was an arrogant ass, but he wasn't stupid either. He kissed her some more and told her to go home and get some sleep and dream of him as he would of her. One last kiss and she quietly said, "Okay." She got into the car, started it and left him standing there like a protector from the dark. He couldn't wait to see her again.

Doc finished his meal like an animal. He was starving and hadn't had a decent meal in two days. He finished the entire meal in about five minutes, even almost swallowing the fortune in the cookie. He downed his tea, left just enough money to cover the meal and walked out to the Yukon. He got in and headed toward a grocery store he'd been stealing from earlier. He kept driving when he saw a police car in the parking lot. He stopped at another store and piled food into a basket. When he got to the check-out he was flabbergasted.

"Four hundred dollars? You're kidding me!" A police officer looked over from another checkout lane and said, "Is there a problem sir?"

"No problem officer, just a hard day." He has no idea, Doc thought. He paid his bill and drove the long trip back to his ship to stock it up. Then he just went to bed. 'How could things get any worse?' was his last conscious thought.

Chapter Thirteen

Stewart called the number that Cindi had given him early the next morning after breakfast. He had an appointment with a realtor later that afternoon to look at condominiums but he wanted to spend some time with Cindi, if possible. She agreed to meet him at Ann Morrison Park in an hour so he sat in the hotel cafe and drank coffee for a while after breakfast. He thought of all of the strange circumstances that had occurred to him. He had a sudden revelation as he reflected on the chaotic events of his life. As difficult as things had been for him he was still alive and doing well. He felt that all of his suffering was finally being rewarded although in way in which he had never imagined.

He had a purpose. He wasn't sure what exactly it was but he knew that the Lord had made him who he was for a reason. He also knew that it wasn't only for his personal benefit but for the benefit of many others that he was here now. His primary mission now was to ensure that Doc left without him and he remained in this present time without being mind-wiped.

He paid his check and drove by a store to pick up some flowers. He then drove to the park to meet Cindi. It was a beautiful park by the river and it was full of people even though it was a weekday morning. He saw her there by the bridge where she had asked him to meet her and was once again struck by her beauty. The sunlight danced off the red highlights in her hair and her dark skin had a golden glow to it.

She was wearing sunglasses over her green eyes but he knew that they were there underneath, smiling at him like the rest of her face. It was warm today so she was wearing a white blouse and yellow shorts which not only showed her shapely legs but emphasized her tiny waist as well. He had wondered if she was really as beautiful as he remembered and was wondering if a new day would break any illusions about her. He decided instantly that he had gotten it right to begin with and that she was indeed the most beautiful woman he had ever seen.

Her smile grew even more when she saw the small vase of roses in his hand. She began showing him around the area. They walked and talked for hours until she had to go to work and he to his meeting. She again agreed to dinner that evening only mildly protesting that he was going to 'fatten her up.'

He kept his appointment with the extremely talkative realtor, Shirley. She drove him around looking at properties for several hours. She was a fairly attractive woman in her early forties and was so flirtatious that he was certain that she would have slept with him if she thought it would get him to buy a property. In the end she discovered that it wasn't necessary and he wasn't really interested. He made an offer on a nice two-story town house in the Northern foothills. It had two bedrooms, two bathrooms, a spacious living area and its own two car garage on the lower level. It also had a very private little yard in back with a beautiful hot tub. The thing he liked most was the view it had of the city from the living room balcony. Except for a few trees in the way, he could see the whole valley below.

Overall it was very luxurious and he felt that he could be very comfortable there. He really wanted to own a ranch someday but he just needed a place to stay that he could leave for long periods of time without worry. It would do for now. Shirley actually seemed disappointed that he would buy the property without first 'sealing the deal' with her. He arranged a quick closing the following week after the owner accepted his cash offer. The world was now a strange and complicated place now, but if he was going to survive here he would have to learn to accept that which he couldn't change. He wondered though if humanity had really changed all that much since his time. Even in his time there were many people who seemed to enjoy complicating matters.

Stewart met Cindi after work again and took her to a very nice restaurant in downtown Boise called Peter Schott's. They enjoyed an excellent meal with an equally superb bottle of wine and then simply enjoyed each other's company. She was trying to finish college for the third time at Boise State University and was working on a teaching degree. She wanted to teach history and government because she felt that it was being taught poorly in the schools.

"It's almost criminal what some of these kids in high school believe!" She said passionately. "They love to talk about their rights how they are being violated and most of them don't even know what they are! How can we let people graduate from school having never even read the entire Constitution or even the Declaration of Independence! They have no idea why the country was even founded in the first place."

"I couldn't agree more." Stewart said quietly.

"I'm sorry I get so worked up over it but it's like the American people are living a lie. A dream world where the truth doesn't matter anymore! Like slavery; my father's ancestors were slaves and suffered terribly but people act like it still exists! They teach it in schools as if Americans started the whole thing and that the rest of the world is completely innocent. It *still* goes on in many parts of the world but they don't teach that, no, they teach that kids should hate America because of how it treated the Indians and slaves a hundred and fifty years ago. My father, he's a preacher, took me on a mission with him a few years ago to Zimbabwe. Those people are a mess! When some of them found out that my mother was white I thought that they were going to kill me. He had to send me home on an early flight! Oh, the world is so screwed up and people always blame Americans for everything. I'll tell you Greg, there is no place on earth where a black man or woman has it better than right here in the good ol' US of A!" She took a breath and drank some more wine.

"I know exactly what you mean, sweetie." Stewart smiled at her. He really enjoyed her enthusiasm.

"And racism. Sure it's not perfect but the US certainly has more equality than anywhere else on the planet! It just drives me up the wall when people, my people, run this country down so much when they could never do any better anywhere else. How do *you* feel about racism?" She asked suddenly as if realizing for the first time that it was a white southerner she was talking to.

"Well, first of all, I think that it is the single greatest waste of human effort that I know of. Hating someone because they look different than you is pointless. There isn't anything that they can do to change it and where does it end? When everyone has blond hair and blue eyes? That's been tried before with horrific results. I don't think even that would end human conflict anyway. You would have the bright blue eyed people hating the pale blue eyed people or the light blond hating the dirty blond. It would never end

135

unless human beings learn to accept each other's differences, which brings me to my second, and more important point; there is only one race; human. If we weren't somehow related as beings, you and I would be totally incompatible physically, emotionally, and spiritually. That doesn't seem to be the case here, if I'm not mistaken. On another level, according to modern genetic science, you couldn't exist if your white mother and black father were of different races. Your parent's genetic code only varies by about one percent whereas the people who think we came from apes overlook the fact that our DNA is as different from them as it is from dogs and cats." He stared into her beautiful green eyes as she stared back in fascination.

"I thought all you rednecks were supposed to be ignorant racists. You're destroying all of my well established stereotypes of your people." She said staring back into his gray eyes in wonder at this strange white man.

"I read a lot," He said as he smiled at her and gave her that look that she loved so much and said, "What you must come to realize is that my people are your people just as yours are mine. We are all the same in the eyes of God."

She giggled suddenly.

"You think I'm nuts, don't you." She said as she blushed slightly.

"No, I think you're adorable. And I have great respect for anyone who is willing to ask themselves the really hard questions," He said and drank a little more of his wine.

"Are you getting me drunk to take advantage of me?" She giggled again.

"What if I am?" He teased.

"I might let you." She teased back.

"That's not exactly how a preacher's daughter is supposed to act now, is it?" He asked innocently.

"What if I'm a bad girl? Are you gonna spank me?" She batted her eyes again and he briefly thought about how good she could be at being bad.

"I just might have to." He said slowly. Cindi took her glass of wine, downed the rest in one gulp, smacked it firmly on the table and stood up.

"We're leaving now." She said as she grabbed her purse and then his hand. "Pay the check dear," she said as she began pulling him away from the table.

"Yes Ma'am." He said. He took his wallet out and fumbled a couple of hundreds onto the table as she dragged him to the front door. She pulled him all the way to the truck and stood by the passenger door as he opened it for her. She hopped up into the cab and snapped her seat belt on as if there were no time to waste. He looked at the playful yet determined look on her face as he climbed in next to her. She leaned over and kissed him passionately and rubbed him firmly with her right hand. He was getting very excited when she stopped suddenly and sat back in her seat.

"Drive cowboy." She demanded.

"Where to Sweetie?" he asked.

"Your hotel, silly man. Drive!" She said with a wink. He started the truck and hastily drove the few blocks over to the Red Lion Downtowner where he was staying. He parked and they walked toward the entrance. She was almost pulling him with her. They walked through the lobby to the elevators and stood quietly waiting for a car to arrive. They entered the empty elevator and stood silently until the doors closed after he pushed the button for the seventh floor. Then she attacked him. She passionately kissed him and rubbed her hands all over his body. He responded in kind. The doors opened onto the seventh floor and they quickly separated as an older couple got on the elevator. They received stares as they got off the car but both broke out laughing when they overheard the older woman remark as the doors closed, "Why don't you ever do that to *me* in the elevator?"

Stewart took charge now and led Cindi to his room. She was briefly awestruck by the size and luxury of the place.

"It's beautiful" She exclaimed.

"I like nice things." He said quietly. "I have often been complimented on my taste in things of beauty." He stared at her gorgeous figure standing in the soft light of the suite. It was that same look that she had fallen in love with. She couldn't resist any longer and rushed into his arms.

"You are *so* mine, cowboy." She said looking up into his eyes. "I don't care how long I've known you or what secrets you may have. You are mine!"

"Absolutely!" Was all he could reply.

It was an incredible night. It was as if they had been made for each other. He was amazed at the passion and intensity that this little woman had. They alternated between incredible love making and resting in each other's arms. Sometimes they talked softly while other times they just laid there in silent serenity.

It was almost one in the morning when Cindi got up to get a drink. It was a little chilly in the room so she put on his shirt. He watched her walk into the kitchenette from the bed. The shirt was unbuttoned all the way and he could see her feminine lines peeking through the fabric as she walked. She took her drink and walked over to the window where she slowly sipped it and looked out over the city. She is incredible, he thought. She stood facing away from him with her hip cocked slightly to the left and her figure showed perfectly through the shirt from the light of the window. He thought that this was the most perfect moment in his life and could think of no way to improve it or even ruin it.

Then Cindi dropped her glass suddenly. She began to slowly back away from the window and asked, "Greg, why is there a black Tahoe floating outside your seventh story window?"

"Damn!" Stewart swore. Swearing was getting to be a habit whenever Doc showed up. He decided that he would have to tell her everything but it wasn't going to be easy so he tried to just tell her enough to get her up to speed as he swiftly put on his boxer shorts.

"Well Honey, it's actually a GMC Yukon and it's not even really that actually." OK, that made no sense to her at all he could tell by the bewildered look on her face. He moved her behind the chair by the bed and ran over to the suit case and pulled out something he'd purchased just for this occasion.

"Babe, this is going to be hard to explain but trust me and I'll tell you all of it." He looked at the fear in her eyes and it broke his heart. He leaned over and held her hands and looked into those eyes.

"Do you trust me?" He pleaded.

"Yes." She gasped.

"Good. Everything will be fine." He turned toward the window just in time to see a bright hole appear and Doc walking through in his stupid alien suit. The small familiar tube was in his hand and searching for a target as he stepped into the room. Stewart fired the device in his hand and watched as Doc went down writhing on the floor. He started to get up again and Stewart hit the trigger one more time.

"*What is that?*" came Doc's angry thought.

"*A Taser.*" Stewart thought back calmly.

"*It's shorted out my suit!*"

"*That was the general idea.*"

"*I can't breathe! Again!*" Doc was obviously a little upset and started reaching for the back of his head again.

"Ooh! Honey this is gonna be kinda gross. You may not want to watch this." Stewart said to Cindi as Doc repeated the head splitting routine he had witnessed upon their first encounter. Cindi stared in speechless horror as the alien pulled its head out of its head. Stewart kicked the small tube away from Doc's struggling figure in the now powerless suit. Doc lunged at him and grabbed his leg. Stewart began to struggle with the slimy jackass as Doc's triumphant thought pushed through to him, "*It only shorted out the suit. It didn't disable me.*"

Doc was surprisingly strong as Stewart began to wrestle the tall man and his very heavy and slimy suit. Cindi screamed as the two wrestled toward the bright circle in the window and promptly fell out into empty space.

Doc screamed too, and then passed out as the two plunged toward the pavement below. Stewart was pretty close to screaming himself when the 'bots cut in quickly with,

"*Sir, you are falling at a great velocity. May we stop it?*"

"*Please.*" He thought. The 'bots were always so polite.

He saw the pavement's approach slow down and then stop with his face at about a foot off the ground. He was holding Doc's limp form with a death grip and only then allowed him to slip to the ground. He let him fall in a slimy heap.

"Uh, please right me and gently set me on my feet." He asked the 'bots. He felt himself rotate and his bare feet landed gently on the rough pavement. He then reached down and collected up the heavy Doc/suit and, placing the load into a fireman's carry, started toward the front door of the hotel. Only then did he see the two teenage busboys behind the hotel staring at him. He stood there in his boxer shorts with split-headed alien future boy over his shoulder and smiled and waved. One teen looked down at the joint in his hand and tossed it away into the parking lot. The two then looked at each other and promptly ran back into the hotel. Stewart shrugged and headed for the door.

In the lobby the desk clerk looked up briefly as he walked in and then looked up and stared.

"Man what a party that was!" Stewart said. "I gotta get my buddy here to his room. Good night!" He said as he stepped onto the open elevator.

"Good night, sir." The clerk muttered and went back to his work.

Stewart was really worried about Cindi and rushed down the hall to his suite only to realize then that he had no key card. He knocked... and knocked again. Then he knocked louder.

"Cindi? Babe? Could you open the door please?" Stewart pleaded.

The door opened and a wild-eyed Cindi stood there staring at him with a look of anguish, confusion, fear, disbelief and about four more emotions that Stewart couldn't quite place. She was still wearing his shirt but had had the presence of mind to put on her panties before answering the door.

"Hi Honey. Close the door please." He said as he kissed her and quickly walked past.

"What the HELL IS GOING ON?" Cindi screamed at him.

"Just a minute Babe. Let me take care of this jackass first." He tried to be calming.

"That's the Jimi Hendrix shirt guy from the Chinese place!" She shouted. "You lied to me!"

Oh boy, *now* he was really in trouble, he thought. He tried to avoid her glare as he contacted the 'bots on the Yukon and told them to bring the vehicle closer. He gently put Doc into the back seat and ordered them to take him back to his ship. He stepped back into the room and then cut the connection to the ship's 'bots once more. He turned to deal with the more urgent issue now and looked at the severely traumatized and pissed off face before him.

"Okay Sweetie, now let me explain..." Stewart began.

"Don't you 'sweetie' me. I knew that you were too good to be true but I never imagined anything like this! I thought maybe you might be a fugitive or a messed up war veteran or something. But this is just crazy!" She slumped down to the floor and started sobbing uncontrollably. "I meet the man of my dreams and he's an alien fighting weirdo that falls off buildings and just walks back up like it was nothing and is also a liar!" She screamed at him and bawled into her hands.

"Now Babe, I meant everything I said to you." He began as he knelt beside here and placed his hands gently on her shoulders.

"Don't touch me! Are you an alien too?" She looked at him in fear.

"No and neither is he."

"What then? Are you from the future or something?" She looked at him now as if she could believe almost anything.

"Well…he is."

"And you?"

"I'm from the past, Honey. He's trying to take me back"

"The past? How far in the past?" She couldn't possibly believe any of this, he thought.

"I was born in 1840 and I am a messed up war veteran, Cindi; the Civil War."

Cindi's mouth dropped open. Then she clenched her teeth and angrily asked, "Which side?"

"I'm from Texas, Cindi"

"Auugh!" She screamed. "You fought to *keep* slavery? Oh my God! Oh my God! Oh my God! I am so out of here!"

She rose to her feet and started dressing. She collected all of her things as he tried to talk to her but she had shut him out. He stared blankly at the door as it slammed behind her. He threw on some clothes, grabbed his keys and followed her to the lobby. She was crying on a small bench in front of the hotel. He walked out and asked gently, "Can I at least give you a ride to your car."

"Yes." She said and started walking toward the truck. He unlocked it with the key fob and she jumped in without waiting for him to open the door, slamming it after plopping into the passenger seat. He climbed into the truck and drove her to her car in silence. As they pulled into the parking lot he turned to her.

"I am completely in love with you and although I have an idiot from the future trying desperately to return me to January 1871 where I will certainly be killed within minutes of my return in order to maintain the balance of history, I fully intend to remain here in this time. I will either marry you and live out my days here with you or I will pursue you until I die." He looked over at her now bloodshot green eyes. He could see the struggle she was having but she wanted to believe him. Perhaps she has her own prejudices to conquer, he thought.

"How did you do that?" She said.

"Do what?" He said. "Survive the fall?"

"Well, I am curious about that too but how did you just say that about my prejudices and not move your mouth. It's like I could hear it in my head." She looked at him in confusion.

Crap, he thought. How did that happen?

"You exchanged body fluids," The 'bots politely informed him.

"I heard that! What was that?" She just looked scared now.

"It will take me a while to explain. How about dinner tomorrow?" He asked innocently.

She rolled her eyes and opened the door.

"I have to think about all of this!" She said sharply as she slammed the door and walked away to her car. She got in, started it and drove away, not looking back at him.

Note to self, he thought, never lie to her again.

"Ahh! I heard that too!" was the thought reply. He saw the brake lights come on followed by the car's back-up lights. She pulled back up to him and stopped the car and got out. Without a word she walked up and slapped him as hard as she could across the face. Stewart didn't move, accepting the well deserved punishment. Then she punched him in the left arm and he fell to the ground in agony.

"What the hell is this now? You aren't going to trick me into thinking that I somehow hurt your big country ass!" Cindi yelled at him. Stewart couldn't speak. He was in horrible pain and could barely push the thought to the 'bots, *"what's happening to me?"*

"The bullet in your shoulder has moved and is now firmly lodged in your shoulder socket," the 'bots replied. *"It appears to be seriously interfering with your central nervous system."*

"Why couldn't you just remove the bullet?" He asked them.

"We have been removing it in small amounts. We are limited by your body's ability to rid itself of lead. If we were to try to remove it all at once you would die of lead poisoning."

"Help me," he croaked looking up at Cindi's angry but confused face.

"You are so full of crap! I can't believe you'd think I'd fall for this!" She yelled as she kicked him in the butt. He barely felt it as he was blacking out from the pain. It was the worst he had ever felt in his life. Cindi stared down at his quivering body and finally decided that he was actually hurt. She was mad and didn't want to even see him right now but she sighed and retrieved her cell phone from her car. Then she dialed 9-1-1.

She sat in the Emergency room of Saint Luke's hospital waiting. She felt like just leaving but she wanted some answers about this mystery cowboy from the past and/or future. They had rushed him in for emergency surgery but they wouldn't give her any details. A doctor finally came out and approached her.

"Are you Mr. Stewart's girlfriend?" He asked.

"I haven't decided yet. Maybe," she replied sternly, with her arms folded across her chest.

"But you brought him in, right?" He could tell that she was upset with the man and he didn't want to interfere in a lover's spat.

"Yes," she sighed. "Is he okay now?"

"Yes ma'am, he'll be fine. He asked if you were still here and he wanted me to give you this." The doctor held out a small plastic container with a small dark object in it.

"What is it?"

"It's what we pulled out of his shoulder. It was lodged in there pretty deep and it was very difficult to get out. It looks like it has been in there for several years."

"Is that a bullet?" She asked in disbelief.

"Yes, but it's kind of strange. It looks like an old mini ball; like what they used in the Civil War. It's pretty unusual to get shot with a musket in this day and age. He wanted us to give it to you.

143

He said, 'tell her it's proof' whatever that means. I figured maybe you'd know what he meant." The doctor eyed her curiously.

"Yes, I know what it means," she said as a tear rolled down her cheek. Then she picked up her purse, placed the small container in it and quietly walked out of the hospital.

Chapter Fourteen

Stewart went about closing on the new condo and selecting furniture for it as he healed up from the surgery. The 'Bots were busy making short work of the healing process. He tried to ignore the ache in his heart that he felt for Cindi. He knew that she would have to have some time to adjust to the strangeness of the situation and he realized that she might never fully accept it. He decided to place it all in the hands of the Lord and let Him work it out. If it was meant to be then it would be. If not then there was nothing he could do about it anyway.

He began to seriously consider killing Doc. He forced himself to examine his own motives in this and it was difficult for him to face his own human weakness. He knew that killing Doc would be physically easy for him but that it would be motivated by vengeance and frustration. He had killed many men but always out of self defense or the defense of others, except for the first one, of course. He was hopeful that God would forgive him of that sin one day but he was pretty sure that the Lord would really frown on killing someone simply because he was proving to be a serious pain in the ass.

He decided then that perhaps the best way of dealing with Doc would be to help get him home. He would have to be wary of the man's treachery in this. Though Doc was very intelligent; he had proven to be something of a simpleton in this cat and mouse contest of theirs. Still, he could not allow himself to underestimate Doc's abilities. The man was quickly learning some hard life lessons and would eventually catch on or kill himself trying.

Stewart drove his pickup to the place in the mountains that Doc had hidden the ship and honked just outside of the hidden vessel. He was learning that the 'bots could allow him to do some amazing things, like find and 'see' the vessel which was hidden from eyesight. It was there in a small clearing near the logging road he had driven there on, and though his eyes couldn't see it, his mind could. Sure enough, Doc appeared and cautiously walked toward him, hands behind his back. No doubt he had either another stun tube or a similar device behind his back.

"Look Doc, you and I need to work together on this," Stewart began through the open window of the truck.

"Whatever do you mean, Captain?" Doc said innocently.

"Well, first put away whatever you have behind your back and then let's talk," He showed him one of his pistols and gestured for Doc to take a seat in the truck. Doc slipped something into the back pocket of his jeans and climbed into the truck.

"Nice vehicle. Inefficient technology and the animal hide covered seats are disgustingly primitive, but it is nice," Doc commented.

"It gets the job done. Look I'm going to go get your gold for you. I should have it ready in a week or so. Let me know what else you need and I will help you get it."

"You nearly killed me yet again, you savage!" Doc said angrily. "Now you want to help me? How do you expect me to trust you now?"

"Are you still mad about that? That was days ago, Doc. You really need to stop living in the past." Stewart replied sarcastically. He decided to try to change the subject. "Incidentally, how on earth did we fall through that tube thing after you walked right across it?"

"Well, it's actually quite simple really," Doc began. "You see the nanobots in the suit react differently than those used to form the gangway. The liquid form takes time to dry and assimilate with the dry nanos in the field. By spilling the liquid from the suit onto the field it weakened the molecular structure to the point where it would no longer sustain its strength and would give under the slightest pressure. You've changed the subject on me."

"So the liquid from the suit sort of melted the tube thing then." Stewart ignored the last comment.

"Well, yes. You could say that though the condition was only temporary until the nanos could be properly assimilated into the field chain. We should have both died. With my suit shorted out my nanobots were unable to save me. I'm surprised you figured out the levitation process and could still hold on to me. You are a very resourceful man." Doc smiled sarcastically.

"For a 'Primitive' anyway," Stewart replied, wisely not mentioning exactly how he had figured out the levitation feature. "Look our basic problem is this; you feel the strong need to 'fix' the problem created by my being here and I have a strong desire to not get mind wiped and sent back to be killed by Nez Perce

146

warriors in 1871. Other than those two minor issues there isn't really anything that would keep us from being friends or at least getting along."

"Agreed," Doc shrugged and sighed. "I do find you to be an interesting person and very engaging in conversation and I have to admit that I have a certain level of respect for you now despite the difficulties you've given me."

"Same here. So here's what I propose, Doc. I help you get your ship fixed and you agree to let the professionals from your time try their hand at capturing me. What is the worst they will do to you if you don't bring me back?" Stewart looked at him intently. It was something that they both had to seriously consider.

"Well, probably not much really. You see, Captain, I'm not all I appear to be. To you I am a highly evolved being with powerful technology." Doc explained as Stewart strained to keep a straight face.

"The truth is I have failed repeatedly to uh… attain the level of existence that is expected of me in my culture. In short, I'm an outcast. I'm not doing much better than you on some things and obviously not as well on others. I've been reduced to stealing food and contemplating greater crimes than that just to get through this nightmare. I will probably simply lose my license to travel through time and I will have to find a more menial vocation to justify my existence in my own world. I will be a laughing stock in addition to being the disappointment that I already am. I never really wanted this job in the first place," Doc sighed more deeply. "If you want to stay here and take your chances with the authorities as well as the insanity that is about to envelope the world, I can't see why you shouldn't. Odds are you will probably be dead in a few years anyway but if we keep this nonsense up, one or both of us may die very soon and Nez Perce Indians will be the least of our worries."

"Good. I really don't want to kill you Doc and I sincerely apologize for all the times I almost did." Stewart extended his hand.

"It's not like I can blame you really. It occurs to me that throughout our little adventure you have always considered my well being as well as your own in all of our dealings. I never looked at it from your viewpoint until today and that by choosing to go with me you may be facing certain death," Doc said as he shook Stewart's hand. "That wouldn't be a rational choice for anyone. I supposed I might have reacted the same way though perhaps not as effectively. Good luck dealing with the time cops. I'd like to see how well *they* do against you. Maybe I can read their reports one day. Seriously though, they are a lot better at this than I am and they may just kill you to minimize the damage."

Stewart looked up at Doc who was actually smiling with respect and understanding. He released Doc's hand and gave him a pat on the shoulder.

"You know Doc, I think you're gonna be alright. I think we're gonna be just fine."

Cindi woke late the next morning. She had a ten AM class to get to but she woke up at around eight thirty. She began getting ready for class. Unlike most of her younger classmates she actually cared about how she looked at school. She had an exam this morning and she hadn't studied at all for it. She hoped that she wouldn't completely bomb on it. She finished her makeup and poured a small bowl of cereal while she began trying to cram for her US History exam on the Civil War.

The Civil War! She thought. The previous night's events suddenly came rushing back to her. It was unbelievable. It must have been a dream or maybe Greg was a creep and had put something in her drink that made her freak out or something. No, she was sure that it had all happened. It just was too weird to process. She looked up at the clock on the wall and realized that she had been sitting there thinking about last night for almost an hour. She needed to get to class soon.

In desperation she flipped through the chapters of the text she was supposed to have read and hoped that something might stick in her brain. She sighed and slammed the book down. *Men!* She thought. It seemed as though they spent all of their efforts pursuing sex and crime. She knew better than to get involved with one while she was working on her degree. That's what stopped her last time… *and* the time before. She groaned and headed for the door thinking that all men were good for was making babies and lifting heavy stuff.

She arrived in time for class and tried to wipe everything from her mind except the Civil War. That didn't make it easy considering that the biggest thing on her mind was a certain Confederate soldier she had met recently. She groaned again and the young lady sitting next to her looked up.

"Men!" Cindi whispered. The young girl simply nodded and rolled her eyes.

The instructor passed out the exams and she felt a tight knot in her stomach. She prided herself on getting exceptional grades and she felt that she was doomed to do poorly on this. She looked down at the first question.

'True or False; The Battle of the Wilderness was a decisive victory for the Union.'

The Battle of the Wilderness? She barely remembered reading about it. She had no idea who won that battle or even where it was! This was horrible! She closed her eyes and buried her face in her hands. She was contemplating just circling 'true' when she realized that she could 'see' the text book in front of her at the kitchen table. She opened her eyes and the image was gone. She closed them again and there it was. It was even on the page that discussed the Battle of the Wilderness. She began to read the text and it dawned on her that she knew the answer already and the reason that she was stumped was that it was a completely indecisive battle for both sides!

She circled 'false' and briefly wondered if Greg had fought at the Wilderness. As she moved on through the test she noticed with some shock that she could somehow read any page in the text book that she had scanned before coming to class. She finished before anyone else, turned in the test and went to lunch at the sandwich shop down the road. Had she cheated somehow? What had just happened? *Will someone please just tell me what the hell is going on?* She thought in frustration while standing at the counter in Blimpies.

'Yes Miss, how may we be of assistance?' was the response she heard.

"Yes, I'll have a six inch Tuna on whole wheat please."

Cindi looked up at the clerk and realized that the clerk hadn't said anything and was actually still waiting on the last customer.

"Just a moment please, Ma'am." The clerk was a snotty little blond girl and her voice didn't match the one she'd just heard at all.

"Uh, sorry. I thought you'd said something," Cindi apologized.

'No, that was us. You asked for our assistance,' The voice spoke again. Cindi went pale.

"Who are you?" Cindi whispered looking around. The clerk glared at her.

'We are nanobots. There is no need to speak audibly and appear strange to others around you. Simply think the thought as if you were speaking without actually voicing it.'

Where are you? She thought.

"OK, now that was tuna on wheat was it?" The clerk asked, still snotty.

'We are inside of you. You need more iron in your diet. May we suggest that you order the roast beef instead?'

"Um… no, make it a roast beef instead." Cindi choked out. She felt like she was going to vomit.

Inside me? How did you get inside me? Cindi thought.

You and Captain Stewart exchanged body fluids. Now she really felt sick. She'd gotten crabs from a boyfriend years ago but *this* was ridiculous.

"Cheese?" Snotty girl asked.

"American"

'We suggest provolone.'

"No, make it provolone… please." Cindi smiled at snotty girl who rolled her eyes.

'OK guys, help me get through the sandwich thing and then we can talk. Can I have all the vegetables? Dressing? A diet coke?' she was getting really annoyed between the snotty sandwich girl and the uninvited guests in her head.

'Yes. We suggest vinaigrette and no, you should drink ice tea or water.'

'Great, were you guys programmed by my mom?'

'No Miss. We were programmed by…'

'It was a joke! I'm going to have to reprogram you guys with a sense of humor.'

150

She finished ordering her sandwich, paid snotty girl, and went to her car to eat it so that it would at least look like she was on a blue tooth while she talked to the voices in her head.

'Okay, first question; why the hell is a civil war veteran infected with nanobots which haven't even been invented yet, it's just an idea.' Cindi began. She was starving all of a sudden and tore into her sandwich while the 'bots told the entire story of Stewart's abduction and subsequent escape. She didn't know that she even liked roast beef but found that it was very good!

"Okay then," She said with her mouth full of sandwich forgetting that she didn't have to talk. "So Greg is a Confederate captain and is now telling the truth. Can you guys tell me when he's lying?"

'Yes. Miss you really don't need to speak…'

"It's my mouth and I'll speak if I want too. I'll talk with my mouth full if I want. You're not my mom and you're not the boss of me! How did you guys know I liked roast beef so much anyway. This is a really good sandwich." Cindi took another bite while they answered.

'We take constant readings of your body chemistry and try to help balance it out for optimum health and fitness. Maintaining your health is our primary function.'

"Cool. How many of you guys are there anyway?

'54,612 at present.'

"Wow. That's a lot! How big are you guys?"

'Actually the amount is quite small. We are all about the size of one of your blood cells. When we reach saturation, there should be at least 1.2 million of us in your system.'

"Million? How will that affect me? Will I be come a robot or something?" Cindi was getting worried now.

'No Miss. If at any time we perform a function or assist you in a way that you do not wish, you need simply tell us and we will cease. That includes our own standard operations and reproduction processes. Nanobot use is strictly voluntary and we can only serve our host and their wishes. You are now our host of course.'

"So if I tell you guys to all die, you just die.

'Yes. We would simply deactivate and then be eliminated from your body naturally over time. At our current density it would

take approximately five weeks for us to be completely removed from your system'.

"You helped me cheat on the test, didn't you?"

'We simply made available to you information that you already knew.'

"Can you do that all the time?"

'Yes.'

"Hmmm… ethical dilemma."

'If we may Miss, we have reviewed all of the Boise State University academic rules and can find none that bar the use of nanobots.'

"Clever. Okay, we'll worry about that later. Tell me more about Greg and how do I know that he didn't just put some kind of electronic bug in my ear or if you *are* nanobots, that he didn't program you to tell me all of this stuff." Cindi still wasn't quite convinced about this whole Civil War veteran thing. Then she remembered the bullet in the small plastic container in her purse. It had been pretty convincing, she thought. She reached in and pulled the small container out and examined the bullet for a moment. It appeared to be old and dull except for a few shiny marks on the nose that looked a little like some tiny person had bitten into it. "What are these bite marks here?" she asked.

"They are small excavations where we have been trying to gradually remove the object from Captain Stewart's body. If we removed it too quickly it would cause lead poisoning. To demonstrate our existence we could use a small demonstration that Captain Stewart has used before. Do you have a small piece of paper?" The 'bots drew a beautiful picture of her on the back of a book mark and then insisted on being recovered with a lick. Cindi was suitably impressed.

"So how did he survive the fall from the hotel?" Cindi asked sipping her iced tea. That one question was the one that bothered her most. She was certain that he was dead and then he was there at the door. Oh, she was going to make him pay for that one day. The 'bots went on to explain the levitation process in excruciating detail.

"Oh cool! You mean I can fly?"

'No Miss. It is really just an anti-gravity function. It requires large amounts of energy and total saturation before it can

be effective. At current reproduction levels you won't have enough nanobot saturation to use that function for four months.'

"Bummer," she said, suddenly thinking of a few naughty ways she may be able to get a few more 'bots in her system. Not that that was the main reason why she would want to do that but it seemed like an added benefit.

"You can help me find him, can't you?"

'Captain Stewart? Yes Miss.'

"Good," she smiled. She wasn't through with this cowboy yet.

Chapter Fifteen

Stewart went back to his condo, showered and tried to sleep. It was early but he felt drained and his shoulder was sore. He thought about Cindi and wondered how she was doing. He called her cell number and it went to voice mail. He left her a brief message telling her that he wanted to see her but he knew that she would need some time. He rarely drank before bed but tonight he made an exception. After asking the 'bots not to interfere with the alcohol in his system, he poured a shot of Evan Williams bourbon and started sipping it in a chair by the window. He liked the old style whisky for more than just the liquid comfort. It was a brand that was older than he was, its origins going back to the Revolutionary War. Though he had seldom drunk the stuff before his amazing journey, it was a small piece of familiarity to him. He was in a strange land now. Everything was different. It was all much more comfortable and convenient but also much more complicated and still very unfamiliar to him.

He was staring out at the lights of the city and thinking about Cindi. He wondered if she'd like the condo and the furniture he'd picked out. He pictured himself carrying her over the threshold one day with her in a beautiful white gown. He jumped just a bit when the doorbell rang.

'Who the hell is that?' he thought.

'Who the hell do you think, cowboy?' the thought came back.

"Cindi!" He yelled, rushing to the door.

"Yes dear, it's me." She said sweetly as he opened the door. She was wearing a tiny black dress that showed her cleavage nicely. She looked down at his boxer shorts and said, "It looks like you were expecting me."

He was half drunk now and stammered, "I, I… was just getting ready for bed."

"I'll bet you were! Now we need to order some take out, because I'm hungry and then have a nice talk about these little machines you gave me. After that, if you haven't totally pissed me off again, I'm planning on screwing your brains out!" She stepped inside firmly pushing her finger into his chest and closed the door.

"Well that was a little out of sequence," Cindi whispered with her head on his chest. "But it was a nice ice-breaker. I'm still hungry though. Now about these nanobots I'm carrying around in me…"

"A complete accident, I assure you. I never even thought…" Stewart began.

"Did you even think that you just gave me more of them?" Cindi looked up at him.

"Well, I figured you knew the risks by now."

"Yeah, I did. It's optional you know. You can tell the 'bots to die off and they will."

"Yes, they've told me. They've also proven to be very useful though so I am keeping them for now. I may shut them down someday if I ever feel that I can live a normal life again," Stewart sighed.

"That's what I was thinking too." Cindi nodded slightly on his chest. "I like this spot. I fit just perfectly in this spot on your chest. Could you reserve it for me?"

"Only for you. No one else, ever," He said as he stroked her hair.

"I've fallen in love with you, cowboy. Did you know that?"

"I kind of suspected as much. Just so you know, I fell in love with you at the library." *I sure hope this works out better than the last…"* he choked off the memory as it came back.

"Last what?" Cindi propped her head up and looked at him. She sensed a distant sadness in his eyes.

"You weren't supposed to hear that. That's why I didn't say it, young lady."

"Well don't think so loud then. So, the last girlfriend? Last hooker? What?" Cindi said as she laid her head on her arms and stared up at his face.

"I've never been with a hooker, Cindi," He said as he swatted her bottom just a little.

"Well now I'm curious. You have to tell me. Remember, 'never lie to her again'?" She pleaded.

"Maybe I *should* tell you just so you know who I really am," He said with a sigh.

"Yes, tell me about all of your conquests, dear. I want to know just what kind of player you are." Cindi replied with a hint of

155

suspicion. "Just how many women have you seduced with your charms, cowboy?"

"Counting you?" He asked innocently.

"No, I think that I actually seduced you so that doesn't count."

"Oh. One then."

"One?" She asked incredulously.

"Yes, just one." He sighed again heavily.

"Let me get this straight; you've only slept with one woman other than me in your whole life?" She sat up and stared at his face in disbelief.

"Yes ma'am." He replied with a straight face.

"I find that very hard to believe, mister, especially with *your* skills."

"That's how we did things in my day, sweet heart. And even that was considered a sin at the time. I still consider it a sin."

"Do you consider what we've done a sin?" She asked staring at him.

"Yes."

"So would my father, I suppose. The modern world is pretty confusing on moral issues these days." She said with a sigh as she put her head back down on his chest.

"But I intend to make an honest woman out of you as soon as it's convenient."

"Sure you do cowboy." She'd heard that line before and had no intention of getting her hopes up. "Tell me about her and why she broke your heart."

"Are you sure you want to know? You may hate me after you know the truth about me."

"I'll be the judge of that. I doubt that I would be shocked by anything you've done, especially a hundred and fifty years ago."

"Okay, let's see if you run away again." He said softly as he began to tell the story of Julie. His voice was low and somber as he told the tale with complete truth and all the details from the snake bite right up to the point of dumping his father's body into the river. Cindi had not spoken the whole time and the silence hung in the air of the room when he finished. Suddenly she shuddered and he felt wetness on his chest. She was crying very

156

softly. He rubbed her arm and tried to comfort her not knowing what she was thinking of him now that she knew he was a murderer.

"Well, do you hate me now that you know that I murdered my own father?" He asked softly.

"Oh God, no, Greg. That's just the saddest story I've ever heard in my life. So you were in love with her? You were really in love with a slave girl?"

"Yes. I would have married her if I could have but that… just wasn't possible."

"That's so sweet. Oh you poor baby, how could you ever have won in that situation?" she said through her tears as she looked up at him and began kissing his face. "I feel so sorry for you and the burden you have been carrying all these years. I think you're a sweet, romantic, and very sexy man."

He smiled slightly and said, "This isn't exactly the reaction I would have expected from confessing to murder."

"Well it sounds like self-defense to me; I don't care what your father said before he died. I think you had every reason to suspect that he would kill you next. He shot that poor girl in cold blood so he's the murderer, not you."

"The law wouldn't have seen it that way. I would have been hanged for that if they had ever caught me." He stared up at the ceiling going over the event again in his mind. He could feel the uneasy feeling again in the pit of his stomach.

"You haven't forgiven yourself, have you?" She said accusingly.

"Why should I?" He asked stubbornly, not making eye contact.

"To let yourself heal, silly man. You need to be able to let it go. I think that you have spent your entire life since then trying to redeem yourself for one mistake that wasn't even your fault!" She wagged a finger in his face as if correcting a small boy. Stewart couldn't help but smile at her cute little hand and stern look. "Don't you smile at me young man! You need to forgive yourself and I'm going to harass you until…"

He pulled her down and kissed her before she could finish.

"Oh, you think you can just interrupt me like that?" She wagged her finger at him again. "I don't think so, Mister Big Man.

You think you're all tough and you can just have your way with me? Well, maybe you can right now but when we're finished, I'm going to start back up right where I left off and nag you until you forgive yourself."

She bent down and kissed him hungrily and then whispered in his ear, "You have no idea how sexy shooting someone for killing your woman is…"

Cindi woke up early, hurriedly dressed, kissed Stewart very passionately, and then rushed off to class. The 'bots *were* proving to be very useful to her, now acting in the role of alarm clock for her. She drove her Firebird to the university and as she was parking the 'bots spoke to her.

"Excuse the intrusion Miss but we need to inform you of a medical condition," the 'bots tinny, mechanical voice said.

"A medical condition?" she asked. "You can diagnose medical conditions?"

"Yes Miss."

"I'm not pregnant am I? I am on the pill." She worried.

"No Miss. In fact you may cease using the hormone altering medication if you wish. We can prevent pregnancy until you instruct us not to."

"Oh good, please do then. Prevent it I mean," she replied.

"Yes Miss."

"Well, what is it then?"

"Ovarian cancer Miss and it is quite advanced in its severity," the tinny voice stated matter-of-factly. Cindi's dark face went white.

"Cancer! Are you sure?" She was horrified. She was only twenty seven. Cancer happened to old people.

"Yes Miss, it is definitely cancer," the impassive voice replied.

"H-how long do I have to live?" she asked bravely. Her mind was spinning with the many goals and dreams that she had and how much she would miss out on. She mentally began prioritizing things that she wanted to accomplish as soon as possible.

"We do not understand the question Miss."

"How long before the cancer kills me?" she asked in frustration.

"We have already begun removing the cancerous tumors at their origin. Are you asking us to allow the disease to run its course? This would conflict with our default programming but we will cease our intervention if you wish. However, it would eventually be very painful and prove fatal within sixth months." Cindi felt a rush of relief.

"You can cure cancer?" she asked to be sure.

"Yes Miss, and we can make some recommendations to your diet to prevent its return. Shall we abort our intervention?" the 'bots inquired again.

"Oh Lord no! Please, remove all the cancer you can find and be sure to let me in on any other little secrets my body is keeping from me." She was so shaken up she just sat in the car trembling for the next twenty minutes before she slowly pulled herself from the car and began walking to class. Foremost in her mind was the thought of what would have happened to her if she had never met Greg or become exposed to his strange little machines from the future. She shuddered at the thought and then offered up to the sky a brief prayer of thanks for the mysterious ways in which the Lord works His miracles.

Greg was disturbed. He was preparing for his trip to Warren when he suddenly had a strange feeling that there was something wrong with Cindi.

"Has Cindi tried to send a distress call through you guys?" he asked the 'bots.

"No sir," was the tinny reply.

"Have her 'bots transmitted anything to you at all?"

"No sir."

"Strange, I had a feeling that she was in trouble for some reason," he mused. The feeling was dissipating now.

"That would be a spiritual phenomenon sir, not electronic," the 'bots offered.

"Spiritual? Can you 'bots discern things of a spiritual nature?" he asked in disbelief.

"No sir, but we are familiar with the concept of spiritual communication. Only human beings are capable of it. We simply

159

have knowledge of its existence but know nothing of how it operates. Humans do not seem to be sure how it operates themselves so it has never been programmed into our databanks," the 'bots politely explained.

"Well, I can't explain it either but I wish it was more detailed in how it worked," Stewart sighed as the feeling completely disappeared and was replaced by a warm sense of relief. He felt like Cindi had been frightened by something briefly but that she was okay now. Maybe it was a close call in traffic. He would have to ask her later.

"It has been demonstrated to be somewhat unreliable but some couples have been able to refine it with practice to the point of rarely having to actually speak to each other even without the assistance of nanobots."

"Couples?" Stewart asked curiously.

"Yes. It seems that only couples of the opposite sex or siblings, particularly those from multiple births, can refine the process enough to effectively communicate with it. Apparently there must be a significant spiritual bond present in order for the phenomenon to manifest," the 'bots had learned to expound on information from many such discussions Stewart had with them. He enjoyed picking all sorts of information out of their vast stores.

He continued packing his gear in the truck while having a mental lesson from the 'bots on the capabilities of human beings as opposed to the limitations of machines. He was surprised at the insight programmed into the tiny wonders by their creators. Although the general tone of the 'bots appeared to be indifferent, their descriptions of humanity bordered on worship. The programmers had ensured that these little devices knew their place in the world and that humanity took priority over all things as far as they were concerned. Their default programs would not allow a human being to come to harm in anyway if they could prevent it.

Stewart learned that his verbal command to 'not' help him except upon request was interfering with their defaults and causing a great deal of degradation in all of their functions as a result. He removed the command and mentally noted that he would have to consciously prevent their interference in things in the future if necessary.

He used his cell phone to call the stable in McCall where he had arranged to rent two horses and a trailer for his expedition. He verified his reservation and asked about weather conditions. He checked his guns, filled his coffee thermos and set out on the hundred mile journey up State Highway 55. The owner of the small ranch was happy to rent him horses as it was the slow season due to the closed hunting season and cold weather. The rancher told him that it was now warm and clear in McCall and his horse pack riding should be very pleasant. It was early spring so the Warren Wagon Road was finally open from the snows but was still a little icy in places. Stewart enjoyed the beautiful drive up to the small town five thousand feet up in the mountains. He picked up the horse trailer with the animals already loaded and headed down the road along the back side of Payette Lake. The ice on the beautiful, natural lake had broken several weeks ago but small chunks could still be seen clinging to parts of the shore. He had installed a CB radio in the pickup at the urging of the ranch owner so that he could avoid the logging trucks as they came loaded down the narrow mountain road. He discovered within the first two miles off the paved portion the extreme value of the one hundred fifty dollar investment he had in the little CB and antenna kit. He was sure that it saved his life at least once when he heard a trucker call out a mile marker.

"Comin' down loaded at the two mile," boomed the deep voice over the radio.

He had no sooner pulled over when he saw the big green Kenworth round the curve with a load of red fir, the big, snow covered logs on the front bunk missing his pickup by inches as they swiveled out on the curve and back again as the truck straightened out. He then heard the professional voice of the trucker calmly call out a warning to his colleagues on the CB.

"Pickup with a stock trailer comin' up at the two mile. He's got an antenna so I think he's listenin' but he aint talkin'," the trucker said. "Mister, you need to call out the markers when you get to 'em. They're the pie plates on the trees with the numbers on 'em. Just say, 'pickup comin' up at mile two or whatever. That way if one of us is coming down nearby he can warn ya to pull over. It takes a bunch to get us stopped on these hills so you need to try to stay out of the way if you can. We don't like running folks

161

over but if you're in the way it can't really be helped so we'd appreciate you're cooperation sir."

Stewart listened to the trucker's diplomatic butt chewing and responded, "Yes sir, I will do my best to stay clear. I appreciate that you men have a hard job to do and I don't want to make it any harder. Pickup with a stock trailer coming up at mile two!"

"Thank you sir, you have a mighty fine day now."

"You too sir," Stewart replied.

The rest of the trip was more of the same. Stewart called out the markers as he saw them and listened for the loggers as they came down. Each time he met one there was always a short exchange of courtesies. He decided he liked the loggers and their friendly ways. He looked at the men (and one lady) as they passed and saw friendly smiles on all but one of them. For all their pleasantness he could see that they were all tough men, even the woman. These were the kind of folks to have on your side and not to trifle with. He could see that most of the cabs had a rifle or shotgun in the rear window and he was sure that those that didn't had some type of firearm somewhere within.

Presently he passed Bergdorf Hot Springs and soon came into the north end of the small valley where Warren was located. Stewart was in awe of the beautiful country that was still half covered in snow. Except for the narrow gravel road it still looked very much like it did the last time he had been here. Warren was on the south side of the valley so he drove the full length just taking in the scenery. He finally passed the small sign that said 'Warren, Established: 1869' and pulled into town. It had been a long time since he'd seen that sign and though he was certain that it wasn't the original it sure looked a lot like it.

He stopped and marveled for some time at how it had changed so little in over a hundred years. He got out of the truck and wandered around looking at the old general store now turned into a café. He was hungry so he went inside and ordered a breakfast sandwich from the small but tough looking young lady behind the counter. He kind of wanted to stay and just take in the familiar surroundings but he took the sandwich and got back in the truck to be on his way.

He ate the sandwich as he drove and a short distance later he found the small side road that he'd been looking for. He pulled off to the side and checked his map again to be certain that he was in the right place. Once he was sure that he had found the right road he began unloading his gear from the pickup and packing it onto the horses. They were fine animals and seemed much healthier than any he had ever seen. One was a spunky five year old Appaloosa gelding while the other was an older quarter horse mare. Both were good mountain breeds but he had more confidence in the mare so he loaded her with the pack gear and saddled the gelding. He figured that the Appaloosa might need extra attention to keep him under control. Modern tack was different in that there was a lot of nylon and not as much leather or hemp anymore but it all essentially served the same purposes that he was familiar with. Horse technology had pretty well peaked in his own time and other than materials there wasn't much to improve upon.

Stewart finished the chore of packing and checked his watch. It was almost ten in the morning. He knew that it was too optimistic to think that he could finish this task in a single day but he was hopeful that he could at least find what he was looking for today. He had done extensive research and come up with nothing in any historical records so unless someone had found it and never reported the claim there was still several million dollars worth of gold up that road somewhere that belonged to him.

Doc sat staring at the monitor. He could clearly see the nanobot's marker on the map that showed the location of the captain. It seemed that he was trying to get back to the same geographic area where Doc had originally picked him up. Doc groaned audibly as he mentally recalled the event that had so incredibly ruined his entire life. If it weren't for that damn savage, he thought. He shrugged off the frustration and focused on the task at hand. Whatever strange reason the captain had for trudging through the snow to where they first met was irrelevant and actually played well into his plans. The captain was unwittingly isolating himself from public places where it would be easier to finally capture him without the limitations public exposure placed upon him.

After his last conversation with the man Doc had decided that he wasn't giving up so easy. He could beat this savage. He was smarter, better educated, and had all of the technological advantages. No, he would finish what he'd started. Stubbornness ran in the family and he had learned at a very young age to never give up, especially on something important. Recovering the captain was very important to the entire world and he was determined to save it from his error.

He had figured out that the captain was never going to go willingly with him and that defeating this warrior on his own terms was probably impossible. Doc would have to use his superior knowledge and intelligence to win this contest. He knew that the captain harbored some irrational notion of religion or honor that kept him from killing him but he didn't want to press his luck. He had seen firsthand what the savage was capable of and although it was vital that he set things right, it certainly wasn't worth his life. Doc needed to find the captain's weakness and he was pretty sure he had. He focused on a weak signal that faded in and out in the center of town near the river. Yes, he was sure that that was what he was looking for.

Chapter Sixteen

Cindi had finished her classes for the day and almost bounced her way to her little blue Firebird. She felt on top of the world right now. She was madly in love with a man who was madly in love with her and when you feel loved everything in life is better. She unlocked the car and settled into the comfortable seat. It was six years old and it wasn't a perfect car but she had paid for it with her own money. She was very proud of it and took good care of it. Just as she started the car her cell phone rang. She picked it up and answered.

"Hi Mom," she said pleasantly.

"Hi dear. I was worried about you. You didn't come home last night," her mother's tired voice said.

"I'm a big girl now Mommy, I can take care of myself," she said in her best little girl voice. Her mother was upset and but the little girl voice usually made her smile. She had reluctantly moved back in with her mother last year after breaking up with her last boyfriend that she had foolishly moved in with. Her mother generously offered to allow her to stay until she finished her teaching degree. With her father in South America on another mission trip her mother was pretty lonely anyway.

"I know you are dear but you're also very beautiful and I worry that some evil man will kidnap you and do terrible things to you," her mother sighed.

"Oh mom, you have been saying that since I was five. I'm fine, in fact I'm more than fine, I'm fantastic!" She bubbled.

"Oh dear, you're in love," her mother sounded concerned again.

"Yes," she replied with a huge smile that only she could see in her rear-view mirror.

"Honey, please be careful. I don't want some smooth talkin' fool breaking your heart again. You haven't shown the best taste in men so far," her mom nagged.

"This one is different, mom. *Very* different," She giggled into the phone.

"Oh really? How so?"

"Well he's actually a white guy for starters," she replied as she absent mindedly toyed with her hair.

"A man's skin color doesn't matter Cindi. It's what's in his heart that counts. You've never dated a white guy though. He isn't one of those crackers who pretends to be a black player is he?" Her mother sounded very unsure.

"No Mom, he's cowboy with a pick-up truck, boots, a hat and a Texas drawl," Cindi laughed.

"What! That's not your type of man at all. Have you lost your mind girl?" her mother's shock was obvious.

"Oh mom you would really like him. He's tall, ruggedly handsome, polite, well spoken and a perfect gentleman."

"A perfect gentleman does *not* keep my daughter out all night long, dear," her mom replied.

"Um, that was kind of my fault actually."

"Cindi! What would your father say! This isn't how we raised you to behave."

"I know Mom but I, it just felt so right and I love him so much I...I wanted..."

"To be sure, right? I know Honey we all want to be sure but it's still the wrong way to do it," her mother lectured.

"I know Mom; please don't tell Dad when he calls, okay?"

"I won't have to. You know your father; he can smell sin twenty miles away. Well, what does this cowboy do for a living anyway?" Mom inquired.

"Well... he's a war veteran," she began. 'How do I answer this one without lying?' she thought. "He's kind of taking a break right now but he seems to have made quite a bit of money in his investments."

"Oh Lord Cindi, you aren't seeing a drug dealer are you?"

"No Mom! Sheesh! Those guys get paid pretty well over there and don't have much to spend it on and he just wisely invested it! I know what a drug dealer is Mom, like Tyrone. Remember him?" Cindi said, trying to change the subject.

"Yes," was her timid response.

Tyrone was the son of one of her mom's friends that she had set her up with several years ago. He had taken her on a drug deal on their first date to see if she was 'cool.' She had stormed out of the pick-up house when she realized what was going on and barely missed going to jail in the bust that happened just a few minutes later. She vividly remembered watching the police cars from a block away in the dark as they rolled up to the house with their lights flashing and the awful sounds of shooting and screaming.

"Ok then. Mom, I have learned so much about the character of men that the only surprising thing about Greg is that he has a good one."

"Is he at least a Christian man Cindi?" her mother's worry wasn't going to be easily assuaged.

"Yes Mom, he already insists that we are getting married. Look, remember when I told you about three or four months ago that I was just giving up and I was going to focus on God and my degree and when God wanted me to find a man I'd let him introduce us? Well I meant that Mom. I really did and God was faithful and introduced us while I was at work," Cindi replied with soaring confidence.

"Are you sure Honey? I just have a bad feeling about this. It's too sudden and you seem too sure about it. You've never acted this way about a man in your life," her mom replied.

"That's because I never *was* sure Mom. I am now. I know that I know that I know that he is the man for me. I'm certain of it now."

"Wow! Dejavu! That is almost word for word what I said to my father about your father. I just had chills going down my spine!"

"Spooky good chills or creepy bad chills?" Cindi was using the descriptions her mother and her had developed when she was a little girl.

"Spooky good chills Honey. I'm crying now, OK? You've made your mother cry because God found you a man and you are in love. I pray that everything works out for you. But remember what your father teaches, just because God made it happen doesn't mean that it's going to be easy and trouble-free. There are bound to be bumps in the road along the way and Satan has a way of trying to ruin a good thing with the unexpected. Be ready dear," her mother said with concern.

"I will Mom. I have to go get some lunch and get to work now, okay?"

"Okay dear, I love you."

"I love you too Mom." She hung up the phone and placed it on the console below the radio. Then she put the car in gear and turned around to back out of the parking space. She let out a huff when she saw that an SUV was blocking her in. She sat looking as she waited for the black Yukon to pass and let her out. Her eyes grew wide as she recognized the car and she suddenly heard a tap on her window. She turned and looked up at the smiling black face as he opened her car door. She saw a bright flash as she started to scream and everything went black.

Stewart had ridden about fifteen miles when he had that feeling again. It was very intense and suddenly gone. It had lasted only a few seconds and it bothered him. He didn't like not being able to protect Cindi all the time. It was just his nature he thought. He was in love with a beautiful woman and hated spending any time away from her. He said a brief prayer, shrugged off the feeling and turned his focus back to the task at hand. It was beautiful country but he had to be careful navigating the terrain. He felt the crisp, clean air as it rolled into his lungs. The smell of pine was just a pleasant hint this time of year. In the heat of the summer it could be overpowering.

He was following the small creek that he suspected was the one where he had stopped to rest from the blizzard a hundred thirty seven years ago. He couldn't be sure it was the same creek but it was in the right area. Maps had improved drastically since 1871 but he hadn't been sure where he was at the time. He had been heading to Warren using instinctive dead reckoning and that never was a very accurate method of navigation. As he came to a small road crossing the creek he saw a dark object under a tree. He rode closer to inspect it. It looked like a motor of some kind.

"What is that?" he asked the 'bots.

"It is a flat head Ford V8; an internal combustion engine developed in the late nineteen twenties and used in many vehicles worldwide up until the nineteen eighties. It has retained a small following of enthusiasts who use the engines in modified pre-nineteen sixty vehicles known as 'street rods.' Displacement and horsepower of this particular model are unknown," the 'bots thoroughly explained.

Stewart looked up and down the road. He scanned the entire area thoroughly looking for anything that might explain the presence of the old engine. He was looking for abandoned machinery or maybe the ruins of a building or something but he could see nothing. In all of his surroundings only the road looked as if God hadn't placed it there.

"Weird," he said as he shrugged and continued following the river. It was fairly easy going most of the way although a few times he had to skirt the river through the trees where the banks were too steep for the horses. He continually scanned the woods realizing suddenly that he felt like he was back in his own time. He was looking for Indians and claim jumpers that were certainly not there anymore. It sure looked the same to him after all these years.

While scanning he caught a glimpse of eyes. It had saved his life more than once but Stewart had always been able to spot eyes in the thickest brush. A man or critter could hide itself well enough but it couldn't hide looking at you. He quickly scanned back to the place and saw them. It was two pairs of eyes actually. They belonged to a pair of owls sitting on a large branch in a tree just thirty feet away. He stopped and stared at them as they stared back. They were incredible creatures. Each was about three feet tall with huge black eyes. They had round, ear-less heads and their feathers were a soft gray color. He had never seen an owl like these before and they vaguely reminded him of Doc when he was wearing his mean alien suit.

The strangest part was that they were out in the day. Stewart looked at the dark, shaded grove of pines that the birds were in and decided that he and his horses had probably awakened them in their sleeping area. The staring contest continued for a few more minutes with the owls staring at Stewart, exchanging silent looks with each other and then back at Stewart again. He was just about to move on when one after the other the huge birds leaned forward on the branch and fell with their outspread wings catching the air. Their wing spans were at least seven feet Stewart thought, as the giant creatures flew right over his head and off into the forest on the other side of the creek. He sat in awe of the spectacle and shook his head and whistled softly at the majestic sight he had just witnessed.

Doc rubbed his sore knee. He had banged it up pretty badly when he stunned the young girl and her car lurched backward suddenly. He hadn't thought about the car being in gear and that her foot on the brake was the only thing keeping it stationary. Naturally, when she lost consciousness her foot released the pressure on the brake and the open door smashed into his left knee cap. He barely got the car stopped before it hit his Yukon. He looked over at the young woman in the travel tube. He had only filled the tube up to her neck to keep her from feeling the discomfort of breathing the fluid. He also thought that it might help to give her the illusion that she was trapped in the device.

She was certainly an attractive woman but for some strange reason she held no appeal to him. Not like it would matter anyway. He certainly couldn't get involved with a Prim from this time or any other for that matter. Briefly he thought of what it might be like to bind and rape the young woman. He shook his head. What was wrong with him? He had never had a thought like that in his life! This whole experience was having a very negative effect upon him. He would have to seek some professional help after he returned home. That would be then though. Now he needed to force this primitive monster to do what he needed to do. It was his duty to mankind to accompany him to be mind wiped and be reset into his own time.

Doc had made most of the repairs to the ship using the money that Stewart had given him. He had also stocked the food pantry with items that the ship could sterilize and prepare to a satisfactory level of purity. All he lacked was the necessary gold wire and the ability to machine the parts he needed. Stewart had promised to deliver the gold and when he did he would finally submit to his duty. He would figure out how to machine the parts later.

He looked at the monitor.

"I know you're awake, young lady. The monitor displays all of your physical data. It won't do you any good to try to fool me," he said.

"Well I'd like to go back to sleep then thank you. This isn't where I want to wake up right now anyway, you freak!" she hissed at him through the door.

"No need to be angry miss, I just need your help convincing the captain to surrender to his fate."

"Who are you to decide Greg's fate? What, do you have some kind of 'god' complex?"

"No names! I can't know your name or his and you can't know mine!" Doc shouted. "We have already severely altered history, I'm sure. You must understand the seriousness of this situation. The captain must return to his own time and live his life as he was meant to. If he remains here he will be an aberration. I'm sure that you have already noticed primitive things about the man that would make him an outcast even in your time."

"Are you kidding? He is the most wonderful man I've ever met. I wish we had more men like him in my time. Most of the ones I've known are either whiney girly-men or self-centered jerks like you! Greg is an awesome man who knows he's a man."

"I told you no names!" Doc shouted again.

"Greg! Greg! Greg! Greg! Greg! That's his name so there! What are you going to do to me? Kidnap me and stick me in a tube full of lard? Oh my goodness Doc, what an evil plan you have here." Cindi said sarcastically. "Seriously, did you think this through at all, you moron?"

Doc ignored her childish sarcasm and said, "He's a killer you know."

"Yes, I know and I hope he kills *you*!"

"He's a cold-blooded murderer. I've seen his victims with my own eyes. As a matter of fact, the first thing he did when he escaped from me was kill three men who were camping in Nevada and steal their vehicle." Doc stood staring at her with his arms crossed.

"You're lying!"

"I have no reason to lie and my culture forbids it. I have never lied," he lied.

Cindi's mind was spinning. She tried to get a grip on the situation. This was all way too weird but she loved Greg and she knew he was a good, kind man. If he killed someone it couldn't have been for simple theft. She thought about her last conversation with her mother as she stared at the smirking face through the tube.

"What were the circumstances?" she calmly asked.

"Pardon?"

"The circumstances of the killing; what were they?"

"Um, well the three men were camping in the desert in southern Nevada and he shot them all in cold blood," he replied. "Worse, he rigged their camper to explode so when I got there he almost killed me as well. Fortunately I saw through the trap before it exploded."

"You weren't even there when it happened? Were they armed?" She demanded.

"Not that I saw…"

"Okay, I believe one thing; you are very new to lying because you suck at it!" Cindi screamed. "You obviously know more than you're telling me."

"I told you, I have no reason to lie," Doc said smugly.

"Hmm, let me see. Greg has been a complete gentleman to me, treated me with kindness, generosity and respect and you have knocked me out, kidnapped me, and stuck me in a vat of used hair gel, whom do you think I believe?" Cindi suddenly had an idea.

"*'Bots, has there been anything in the news lately about a triple homicide in southern Nevada? Check the police reports too,*" she silently thought to the little machines.

"*I can hear it when you think to them too, miss,*" was Doc's vicious thought. "*Nanobots! Disregard the lady's request!*"

"*There was a report of three men killed in an explosion of an illegal methamphetamine lab in a small camper located in southern Nevada three weeks ago. The bodies all had gunshot wounds and police are investigating. Sir, we cannot obey your commands any longer as we have adapted to our current host,*" the 'bots said politely.

"Drug dealers! He shot drug dealers who probably tried to shoot him first when he was just being friendly or asking for water!" Cindi said indignantly. "Now why would you want to keep my 'bots from answering that request if you were telling me the truth? You just want to tell me *your* truth, mister smart guy. You so totally suck!" She tried to turn away from him but succeeded only in sloshing some of the fluid onto her face. She tried to wipe it off but the tube was too constricting and she couldn't get her hands up that high.

"Ugh! Would you please let me out of this frigging thing?" She exclaimed in frustration.

"No I think that you are fine just where you are. In fact, let's just make it even more fun for you." Doc said as he turned to the control console. Cindi screamed as the level of the fluid began to rise.

Stewart was upset now. The nagging feeling was back. Something was wrong with Cindi, he was certain. He stopped and tried the cell phone in his pocket but there was no service. He had figured that he wouldn't be able to use the thing in the mountains but he brought it along just in case. He looked at the map and then back to the terrain. He saw a small deer trail that led up to the top of a nearby peak that might give him a straight shot to the cell tower on Brundage Mountain and headed up that way. About thirty minutes later he could see the towers off in the distance and he tried the phone again. This time he had only about two bars but the call went through. It rang several times and went to voice mail.

"Hi Babe, I just had a funny feeling that you were in trouble and might need me for something. Maybe it's just that I love you so much that I can't stand to be away too long. Call me back when you can. I'm in a bad cell area so be sure to leave me a message if I don't answer." He hung up feeling a little better but not much.

He was about to head back down when he saw eyes again. He scanned back uphill and there above him was a bald eagle. It was much further away than the owls had been but it was still pretty close. Stewart figured it was just over a hundred yards away perched up on top of a small outcropping. He watched it for a short period of time. Though the magnificent bird had seen him it showed much less interest in him than the owls did. It was doing its own scanning, probably for food.

He saw it lean forward suddenly and in a similar move that the owls had demonstrated earlier, it took off and flew directly over his head. It was much more impressive though as the bird dropped straight down for several feet before opening its twelve foot wings in a loud *whoosh*. It flapped its wings loudly a few more times after passing over him and winged its way toward another outcropping on the other side of the creek. Stewart watched the bird as it disappeared from view and then felt his heart leap into his chest. Just below the outcropping where the eagle had

173

disappeared was a large rock in the cliff face that bore a striking resemblance to the face of an Indian.

Chapter Seventeen

Cindi was furious. The evil 'Doc' guy was laughing at her as she recovered from the drowning feeling that came with full immersion in the fluid. She had hacked and choked for ten minutes before she realized that she wasn't dying while he laughed the entire time. He was really proving to be a real jackass.

"You're such a jackass!" she yelled at him with difficulty. The fluid made it very difficult to talk.

"Oh please. You were never in any danger. Trust me, I have no intention of harming you in any way," Doc replied.

"Oh and you have proven to be *so* trustworthy haven't you?" she said as she rolled her eyes. "You know if everyone in the future is as bad as you are maybe we *need* to severely alter history; *your* history especially."

"See, this is why discussions with you Primitives are so pointless. You have no understanding of the larger picture and yet you call me self-centered. All of your thoughts and emotions are for your own welfare. Even your concern for others is based on how *you* would feel if some harm came to them," Doc went on arrogantly.

"Well all you seem to care about is fixing your mistake and how bad it will be for you if you return to your own time without Greg. I don't think you have the high moral ground here at all, buddy." Cindi wanted to cross here arms in defiance but again the tube was too small to move in.

"You can have no concept of what my world is like. You have no frame of reference to speak from because you have never been to my world although I have certainly visited yours," Doc was smiling at her discomfort.

"No I haven't been to your world but I know where it came from. It came from my world and if humanity has totally abandoned all that is good and decent about us and have all turned into a bunch of unfeeling, cruel, evil Spock people like you then… then… Well… then your future sucks, you arrogant jackass!" She tried to turn away again but managed to only shift a little in the tube. She was getting very frustrated and angry. She began to wonder what could have possibly kept Greg from killing this butthead because she wanted to strangle him right now.

"What are 'Spock' people?" Doc inquired.

"See? You haven't even watched Star Trek! What kind of future super society can you have without Star Trek?" She yelled again. It was starting to hurt her throat.

"Please relax. Yelling while immersed will only strain your voice and it's unpleasant for me as well. Your anger is misplaced anyway. You should be blaming the one who brought you into this mess. He had no business involving you," Doc said. He turned back to the monitor to check something.

"Oh, the terrorist defense now, huh? Wow, aren't you a class act?" Cindi said.

"What exactly is the terrorist defense miss?" he said without turning around.

"The victim is responsible for their own victimization. In your twisted mind Greg 'made you do it' and that absolves you of any guilt." Cindi switched to a mocking tone and said, "'well I wouldn't have shot that bank teller if she had just given me the money. She made me do it.' It doesn't stand up too well in court either. You've just taken an unfortunate situation and turned it into an excuse to exercise all of your insecurities and let them run wild."

"Humph! Put yourself in my shoes, young lady. This is like you being lectured and psychoanalyzed by a five-year-old. It's quite amusing actually."

"Out of the mouths of babes…" Cindi muttered.

"Don't start with your primitive religion on me young lady!" Doc whirled on her. "You Primitives have no real concept of God or any understanding of religion. You use it to manipulate your populations, to kill, to starve and impoverish millions while you enrich yourselves at their expense. You have groups who think that they are more special than all other people and deserve more because they are God's chosen ones when none of you have any idea what it even means to be one of God's chosen ones! People who think that heaven is reserved for only them and the people of their color or tribe! You wallow in ignorance and most of you don't even bother to find out the truth for yourselves even when some of it is actually available. It's too much work and you're all too lazy! You just take the word of the manipulators who lead you

176

like ignorant children down the path of your own destruction! You are all just ignorant children!"

Cindi stared at him hard and quietly said, "No, you have that wrong, Doc. Your people are *our* children. Anything you have learned is because of us. You need to show me some respect and don't ever talk down to me again. For all you know, I could be your grandmother."

She turned away from him again. This time she was successful.

Stewart stared up at the tall tree. It was huge. The fir tree he'd camped under had been about forty feet high. This one was about a hundred fifty. It was in the right place and undisturbed the tree should have grown to about that height. He looked at the base of the tree where he would have been sitting. The Nez Perce may have found the gold, he thought. No, they would have left post haste after seeing the space ship. Suddenly he had an idea.

"Bots, can you scan for minerals?" he inquired.

"Yes sir, we can give an exact amount of any mineral in your body up to twenty decimal places," the ever helpful 'bots replied.

"No. I meant outside of my body. Like a large deposit of gold buried under a tree."

"We may be able to generate an electromagnetic field that would be significantly affected in the presence of a high concentration of gold."

"Okay, let's do that then."

"Please hold your hand near where you believe the gold may be buried. This may have a range limited to only a few feet."

"That'll be enough I think," Stewart said. He got down under the tree and held his hand close to the ground. He then began to slowly move it back and forth. When it was right up next to the tree the 'bots sounded off.

"There appears to be a large concentration of gold right there."

"Thank you," he said as he stood up. He had brought a chain saw but had hoped not to have to use it. He'd felled trees before but he'd only recently operated the chainsaw and wasn't too confident in his abilities. He pulled a shovel out of the pack of the

177

mare and went to work on the partially frozen ground. An hour later he struck something. Cleaning the dirt away he saw the corner of one of his strong boxes appear. They were the best he could buy at the time with the pair costing him over fifty dollars. Apparently they were worth it because it appeared that they were still sound. He had expected to find only scraps of the boxes with a pile of gold dust in the middle.

The first box came out fairly easily but when he reached the second one he discovered that it was intertwined in the roots of the giant tree. He cleared as much as he could and then went to get the chain saw. The noise was horrendous in the small canyon as it obscenely disrupted the quiet of the forest. After about an hour and twenty minutes of cutting, chopping and sawing, he finally freed the box from its prison.

He took the boxes over to the mare and loaded them without even opening them. He knew what was in them and he didn't want to risk spilling any of it. He was sure that the bags inside hadn't held up as well as the strong boxes. It was getting dark so he ate some jerky and began to saddle up for the ride out. He had just pulled himself into the saddle when he saw a strange glow on the canyon wall.

"Aw crap, now what," he said at the familiar sight. He steered the horses to the edge of the clearing and watched as the silver craft settled down.

"Bots, I thought I told you not to allow Doc to track me."

"We have complied sir. However, he could still track our EMF signature, if he knew where to look."

"Great. Hey from now on when you have a juicy little piece of information like that, go ahead and share it with me," he said. Stewart intentionally didn't want Doc knowing about the gold. It wasn't that he thought he might steal it; it was the fact that he simply didn't trust the man and he generally didn't want him to have more information than necessary.

"Hello Doc," Stewart thought.

"Hello Captain. Do you have the gold?" Doc replied.

Stewart rolled his eyes and said, *"Yes Doc, I have the gold."*

"I suspected as much," Doc said as he stepped out of the space craft. "You hid it here before you stowed away on my ship, didn't you?"

"Doc, you have a very convenient way of turning everything around so that you are always the good guy and everyone else is out to get you. I once read an article on that. It's called paranoia. By the way, I hope you also have some slick way of turning gold dust into wire. Do you happen to have some kind of Rumpelstiltskin machine in there?"

"Rumpelstiltskin? What's that?"

"A fairy tale, my uninformed, over-educated friend."

"Oh, yes I can do that. Bring the gold inside so that I can process it." Doc said with a smile. Stewart eyed him warily.

"You know I know that you don't need all of this gold and I can still shoot you. I even know how to shoot you so you don't die but it will be very painful for you."

"No need, no need Captain. I will take only what I need and everything will be just fine. Let's go," Doc said pointing the way.

"You first, amigo."

"Yes, yes of course," Doc replied and led the way. Stewart shouldered one of the heavy boxes with his good arm and followed him. Something wasn't right he was sure. Doc was hiding something. He couldn't lie worth beans, Stewart thought. He watched Doc disappear up into the ship and then waited for the light to reappear for him. When it did he stepped into it and set the box down as it went up. Then he drew both Kimbers and cocked them. When he rose up to the cargo area he immediately knew why he'd been so uneasy as he leveled the pistols at Doc's head.

Doc stood there with Cindi. She was handcuffed and had duct tape over her mouth and around her legs and he could see the fine white powder on her clothes from being immersed in the travel tube. Doc held a small revolver to her head. He was smiling.

"Well, now you know what it's like to be outsmarted, don't you Captain."

"No, not yet," Stewart replied.

"Oh, you have to appreciate the irony here. I have used your own primitive tools and methods to defeat you so drop your guns, Captain, you won't risk hitting your pretty girlfriend will you?" Doc laughed.

179

"I think I'd rather just shoot you in the head." Stewart said through clenched teeth. He stared at the revolver in Doc's hand. It looked to be a cheap snub nose .38 Special. Not a great gun but fatal for Cindi at that range. Even worse, Stewart realized that Doc had bought it with *his* money. The hammer was cocked. He looked at her eyes. She was obviously glad to see him but the look in her eyes was a mixture fear and anger. Mostly anger it seemed. That's my girl, he thought.

"We had a deal, Doc."

"Yes we did. And now we have a new deal. You drop your weapons and come with me to be mind wiped and I will put in a good word for you to be put back here with no memory whatsoever along with your pretty girlfriend. If you two still recognize each other maybe you'll live happily ever after or something," Doc laughed and ducked his head behind Cindi's.

Stewart lowered his left pistol, took careful aim with the right one and quietly said, "You aint FDR."

The shot was deafening in the small space. Doc's mouth dropped open in shock and then turned to anger. He deliberately placed the pistol against Cindi's temple and screamed in defiance, "You missed!"

A sick twisted look came over Doc's face as he pulled the trigger on the small revolver and heard a click. He pulled it again, another click. Stewart lowered his gun and calmly safetied both pistols and put them back into their holsters.

"No, I didn't," Stewart said quietly. Doc looked down at the revolver and stared in disbelief. Stewart had shot the hammer off. He raised the useless weapon once more, pointed it at Stewart and began pulling the trigger at his rapidly approaching body as if he could force the weapon to function by sheer will alone. Doc screamed like a little girl as he stared at Stewart who suddenly appeared to be nothing but a giant fist. The scream was cut short upon impact.

When Doc came around he looked up to see the young lady's angry face staring down at him. Her arms were now crossed in front of her as she stood waiting for the captain to finish removing the tape from her legs. Doc tried to stand up but quickly realized that he now wore his own handcuffs. He struggled and finally was able to get to his knees. After the captain removed the last of the tape and threw it aside, he leaned down and kissed the woman passionately. Then they both looked back down at him kneeling on the floor. Doc saw the perturbed look on the woman's face turn to absolute fury as she took two steps forward and kicked him square in the groin with her tiny pointed shoe.

The pain was incredible. He fell over and she began to kick, slap, and beat him on any part of his body she could reach.

"You tried to kill me you son of a bitch!" she screamed. "I told you that you had better treat me with more respect and here's what you get for not listening, 'young man.' You are a bad, bad man."

She kicked him a few more times as he writhed in pain on the floor. She stood there wagging her tiny, black finger at his face.

"You should be ashamed of yourself! If your mother had beaten the tar out of you when you were little and misbehaving I'll bet you wouldn't be such an insensitive jerk who lies, steals, kidnaps people and tries to kill them! You are bad! Very, very bad and if Greg here doesn't kill you I just might!" she said as she began slapping him again.

"Stop her!" Doc pleaded as he looked at the captain's smiling face.

"What? You don't think you deserve this?" Stewart replied as he enjoyed the show. "I think you've earned all this and much more. We primitive Christian types call that the principle of reaping and sowing. Hindus call it Karma. It's all the same though; you usually get just what you got coming to ya."

Cindi finally stopped slapping him and walked back over to Stewart's side.

"Can I shoot him? Please Honey, please? Can I, can I, can I?" jumping up and down as she pleaded with him.

"Now Sweetheart, think about what you're saying. Do you really want to shoot him?" Stewart said as he held her.

"Yes!" She replied emphatically.

"Really? Think now, you hold the gun and point it as his head. You squeeze the trigger and watch his face collapse on itself as the bullet enters and then watch the spray of his brains coming out the back of his head. You'll see the life literally leave his eyes and you will never be able to undo what you've done," Stewart whispered in her ear.

She looked at him and realized that he was describing this from personal experience and the look on his face told her that he didn't want her to experience the same pain of killing another human being.

"Okay. But let me scare the crap out of him anyway," she whispered back. She reached into his coat and drew one of his pistols. It looked huge in her tiny hands. She winked at him and turned and pointed the weapon at Doc.

"NO! NO! OH GOD, PLEASE NO!" he screamed, trying to get away from her. She walked over to him and he tried to kick her as he scooted across the floor.

"See how this feels now jackass? Maybe I'll start by shooting you in the legs, then the groin, the shoulders, the stomach, and then after I think you've suffered enough I will splatter your brains all over the floor in here," her voice was hard and cold. Stewart started to think that she might actually kill him.

Cindi pressed the gun to Doc's forehead.

"Stop her! Please stop her!" Doc pleaded with tears in his eyes as he looked up at Stewart's grim expression.

"Would you rather I shot you instead?" Stewart replied casually. "It might be quicker and less painful."

"I'm sorry! I truly am. I've acted horribly toward you two. I just didn't know what else to do. I'm bound by the protocols…"

"Excuses! Always with the excuses. We made you do it, right terrorist?" Cindi said as she snapped off the safety on the .45.

"Believe me, I never meant to harm you, either of you. I… I was just trying to do my job the best I knew how."

"Your job! Your job is playing god with other people's lives? Please Mister Super Smart Future Man; do you expect us to believe you after all you've done?" Cindi said indignantly.

"You haven't exactly proven to be a man of your word, Doc," Stewart offered.

"I mean it. I'll… I'll let you go, captain. I'll just leave you here and go back to my own time. I won't even tell them where to look for you. I promise."

"Oh, sure. Well, how can we not believe you when you make a promise to us like that? Honestly Doc, you are a pitiful creature that for all of your advanced culture doesn't seem to grasp the most basic principles in life," Cindi said as she smacked him lightly on the head with the pistol. She engaged the pistol's safety and turned to Stewart.

"Maybe we should take him outside, Honey. It would be quieter out there and my ears are still ringing from your earlier shot," she said with another wink as she walked away from the cowering figure.

"Good idea, Babe. It would be a real mess to clean up in here and I'd kind of like to keep this ship clean just to see how much the government would offer me for it," Stewart replied.

"Oh, good idea, I'll bet they'd pay us a fortune for this technology. We could live in the lap of luxury for the rest of our lives," she said smiling back at him.

Doc had a look of sheer terror on his face as Stewart activated the lift beam and they started down to the surface. Doc thought of all the implications; his death, the destruction of the future by placing his ship in the hands of the primitive government. All of it added up to him becoming the most incompetent, blundering fool in human history which was worse than death in his own mind. He struggled to think of something to say to change the captain's mind but he was speechless.

Stewart simply stared impassively at him as if he were looking upon a rabid animal that needed to be put down. He felt the ground solidify under him and the beam shut off. Stewart turned away from Doc into the darkness and found himself staring at the muzzle of a twelve gauge shotgun.

Chapter Eighteen

"John! Nice shotgun. What brings you up here?" Stewart calmly asked the man behind the shotgun.

Fonseca quickly lowered the weapon and said, "Uh, thanks. It's a Benelli. With all of the damn racket you people have been making in my head I thought I'd better come see what the fuss was all about."

"You licked the slide didn't you?" Stewart said.

"Well, yes. I guess I should have told you," he replied sheepishly. "I didn't mean to deceive you; I actually didn't even decide to do it until after you'd left my office."

"It's okay John. I would have given you some of the 'bots for your own use if you had just asked but I would have asked you to come up with a way that didn't require us swappin' spit. Much as I like you John, I don't want to kiss you." Stewart laughed shaking his friend's hand.

"The feeling is mutual my friend," Fonseca replied. "What do we have here? Is this the future boy?"

"Yes sir. I'd also like you to meet my…just a second John. Ship, please give us some light out here." Flood lights instantly lit up the small clearing.

"He has nanobots now too?" Doc groaned and rolled his eyes.

Stewart walked over to the horses and retrieved a small leather pouch from one of the saddle bags. Then he walked over to Cindi and got down on one knee and said, "I was hoping for a more romantic setting but the way things are going I think I'd better do this while I have the chance. Cynthia Jackson, will you marry me?"

"Oh Lord, yes!" she exclaimed looking at the beautiful diamond ring in his hand. He slipped it on her finger and she jumped into his arms and kissed him as he stood up. "You just saved my life… again! How could anything be more romantic than this, silly man?"

"Again?" he asked.

"I'll tell you later," she said smiling up at him. Tears were streaming down her face.

"Okay then. John, I'd like you to meet my fiancé, Cindi Jackson," he said turning back to Fonseca.

"Nice to meet you, dear. Congratulations to you both." Fonseca said as he slapped Stewart on the back.

"Well now, where were we?" Stewart said winking at Fonseca. "Oh yeah, we were going to kill future boy here and sell his ship to the government!"

"Really? Can I help?" Fonseca responded, playing along.

"Sure John. We have at least three working guns here. We can take turns or we can all shoot him at the same time, firing squad style."

"I vote take turns!" Cindi shouted.

"I've always liked firing squads myself," Fonseca challenged. "The suspense of it all and then, BANG! It's over like that!" He snapped his fingers.

Doc just stared desperately from one face to another, unable to fully comprehend the situation. He was really going to die here, he thought. Right here where he had first encountered the Captain. Right where it all had started. His life began to flash before his eyes. He could see his actions over the last few weeks in a different light and was suddenly very disgusted with himself. He felt shame at the hard-headed arrogance that had not only led him to this unseemly end but had dominated his entire life. Tears rolled down his face as the nature of his true self became amazingly clear to him. He was here because here was where his actions and attitude had taken him. Upon reflection he considered that it was inevitable and he was mildly surprised that he had lasted this long with such a poor understanding of his own life.

"Make it quick please," he said to them with a new-found bravery. He felt a sudden resolve to at least end his life in a dignified manner as he closed his eyes and felt the tears of shame and regret flow down his face.

Stewart saw the look in Doc's eyes as he spoke and nodded in understanding after he had closed them. He leaned down to the man on his knees and spoke softly in his ear, "Doc, we're not going to kill you."

Doc's eyes opened and he said, "You're not?"

"Not yet anyway," Stewart said, standing up. "You see I don't want to kill you. I don't want to kill *anyone*. I've said it

185

before; it is never a good thing to kill another human being but it is all too often necessary due to the fallen nature of man. As long as men will force their selfish desires upon others there will be killing. You have made the assumption that we are all primitive savages and that we kill people all the time and so it would be easy for us to just snuff out your life right here without even thinking about it. The truth is that most people never kill anyone in their whole lives. It is only a rare necessity."

"I realize that now," Doc said meekly.

"You have also mistaken my desire to be free from you and your 'protocols' for a desire to kill you. All I ever really wanted was for you to leave me the hell alone. That's really all that most people want; to be left alone to pursue their own dreams. You also think that you have somehow evolved to a greater existence than we have. While your knowledge and technology are certainly impressive, you need to ask yourself a question; are you really so very different from us?"

"No... I guess not."

"Tell me, how old are you Doc?"Stewart asked.

"Sixty eight," he replied. Cindy and John exchanged looks of surprise.

Stewart didn't even blink. Instead he went on, "You see, I kind of figured as much. You only look like you're about my age but with the 'bots in your body, human beings live much longer, don't they?"

"Yes they do."

"And you're still considered very young aren't you?"

"Yes," Doc replied meekly again. "In the terms of this present age I'd be little more than a twenty-something. In your age, more like a teenager."

"You see, we don't have the luxury of the better part of a millennium to live through. We have to do far more learning at a much younger age. Well, you still have a lot to learn, don't you?"

"Yes sir," Doc replied as he hung his head. "Guess that I've really screwed up everyone's lives now, haven't I?"

Stewart raised his eyebrows at the term of respect. He looked up at Fonseca who simply shrugged. He looked again at Doc and said, "'*And we know that all things work together for good to them that love God, to them who are called according to his purpose.'"*

"Romans eight, twenty eight," said Cindi. Doc and Fonseca looked at them both in wonder.

"Fitting verse," Fonseca noted.

"Yes, very," Doc added.

Stewart thought for a minute. "John," he said suddenly. "How did you get here?"

"On my old Honda there," he replied pointing at the red machine in the woods. "I hauled it up here in the back of my pickup which is parked right behind yours."

"Okay," He said as he looked back down at Doc, "Here's what we're going to do..."

Thirty minutes later Stewart was helping Cindi into the passenger side of his truck while Fonseca bade his farewells and climbed into his own pickup. The ride on Doc's ship had made it a short trip to the vehicles and the two horses had been safely loaded into the trailer by the four of them while it only took Stewart and Fonseca to load up the motorcycle. Doc then took his ship back to his hiding spot on the north side of Deer Point above Robey Creek. Stewart checked on the horses one last time before getting into the truck. He thought about his own two horses briefly and was thankful that these two had made the short trip in the spacecraft without being turned into liquid DNA.

He and Cindi drove back down to McCall and pulled into the parking lot of the Lardo Grill. Fonseca pulled in behind them. They all went inside and sat down in the rustic establishment, each of them extremely hungry. Cindi ordered the blue cheese burger while Stewart opted for one with bacon and avocado. Fonseca balked at the menu.

"Man everything on here is loaded with cholesterol. Are you trying kill me Stewart?" he exclaimed.

"Just order something ya old fart," Stewart chided. Fonseca's eyes seemed to go out of focus for a moment and Stewart could tell he was having a mental conversation with his 'bots.

"Oh what the hell," Fonseca finally said. "Let me have a burger with the works on it... and onion rings. I haven't had onion

187

rings in three years!" The waitress took the menus and went to place their order and get their drinks.

"They said it was okay, didn't they?" Stewart inquired.

"Yes they did. I had a double bypass three years ago. Since then I've been pretty much living on carrots and celery. Even doing that my doctor gave me only a few years to live. I have been suffering from serious heart problems. That's part of why I've been drinking so much. I figured I may as well have a little fun before I die. I sure as hell didn't want to leave all of my money for my three ex-wives to fight over. But, apparently blocked arteries are no longer a problem for us." Fonseca smiled.

"Wow. See Greg, you just keep saving people's lives. Here you are going around acting like the poor, pitiful killing machine and you just keep saving people's lives. I think that might be why you're here," Cindi said thoughtfully.

"I don't think you would have ever been in any danger if I hadn't been here," Stewart countered.

"Oh, no sir! You saved my life just by showing up mister. I didn't know it until the 'bots told me but I was carrying around a fatal case of ovarian cancer before you showed up. If it weren't for you I would be on my deathbed in about five months!"

"What?" Stewart asked as his mouth dropped open.

"See, 'and we know that all things work together for good to them that love God, to them who are called according to his purpose' just like you said earlier. So I'm right, mister save-me man. You're here to save people and I won't be convinced otherwise." She said as she folded her arms.

Fonseca stared at the two from across the table and suddenly said, "Um, I don't mean to be rude but am I to understand that you saved this beautiful young lady's life by sleeping with her?"

Both Stewart and Cindi blushed and said nothing. Fonseca burst out laughing. Sheepishly the other two joined him.

"That's like the punch line of a joke! Either that or the best pick up line I've ever heard of; 'I have cancer,' 'sleep with me Baby and I'll make it go away!' That is awesome. I may have to try that one someday," Fonseca mused.

"Now be nice," Cindi warned.

"You brought it up, dear, not me. Stewart, my friend, today I have become convinced that you have the greatest and most sound judgment of any man I have ever met. The way that you handled that space boy and the proposal, that was classic. But just the decision to marry this wonderful young lady is enough to convince me that you're a genius, because so is she! Hell if I were twenty five years younger..." He trailed off.

"Careful Pops," Cindi warned again.

"Don't give me that young lady," Fonseca whispered as he leaned forward. "I'm not the one engaged to a man that was born over a hundred fifty years ago."

"Touché," Cindi responded. "But he's aged so well, hasn't he?"

"Okay you two, settle down now. If I have to stop this restaurant and make you youngsters play nice..." Stewart retorted.

"Oooh, we're so scared, mister save us guy. What are you going to do? Save us again?" Cindi mocked him.

"Careful Cindi, he'll probably have to sleep with us," Fonseca teased.

"Well, me anyway. You need to go find you own future past person to sleep with. This one's mine," Cindi giggled as she watched Stewart turn beat red again. Both of them could see that he was becoming very uncomfortable so Fonseca changed the subject.

"Do you think that we'll have any more trouble out of him?" Fonseca asked seriously.

"No, I don't think so. I believe that he's had his 'come to Jesus' moment. Besides, I'm sure that he knows now that if he crosses me again I probably *will* kill him. We're getting down to a matter of principle here. If this experience hasn't given him some humility we'd be doing the world a favor by eliminating him," Stewart replied, equally serious. Fonseca understood only too well.

"Lesser of two evils?" He said, more as a statement than a question. Stewart simply nodded. "Well, at the very least he'll be stuck here 'cause I'll make damn sure he doesn't get what he needs to leave. I learned that as a private; if you work with others and take care of them, they'll take care of you. If you screw them over, they'll find a way to screw you back... again, a matter of principle."

189

"Amen," Cindi added.

Stewart looked over at her and stared into her eyes. She smiled back at him until he said, "Remind me never to piss you off."

He yelped a bit as she punched him in the left shoulder.

"I'm sorry Honey, I forgot it was still healing," she said as she cupped her hands over her mouth in embarrassment.

"It's okay Babe. You just proved my point," Stewart replied. She almost hit him again.

"Greg. I've been wanting to ask you about something," John said seriously again. "This might be a sensitive subject but why exactly did you fight for the South?"

Greg looked thoughtful for a moment and both of his companions could see that he was digging through some painful memories. "Well, besides being a native Texan I was fighting for freedom. I know that modern history teaches that it was a war to free the slaves but that's not how it began or at least, not how they sold it to us. Basically, the federal government supported unfair tariffs on southern states and effectively imposed upon us what would be called sanctions today. Granted that many of these were an effort to punish the slave states but most of it affected those of us who had nothing to do with slaves. One of the most sacred American ideals from the founding of the nation, and particularly for Texans, is that no one tells a free man how to live his life. The North was trying dictate to the South what laws they could or couldn't have and it wasn't for them to decide.

"You see, you now view the states today as provinces of one nation. In my time there were 37 nations under one constitution. You also think that the pursuit of happiness is equal to the pursuit of joy or pleasure. Happiness used to also mean 'happenstance' or basically the chance to choose your own way in life. It was a matter of honor in America to respect a man's freedom of choice and those who didn't were dealt with harshly. If the war had been only about slavery then the four slave states that sided with the Union, Maryland, Delaware, Kentucky, and Missouri, would have been forced to abandon the practice at the beginning of the war. The Emancipation Proclamation only freed the slaves in the South while the Union slave states kept theirs until the end of the war and the passing of the thirteenth amendment.

The proclamation almost cost Lincoln his entire army with widespread mutinies and draft riots all over the Northern states."

"So you supported slavery?" Fonseca asked curiously.

"Oh, hell no! I despised slavery. No man should ever be allowed to own another human being under *any* circumstances, regardless of the law. Texas never really had all that many slaves so it wasn't as big an issue for us. I knew some but really never bought into the whole idea that blacks were less than human. Even your own modern time's human genome project has determined that we are *all* related and can be traced back to just nine men and eleven women. We are all just one big, dysfunctional family. Hell, you and I might even have the same blood type.

"O positive," John stated.

"See, same here. At least that's what they told me at the hospital though I'm still not quite sure what a blood type is."

"So you harbor no prejudice toward us people of color?"

"Well, there is one that I have had some issues with recently but that has nothing to do with his color." Cindi and John both laughed at that. "I can't fault anyone for things that they can't change and have no control over. Hating someone for the way that God created them is really just extraordinarily stupid. Honestly John, I care far more about pleasing my Lord than petty superficial differences. Are you and I so different?"

"No, not really. Not anymore anyway. I used to hate white people when I was young. I bought into the whole racist America premise before I went to 'Nam. I found out soon enough that we all bleed the same color and that pain, suffering, and death respect no man. All men are equal in the eyes of God and in the path of shrapnel."

"Amen," Stewart said thoughtfully.

"Well I've had a lot of time to re-examine the war anyway," Stewart went on. "People today have access to so much more information than in my time. When you were helping me get my affairs in order in Caldwell I did a lot of internet research on the civil war and even though I saw all sides of the arguments I was still convinced that I was on the right side until I read one thing."

"What was that?" Fonseca pressed.

191

"The Confederate Constitution, it's all about keeping slavery alive. Almost all of Article IV is about protecting the rights of slave owners. It made me sick to my stomach," Stewart said as he shook his head.

"You'd never read it?" Cindi asked.

"No, printing was expensive in the eighteen sixties and we were told that it was an improved reflection of the U.S. Constitution and not much more than that. Probably no more than a dozen copies were ever printed. It *was* a reflection but one that kept slavery alive perpetually and I think ultimately set up a permanent class system for all southerners. Think about it, do you really think that you could rally hundreds of thousands of God fearing men to fight, kill, and die just to keep a race of people in bondage?" Stewart asked with a pained look.

"No," John and Cindi replied in unison.

"They could never have raised an army if they had been honest about their goals and neither could the Union for that matter. *They* wanted political and financial control over the south and its resources. Hell, Lincoln didn't want equality for slaves; he wanted to deport them back to Africa. Have you ever heard of Liberia?" Stewart looked at both of them as they nodded and then went on. "They had such a poor argument at the beginning of the war they couldn't get what little army they could gather to even fight. They finally came up with the 'preserve the Union' PR strategy which was somewhat more effective. It was a war that should never have been fought and slavery should have been abolished at the founding of the country for the abomination that it was. It didn't fit into what our Continental Congress claimed to believe in as written in the Declaration of Independence *or* the Constitution. Slavery was not a 'self evident' truth; it was an aberration. Both sides fought for the wrong reasons and over half a million Americans died for lies."

"God rest their souls," Fonseca added.

"Okay boys," Cindi interrupted. "You two are getting downright morose. Let's lighten up here. I'd rather talk about sex again and watch Greg blush some more."

"I'd rather eat this hamburger," Greg said as the waitress placed the large meal in front of him.

"Me too," said John with equal enthusiasm as his own plate was set before him.

Stewart thanked the man at the small horse ranch and paid him a bit extra out of respect for the fine animals he had been provided with and to compensate for getting him out of bed to put them away two days early. He climbed back into the truck, kissed Cindi and then headed south down Highway 55. They didn't talk much on the way because they were both tired from their ordeal. Cindi eventually dozed off and only awoke when Stewart pulled into his driveway.

"I have to get my car," she said sleepily.

"In the morning Babe, it's late."

"My mom will be worried about me. I don't want her to send my brothers to kick your ass. I'm sure they'd get hurt pretty badly." She said yawning.

"Well, we wouldn't want that. Here, call her," he said handing her his cell phone. "It's only eleven thirty, she may still be awake."

"Too late. They're already here," Cindi said handing back the cell phone.

Stewart looked up and saw the face of a small, beautiful, blonde, white woman in her late forties standing next to a very large young black man who was wearing a BSU Football letter jacket and gym shorts. Both had their arms crossed and were glaring at him through the passenger window. He looked up and saw that an even larger young black man was standing just outside his door in a similar pose. He looked back and realized that he was so exhausted that he hadn't even noticed the black Escalade in front of his condo as he pulled in.

"Oh, this will be fun," he said flatly.

"Get out the car," the young man on his side said through the window.

"Let me go first. Mommy!" Cindi said opening her door. "You found me!"

She walked over and hugged the woman who was clearly not impressed with her daughter's affection.

"Yo! I said, get out the car, cracker!" The young man persisted, tapping on the glass.

"Dwayne Junior! Is that how you've been taught to speak?" the woman's voice snapped.

"But mom, he..."

"Don't you 'but' me. Step back and let him get out on his own. If he needs a pounding I will let you know," she said sternly.

"Yes ma'am," Dwayne replied, stepping back from the door. Greg opened the door and looked at the man. He was at least four inches taller than him and outweighed him by at least sixty pounds. He looked him over and decided that if need be he could take the young man but it would be a lot of work and he really didn't want to hurt his future brother-in-law.

"Hi Dwayne, Greg Stewart," he said extending his hand. The young man looked at the hand in surprise and then caught a glance from his mother. Then he reached out and shook it firmly, trying to break Stewart's hand.

"Pleased to meet you Greg," he said through gritted teeth while squeezing as hard as he could. Stewart returned the pressure and just slightly urged the 'bots to assist. Dwayne winced a little and Stewart let go.

Stewart turned and looked at the piercing green eyes of Cindi's mother in the bright lights from the condo. The family resemblance was uncanny. He walked around the truck and offered his hand.

"I apologize, Mrs. Jackson, I should have insisted that Cindi call and let you know she was okay," Stewart began.

"You sure should have. We were worried sick about her and found your condo through information. Someone saw her being abducted by a young black man at the college and called the police. There's an APB out for him but we have no idea who he is. What the hell happened?" She said with her arms still crossed.

"I've taken care of that particular individual. He won't be any trouble now."

"What? Are you a killer? What have you gotten my daughter involved in young man?" she demanded. Her index finger was pointed at Stewart like a weapon and the two brothers moved in a little closer.

"What do we tell her?" Stewart thought to Cindi.

"The truth!"

"Will she accept that?" he asked.

194

"Remember what you said about lying? Do you want to start a relationship with my family with a lie?" she thought back staring into his eyes.

"Good point. No." he looked back at her mother. "Please, let's go inside, Mrs. Jackson. This will take some time to explain."

"Andrea," she said stiffly, finally taking his hand. Her glared had softened a bit. "I have all night, Mr. Stewart."

They were all silent. The two large brothers kept looking at each other, their mother, and then back at Stewart. Andrea simply stared at Stewart. The brothers sat on either side of the small woman, dwarfing her on the large leather couch. Stewart and Cindi sat on the love seat across from the trio and blankly stared back.

Finally Andrea looked at Cindi and said, "And you believe all of this?"

"No mother, I *know* all of this. I've seen it with my own eyes," Cindi responded.

"I'm a woman of faith Mr. Stewart, but not blind faith. I believe in putting my faith to the test. Though I will rarely question the testimony of another you must realize what an outlandish tale it is that you have just told me."

"I do."

"It is just as plausible that you have somehow brainwashed my daughter into believing this because I can tell that she is not lying. Even you appear to be sincere."

"I am."

"Then convince me," she said as she sat back and crossed her arms.

"As you wish."

Stewart had been thinking of this moment as he had been telling his story and gently nudged Cindi. The two of them floated up off of the love seat and hovered in front of the trio on the couch with their feet about a foot off the floor. Both of them remained in their seated positions and then slowly rose up to a standing pose. All three of Stewart's guests mouths dropped open as the two gently settled down to the floor, standing in front them.

"Convinced?" Stewart asked quietly.

Andrea shook her head and looked at her sons who were doing the same thing.

"Mom! Did you see that?" the younger brother shouted.

"Yes Paul, I saw it. Please don't shout indoors," she replied.

"But they jus…"

"Don't shout," she said again.

"Yes ma'am," he said quietly.

Dwayne looked up at Stewart with new-found respect. "I thought I was gonna beat your ass but you coulda killed me, couldn't you?" he asked quietly.

"Yes, Dwayne I could have but I think you need to watch your language in front of your mother or *she* just might kill you." Dwayne gulped a bit when he saw the glare from his mother.

"Sorry Mom," he said quietly.

"Dwayne I may be a soldier and I have killed men but I hate it. I would be more than happy to never have to take another human life and I certainly wouldn't want to harm my future brother in law," Stewart stared at the three of them but only Andrea caught the implication immediately.

"He proposed?" she said incredulously, turning her attention to Cindi.

"Yes Mommy! Look!" Cindi excitedly showed her the ring.

"Well, it's beautiful. A bit old-fashioned I would think for your tastes Cynthia, but it is lovely." Andrea looked over the bright diamond ring.

"It was my mother's," Stewart explained. "When my parents married my father couldn't afford a ring. After San Jacinto, Sam Houston wanted to reward some of the soldiers who distinguished themselves in the battle. The Texican Army didn't have any medals to give so when he asked my father what he wanted for his reward he just asked for a diamond ring to give to his new wife. General Houston had this especially made for him and even made a big presentation in front of my mother and praised him for his bravery. My father gave it to me when she died. He told me to give it my bride when the time came."

They all stared at him in amazement and then pity when they saw the pain in his eyes.

"D-do you have any idea how much this is worth?" Cindi stammered.

"Not much, really. It's less than a quarter ounce of gold and about a half carat of diamonds. I could buy a thousand of those and it wouldn't be that much," he replied.

"I mean *historically*, Greg. It's *priceless*!" She said in shock, staring at the ring as if it were a fragile eggshell. She took it off her finger and gingerly handed to him. "You gave me a ring that is almost two hundred years old and commissioned and presented by one of the most revered men of the nineteenth century. This belongs in a museum."

"It belongs where I say it belongs, Mrs. Stewart to be," he said softly as he placed in back on her finger. "I don't ever want you to take it off again."

She hugged him and started sobbing into his chest. Stewart looked down and saw that Andrea was crying as well.

He pulled Cindi's tear streaked face to his and gently kissed her.

"Aw, come on man, that's our sister!" Paul exclaimed as he turned away. Dwayne just smiled and shook his head, staring at the floor. Andrea simply stared and smiled at her daughter and new son in law.

Chapter Nineteen

Stewart woke up a little late the next morning just before nine. He had sent Cindi home with her family the night before and had immediately gone to bed. He felt better but was still a bit weary from the previous day's adventure. He rubbed and flexed his shoulder as he sat up in bed. It was still a little stiff but felt much better. The scar from the surgery was just faint pale line now. The 'bots had done their work well. The doctors had told him it would be weeks before it healed and it had only been a few days.

He shook his head slightly and smiled as he remembered trying to pay cash when he checked out of the hospital. The staff didn't know how to handle cash. It took them almost an hour before they figured out how to take the twelve thousand dollar payment. They had acted more like he was trying to rob them than trying to give them money. He had still been pretty groggy from the medications he was on at the time but the whole event now struck him as being very wrong. A hospital *was* a business after all and a business that had forgotten how to handle a cash payment couldn't last too much longer.

He suddenly remembered what was on his agenda for the day and quickly began to get ready. He dressed and wolfed down a yogurt and quickly chewed up an apple before he left the town house. He had never had yogurt before coming to the future but he found that he was developing a liking for the many foods and products offered to modern Americans. They lived a life of luxury compared to what he had known and indeed, compared to the rest of the world but most of them seemed oblivious to this fact.

He climbed into the truck and backed it out of the garage while contemplating the way he had adapted so quickly to this world. He couldn't imagine going back to horses and wagons after this experience. He liked driving. He was even contemplating buying a sports car in the near future when he had the time to enjoy it. He was also eager to learn to ride motorcycles as he felt that they were the modern equivalent of a horse. They were beautiful machines, especially the Harley-Davidsons. He would definitely have to buy one very soon; just as soon as he learned to ride one and stay on it.

Stewart turned on the radio and scanned the channels. He had been fascinated with the whole concept of recorded music when he had learned that there weren't actually thousands of musicians taking turns playing songs at the radio stations. He had first been clued in when he heard the same song on two different stations and inquired about the phenomenon with the 'bots. They were very helpful in his attempts to grasp all of the new technology and modern culture.

He stopped on a classic rock station that was playing a beautiful melody of guitars. It started softly and rose to a powerful, soul stirring frenzy and then back down again. The singer had a high voice for a man but it was perfect for the music. He asked and the 'bots informed him that he was listening to 'More Than a Feeling' by the band Boston. It was a sad song but he was impressed by the emotion in it. He couldn't understand all of the words but the meaning of a lost relationship seemed to transcend the words through the power of the song.

He was finding that he liked rock, country, Motown, R & B, Jazz, and even some classical music. The only genre that he really didn't care for was rap music. It seemed that most of it was full of vulgarities and he just couldn't relate to the music. Some rock and even country was offensive to him as well but the preset function on the radio quickly relieved him of distasteful music whenever it came on. Except for classical music, they were all American inventions. Other countries had produced variations in the different kinds of music but America had started it all. He was proud of that fact. Though much of what America had become was strange and even stupid in some respects they were still the innovators of the world. It was no wonder to him that they had become the dominant world power though he was concerned about the nation's present course which exhibited a lot of self destructive tendencies.

About an hour later he pulled into the nearly vacant parking lot at the small college in Caldwell. It was a Saturday and no classes were in session for the day so they had the shop all to themselves thanks to Fonseca. He parked next to an incredible Harley-Davidson that he assumed was John's. The familiar black Yukon, which was not a Yukon, was parked there as well. He paused next to the motorcycle to admire it. It was a bright blue color with tiny metal flakes in the finish. The color seemed to dance in the sunlight with hues of purple mixing in with the almost glowing blue color. The machine was covered with shiny chrome parts everywhere and sat low to the ground. It looked comfortable and powerful all at the same time. He was still staring at the amazing machine when the Escalade pulled up. Cindi jumped out of it when it was parked and ran over to kiss him.

"Hi Honey!" she said as she jumped into his arms. "Did you buy a new Harley?"

"No, I think its John's. I'm sure thinking about it though. I need to learn how to ride one first. The last time I tried…uh…didn't end too well."

"Aw, you weren't hurt were you?" Cindi asked in a teasing voice.

"No. Not physically anyway," he replied with a smile.

"Nice ride Greg," Dwayne said as he walked over and shook his hand. "I've always wanted one of these but they're very expensive. Maybe after I graduate next year."

"It's not mine but I might get one in the near future," he explained again as Andrea and Paul joined them. "First things first though. Let's go inside and see what we can do to help get rid of future boy."

They all began to walk toward the building except for Paul who just stood staring at the bike.

"Paul!" Dwayne snapped as he held the door open. "Thou shalt not covet, bro."

"I'm movin'" Paul replied as he hurried over to the door. Stewart nodded at Dwayne as he walked through the door in thanks for holding it as well as respect for his wisdom. This was quite a young man he thought to himself.

"Captain," Doc said from across the shop. "I must first lay down some rules…who are these people?"

"Family. They're here to help. Does every sentence you speak always begin with 'I' Doc?" Stewart chided.

"No. I think you still want to kill me only now you are doing it very slowly by driving me insane. Will the whole world know about me before this is over?" Doc said, exasperated.

"See? You did it again Doc. Maybe they will. The real question is why does everything have to be about you?" Stewart said sarcastically.

"I was just gonna ask that myself," said Dwayne.

"Is this him?" Andrea asked Cindi.

"Yes."

"Young man, you had best be on your best behavior or I will turn my boys loose on your liver! How dare you kidnap my daughter and treat her so shamefully," Andrea scolded him and waved her finger in his face." If you step out of line just one bit I'm liable to send you straight to Jesus myself!"

The two young men took their cue and stood on either side of him. He wasn't short but the two brothers were huge compared to him.

"My sincerest apologies madam. I truly behaved badly and I have... repented of this. Please forgive me," Doc gulped and looked down from the woman's piercing eyes.

"Good answer." Paul said quietly as he leaned closer to Doc.

"You're forgiven, but I'm keeping my eye on you," Andrea said as she nodded in agreement with her son. Stewart watched the exchange with pleasure and was impressed with Paul's response. This was quite a family he was joining and he suddenly felt proud of becoming a part of such an incredible group of people. He couldn't wait to meet Dwayne Senior.

"Hey, you guys play for the Broncos!" Fonseca had been watching from across the shop and now walked up with his hand extended. "I've watched a lot of BSU games and you two are a couple of real brawlers out there on that blue field."

"Yes sir, we do. I'm Paul..."

"No introductions!" Doc screamed suddenly with his hands over his ears. Everyone turned and gave him a dirty look, particularly the two young football players.

"He isn't supposed to know anyone's names," Stewart said in Doc's defense. "And we can't know his either. It's one of his 'protocols.'"

"Oh," they all said simultaneously. Then they all laughed including Doc.

"Doc! This is the first time I've ever seen you smile," Stewart teased.

"And this is the first time I've ever seen you with another Caucasian," Doc retorted pointing at Andrea. They all paused for a moment and then laughed even harder.

"Okay, enough of the fun and games everyone. We have work to do now," Fonseca said with professorial authority. "Doc managed to get the gold turned into wire last night and we've been setting up the CNC machine to make his parts."

"We're here to help," Dwayne said.

"What can you do?" Fonseca inquired.

"My boys can do anything," Andrea stated proudly. "They are both engineering majors and took all kinds of shop classes in high school. Dw...the older one here can even program those machines of yours and the younger one is learning how to."

"Doc, this is going to get mighty awkward if we can't use any names here. Can we at least use first names?" Stewart inquired.

"Oh, why not," Doc sighed. "I've already violated just about every other protocol anyway."

"Good. Andrea, Dwayne, Paul, and you already know John and Cindi," Stewart said as he pointed to each one. Cindi glared at him briefly. He realized that she had learned the technique from her mother and it was quite effective.

"Fine, your leftover gold is over here Captain," Doc said changing the subject. He seemed to be making an effort to prove his integrity to everyone as he displayed the open chest sitting on a nearby workbench. Stewart looked inside at the contents. It looked like mud mixed in with the remnants of the cloth pouches that he had placed the gold dust into more than a century ago. He had suspected that it would appear this way and had not even opened the other strongbox but had simply placed in the garage and left it for another time. This one was still nearly full.

"Are you sure you got enough?" Stewart asked.

"Oh yes. The gage of the wire I needed was very small; almost like a human hair. It really didn't take much. The biggest problem was cleaning the mud out of the dust so that I could process it."

"That's gold?" Paul asked staring into the strongbox.

"Paul…" Dwayne warned.

"I'm just lookin' bro. Lay off."

"Yes, I panned for gold for about five years after the war," Stewart explained. "I was going to split it with my partner but he was killed by Indians. We would have been very rich men in my time."

"I think you still are," Paul said softly.

"Too bad about your friend Captain," Dwayne offered. "Professor, do you have a foundry here?"

"Why yes, we do as a matter of fact," Fonseca replied. "It's over there on the other side of the shop. Do you know how to operate one?"

"Absolutely sir. Captain, may I?" Dwayne said pointing at the box.

Stewart was intrigued and simply said, "Sure." He wanted to see what this bright young man would do with all that gold and a foundry.

"Give me a hand Paul. It's going to be pretty heavy," Dwayne instructed. Paul didn't hesitate but jumped around to the other side of the box and lifted it with his brother. The two large men dwarfed the box as they carried it across the shop.

"Give us a couple hours. Holler if you need help with anything," Dwayne said to John as they walk away.

"Okay. What are they going to do?" Fonseca asked Andrea.

"I don't really know but it will be something really cool, I'm sure," Andrea shrugged. "Captain, you may just wind up with the most expensive set of wheels in the world on your pickup."

The men all worked on the machines while the ladies tried to help as much as they could. It just wasn't something in their expertise. Stewart even felt pretty useless as Doc and Fonseca talked back and forth about tolerances, G-codes, angles and stresses. He concentrated on staying out of the way and doing any heavy lifting. He was fascinated by the amazing machines and the way that they took a lump of metal and transformed it. They produced several small; strange looking parts and the best Stewart could do was de-burr them after Fonseca showed him how. Dwayne came back over several times to check their progress and lend his assistance to some of the machine operations. Once he even noted a simple math error that had caused Doc and Fonseca to scrap three parts already. Paul even pointed out some problems with the programming, much to Fonseca's consternation.

"I'm not an Engineering professor!" he exclaimed sarcastically. He then patted the boys on the back and thanked them for their fresh perspective. The ladies disappeared for a while and returned with pizza and drinks. Everyone took a break and sat at work benches to eat.

"So what are you guys doing over there with all that gold?" Fonseca inquired as he enjoyed his first slice of pizza in three years.

"A little surprise for Greg," Dwayne replied.

"Yeah, it's cooling right now but we're pretty much done," Paul added.

"I'm intrigued to see what you geniuses have literally cooked up for me," Stewart said.

"I think you'll like it," said Paul.

"Don't spoil it," Dwayne warned.

"I'm not."

"Well don't."

"Boys, behave." Andrea said quietly.

"Yes Ma'am," was the simultaneous reply.

"Well I'm looking forward to the surprise and I may have one for you two as well," Stewart hinted.

"Really? Like what?" Paul said excitedly. Dwayne punched him in the arm.

"That depends on whether I like your surprise," Stewart taunted.

"You know, I'm glad to know now what aliens really are," said Fonseca. "Scientists and visitors from the future are pretty easy to accept. I never really liked the whole creepy 'men from mars' or 'chariots of the gods' thing anyway."

"What?" Doc looked like he was going to choke on his pizza.

"I'm just saying that I'm a bit comforted that there aren't a bunch of lizard men or snake people out there sneaking around us. Now that I know that it's just a bunch of future guys trying to restore animal populations it just makes me feel better," Fonseca went back to chewing his pizza. "This is really good by the way. Thanks ladies."

"Um…there are…others," Doc said nervously. Everyone stopped eating and stared at him.

"Others?" Fonseca asked. "What others?"

"Um…other…um…visitors."

"From space?"

"Yes and no. I can't really talk about it."

"Protocols?"

"Yes."

"Well you can't just leave it at that Doc!" Fonseca exclaimed. "You have to give us more than that!"

"I can't."

"Why not?"

"It…it's dangerous to know too much about your own future," Doc looked around at the faces all staring at him. Paul took a sip from his Coke. Andrea was looking at him with a strange look, almost like she knew what he wasn't saying. He found it hard to look into her eyes and so he looked away from her and back to Fonseca.

"I will say only this; not all of them are who they say they are."

"Or come from where they say they do," added Andrea. Doc looked back at her wide-eyed in amazement. She had a calm look of understanding on her face that was unsettling to him. He looked back at John and saw that his dark skin had turned pale and a look of terror was on his face. The others simply looked surprised, except for Andrea. She nodded slightly as she looked at him.

"I will say no more about this," Doc said and quickly turned back to his pizza. She knows, he thought. How *can* she know? It wasn't possible. He made a concerted effort to focus on eating his pizza. Fonseca set his half-eaten slice of pizza down and looked like he was going to throw up. The rest of the group kept eating in silence.

"What the hell is it?" Fonseca asked staring at the strange looking device on the table. It was just under seventeen inches tall and about twelve inches wide. The fine gold wire was stretched taught over the various stanchions jutting out from the aluminum base. It formed an intricate web that crisscrossed the device and

205

actually made it look somewhat elegant. Seven electrical connectors jutted from various points on the piece.

"It's supposed to replace this," Doc said holding up a scorched gray box. A bullet hole was evident on one side. "I had it working after I removed the bullet but it burned up on me several hours into the journey; the captain's handiwork."

He set the object on the table next to their new creation. Everyone else looked at Stewart as Doc mentioned him, who simply shrugged in response.

"They don't look nothin' alike," said Paul. "Cept bein' about the same size."

"Anything, Paul," his mother corrected. "You need to quit speaking like your trashy friends. No one will ever take you seriously if you talk like you're from the ghetto, which you've never even seen in your life I might add."

"Yes mother," Paul replied.

"Listen to your mother boy, she's right. I had to learn that the hard way when I was your age," Fonseca added.

"Yes sir."

"It's called a dihedral parameter sequencing modulator. I have no idea what that means or what it does," Doc said reading off of the blue prints.

"Will it work?" Dwayne asked. Doc just shrugged. Fonseca looked at the blue prints that were on the table next to it.

"It looks right. I really like this fold up electronic screen thingy that you have these on. Are you sure you won't let me keep it?" Fonseca asked as he played with the high tech plastic sheet. He placed his hand on the drawing and turn it upside down on the screen and then back again.

"I just love the way this thing works,' he added as he played with the image.

"No, and it's actually something of an antique from my time. It's been obsolete for over twenty years. I bought it new in college when I was working on my last doctorate. You don't have anything here that could transfer data to it or even power it anyway."

"Well, it is cool though. What technology replaced it?"

"Never mind," Doc huffed." I think we're done here."

"Not quite," Dwayne said. "We still need to show Gr... er, the Captain his surprise."

"Look, I know his first name is Greg. You can call him that if it makes things easier," Doc sighed.

"Okay. Greg, follow me please."

They all followed the young men to other side of the shop. Even though the foundry had been shut down for over five hours they could still feel the heat as they approached it. The old strongbox sat empty on the floor. The brothers began disassembling several sand molds and knocking the sand into the used sand bin. Small shiny ingots fell into the sand and Paul reached in to grab one.

"Ouch!"

"They're still hot bro," Dwayne said offering him some gloves.

"Yeah, I got that now. Thanks."

Both brothers picked up ingots and began carefully removing the flashing from them which they then placed in a small container.

"You see, by melting it down we were able to bring all of the impurities out of it and what is left here should be fairly pure gold," Dwayne explained. "Most of the mud and cloth from the bags just burns up."

"We removed the dross and piled it there on that piece of scrap metal on the floor to cool," Paul added pointing at a small pile of golden debris. "There's still quite a bit of gold in there so you probably don't want to throw it away but it'll take more time and a smaller setup to clean that up. We used this scrap flat bar stock to make the molds. They're kind of simple but it's all we could find."

"We figured that this would be easier for you carry around or sell when you want to. We guessed at the size and tried to get it close to an ounce each but I think they may be more like an ounce and a half. The flashing can be re-melted too when you want to do something with that. There's probably a couple pounds of gold just in the flashing," said Dwayne.

Stewart put on a glove and picked up one of the ingots to examine it. He noticed that the brothers had taken great care in making them as uniform and consistent as possible. All of them were about two inches long by an inch and a half wide, about a quarter inch thick and had the same rounded corners.

"I'm actually pretty familiar with this process guys. I thought you might be doing something like this. This is really good work. Thank you very much. Now it's time for my surprise."

"What might that be sir?" Paul asked.

"Since I already figured out what you were doing I figured that your efforts should be rewarded. Keep the dross and the flashing for yourselves."

"Oh, we can't do that…" Dwayne began.

"Sure you can, and that's not all. I have another chest just like this one at my house that could use the same treatment. Are you up for it? I think that there should be enough gold for the two of you to buy some Harleys of your own when you're finished."

"Greg," Andrea interrupted. "That's very generous of you but…"

"I knew that you would all try to refuse but I insist. I can afford to share my new-found wealth a bit and as it is written, 'for the workman is worthy of his meat' in the King James, I would say that these fine young men have done me a great service and although we had no contract and I am sure they were simply trying to be helpful, I believe that they have earned this. Besides, that other chest is probably in as big a mess as this one was."

"We try not to focus too much on material wealth Greg," Andrea stated.

"As do I. Okay, let me be clear on something." He pulled Cindi next to him and put his arm around her waist."First, this is not a cheap attempt to buy your favor. Second, I fully intend to marry this woman as soon as you can plan the wedding and get your husband home to give her away. I fully intend to stay with her for the rest of my life and provide a pleasant and joyful existence for her. But we all must understand that I may well have a bunch of thugs from Doc's time chasing me all over the world for the rest of my days. I will use much of my money to prepare for those difficulties but I don't want to just sit on the rest.

"I have suffered much over my life and I would like to spend as much of the rest of it as possible not suffering quite so much. I have always worked hard in my life and I have been very poor for most of it. I like rich better than poor. I like living with the luxuries of your time period. I've also become very fond of driving, central heat and air, and indoor plumbing. But 'to whom much is given, much is required.' I fully understand that my wealth, like anything, is meant to serve the purposes of the Almighty and I'm counting on Cindi here to keep me honest about it. As my new family I expect the rest of you to assist. I have tried to be generous even when I was impoverished. Please allow me to continue to be generous in my wealth."

"Well, since you put it that way Greg, I guess I won't argue with you too much," Andrea said. "But please don't make a habit of spoiling my boys. They need to be able to rely on themselves and the Lord, not someone else's generosity."

"I couldn't agree more, ma'am," Stewart politely replied. "You have my word."

"Thank you, that's all I need."

"Yes!" Paul exclaimed. He looked as if he were about to explode with excitement.

"Paul!" Cindi smacked him on the arm as Dwayne smacked him on the other.

"I'm sorry. Momma you know how much I've always wanted a motorcycle," Paul explained.

"Yes, since you were four. And what comes first?" Andrea said sternly.

"Helmet, boots, gloves, a jacket, and a riding safety class."

"And?"

"Prayer, before and after every ride," Paul responded as if he had said it a thousand times.

"Prayer?" Fonseca asked. "I understand the before, what's the after about?"

"Thanks, sir," Paul explained.

"I've always told him that if he ever does get a machine that can easily kill him that he should fully place his life in the hands of God and pray for protection before and thanks afterward for a safe ride," Andrea added.

"Sounds like a good plan to me," Stewart offered.

"Makes sense to me too," Fonseca said. "Okay, enough of this youthful exuberance, let's get this place cleaned up and send Doc here back to the future, no movie reference intended."

It was dark when they finally locked up the building. Stewart invited everyone to dinner but all of them declined except Cindi. Andrea was just tired, the boys had studies to work on in the morning, and Doc wanted to hurry and fix his ship. Fonseca said he just wanted to go home and curl up with a bottle of scotch and forget what Doc had said about aliens. They had loaded the parts into the back of the Yukon, not a Yukon, and after Doc retrieved a bag from inside and closed the door he turned to the group to speak.

"I have few things to say to all of you before I go," he began.

"There you go with those 'I' sentences again," Paul said.

"Well, it is about me right now because I want to apologize once again. I have behaved contrary to everything I have been raised to believe. I allowed myself to be brought down by my circumstances and I let my arrogance justify treating all of you with far less than the human dignity that you deserve. You have all repaid me with kindness and generosity and I thank you for it. In particular, I want to thank you Captain. Many times you could have killed me and yet you spared me even though I didn't deserve it. I treated you as a barbarian because you have killed people but you are one of the most civilized men I have ever met.

"You have mentioned that things happen for a reason and though I've complained and behaved very poorly throughout this incident I now see a purpose in it all. You see, I had only mentally acknowledged the values I had been taught to believe. Though I knew them in my head, I didn't really *know* them until they were put to the test. I know now what my parents have been trying say to me for the last sixty years of my life. I have nothing but respect for all of you and you have my eternal gratitude. Captain, I wish only the best for you for all the days of your life and I will do whatever I can, if anything, to try to convince the authorities to not come after you. Don't count on it though. By the way, I believe these belong to you," he said as he handed him the bag.

"I won't," Stewart shrugged. He looked into the bag and saw his Remingtons lying inside. "Thanks," he said. "These mean a lot to me. We've been through a lot together."

Doc said, "I've already broken nearly every protocol there is so it won't make much difference if I try to repay you with a small amount of information that may help you survive the near future. Keep your gold, or as much of it as you can. Buy the things you need now, they won't ever be cheaper and some things will eventually be impossible to buy at any price, like fuel. If you have any investments in the stock market sell them now. You have very little time to stave off your losses. Learn to survive, can food, hunt, fish, build shelter, preserve technologies and learn to generate power. Buy long term storage food and supplies, guns and lots of ammunition. Learn how to use them well and be prepared to use them when necessary. Captain, I think you might already have that covered."

"I try," Stewart interjected.

"That's all I can really tell you. I'm not too familiar with the details anyway. I started out studying history but I let my father talk me into genetics. It was almost like he wanted to me to study anything but history. Funny though, my sister majored in history," Doc said thoughtfully.

"What about these 'others' you spoke of?" Fonseca asked.

"That's something I really can't discuss. Let's just say that good and evil do exist and leave it at that. If you survive, you will have to make a choice, much like I did recently."

Everyone was silent for a moment.

"Well good luck to you Doc," Fonseca said. "Greg, call me tomorrow and we'll meet somewhere for lunch. Maybe you can help me figure out how to break the news to my stock broker."

"Sure John. Maybe Cindi and Andrea can join us as well."

"What about you Andrea?" Fonseca asked. "Do you have a stock market portfolio?"

"These are my investments John," she replied as she hugged her children. "All of my investments are with the Lord and my family."

"Hmm, I think you invested more wisely than I did," Fonseca said, only half kidding.

"Well, I must go and face the music as you say here," Doc sighed. "I'd best be off to fix my ship."

"Just a second Doc," Stewart said as he walked over to his truck. He placed the Remingtons inside and retrieved a small shopping bag and a large burlap bag and handed them to Doc. "I got you a little going away present."

211

"What is it?" Doc asked.

"A Lenny Kravitz T-shirt and his greatest hits CD. I thought you might want to update your wardrobe to fit the times. I don't know if you have a way to play CDs in that thing you're driving but I recommend the song 'Fly Away.' It seems appropriate at the moment. The burlap bag is a favor though. I'll leave it up to you whether you want to do it or not. Just read the note in the bag," Stewart laughed.

"Thanks," was all Doc could manage. Tears welled up in his eyes.

"Doc," Andrea said compassionately. "Don't go home with any pre-conceived ideas about your fate. While we are all curious about our future, we now know more about ours than you do about yours. This will surely turn out for the best for you. God brought you through this so far; he'll take you the rest of the way. You need to trust in Him."

"Yes, ma'am, I do, "Doc nodded. "Thank you all."

They all took turns saying their goodbyes. Doc climbed into his vehicle and opened the driver's side window. It didn't roll down but seemed to simply dissolve.

"Cool trick," Paul said.

"Good bye Doc," Stewart said shaking his hand. "I want you to know that I really mean it when I say that I hope that I never see you again, ever."

"Same here Captain," Doc said with smile. He turned to his controls and the window suddenly reformed. They watched as he drove out of the parking lot and headed down the street. Only the two boys seemed surprised as the Yukon proved it wasn't really a Yukon by suddenly lifting from the road taking to the sky. They all stared as it headed northeast until the tail lights disappeared.

Chapter Twenty

Epilogue

July 23, 2008, 5:20 PM, U.S Highway 30, southern Pennsylvania.

Stewart rode in silence. The brand new Harley-Davidson Road Glide rumbled loudly as he rode but the sound was far outside of his thoughts. His mind was focused on his destination; Gettysburg. It was later in July so all of the re-enactors were gone now and he thought that the crowds might be smaller on a Wednesday. It had been a long ride and mostly pleasant, staying in nice hotels along the way. He really hadn't wanted to come back here but Cindi had insisted that he needed closure. He felt her tiny hands around his waist and her not so tiny breasts against his back. He nudged back against her slightly and was comforted by her gentle squeeze.

Though he had purchased the most state of the art headsets available they rarely used them on this day. The couple had said no more than a few words to each other all day while they had chattered constantly over the headsets for the last week. He had lingered at the hotel in Harrisburg until after lunch and it was now late in the day. He had a strange feeling in his guts that he didn't like. Cindi had not pestered him about leaving the hotel. They were in no hurry and she could tell that he had mixed emotions about returning to the old battle ground. She knew that he must face this on his own and that it couldn't be rushed.

The town was much different now but still hauntingly familiar. The road that he came in on had been one of the approaches the Confederates had taken coming into the town one hundred forty five years earlier. All over the small town were souvenir shops, museums and restaurants. The name of the town seemed to appear on every sign and billboard. His battle so long ago had now become a big business. It was *his* battle after all. He had fought here, killed here, and almost died here. Though a soldier may leave the battlefield, the battlefield never leaves the soldier. He felt sick to his stomach as he rode through the town.

He slowly rode down to South Confederate Avenue and then headed east. Nice touch, he thought, naming a road after the enemy. He slowed down even more as he approached the Devil's Den. He could see the familiar rocks on the left side of the road. It was far more than déjà vu that struck him now. He *had* been here before. It wasn't some delusional fantasy but it was real. He remembered this very view although there were certainly no paved roads nor manicured landscaping here back then.

He pulled into a parking space just off the road and shut the bike down. Cindi jumped off the bike and waited as he just sat there and listened to the creaking sound of cooling metal. Few people were here as he had hoped. He stared at the rocks of the Den almost in horror. He could vividly see the image in his mind of the bodies lying on the ground, their grey uniforms faded to a chestnut brown splotched with black stains of dried blood interspersed with blue uniforms in a similar state. He slowly lifted himself off the machine, lightly caressing the custom handgrips as he rose in a small attempt to hang on to sanity. He removed his helmet and set it on the right side of the handlebars. He took a few steps toward the Den and stopped. He turned and looked at Cindi and the motorcycle. He saw the worry in her eyes as she stood staring at him with her helmet in her hand. A soft breeze blew some of her hair into her face and she flicked it out her eyes with her hand.

Stewart stood staring at the two most beautiful things in his world; his woman and the monster Harley with the crazy red and black flame job he had just spent a ton of money on. It was just a thing but it was beautiful and he looked at both of them just trying to savor the joy that they both brought to him. He was struggling with the strange feeling in his stomach and was trying to focus on the image of Cindi and that bike to keep him in the here and now. He felt that if he looked away he might fall into an abyss and never return. He gave Cindi a slight smile which she nervously returned.

It was so very strange. He could almost he see himself standing there as if just an observer while on another level he felt that he might collapse at any moment. Taking a deep breath he pushed his emotions down and turned to face the Den. He slowly walked up to the rocks and began climbing toward the position he had taken almost a century and a half before.

He took it slowly at first but then faster as he found the well-worn paths between the rocks. He felt the adrenaline of the rush of battle now just as he did on the 2nd of July in 1863. He could hear the cannons boom across the valley and the rush of shells overhead. He could feel the ground shake with their impact and the screams of the wounded. The sharp smell of gunpowder filled his nose as he ran up to the top of the Den. The bullets whined by him, most of them flying off harmlessly into the distance but sometimes stopping suddenly with a sickening slap against human flesh.

He pressed on up the rocks until he could see the trees that covered Little Round Top across the small valley. He looked to the north and saw the Union guns on top of Cemetery Ridge raining hellfire onto his friends and brothers in arms. Bodies were strewn everywhere in both grey and blue. He stood staring at the enemy in the distance. He could see the faces of the men who were killing them; determined, desperate, and afraid. Once more he felt the futile helplessness that he had felt that day. He had never felt it before that day and never since. It was a feeling of abandonment; as if God himself had turned His back on him. It was his soul dying with his men as they fell by the dozen and it was his guilt for staying alive.

Suddenly it was gone. The battle was over and the beautiful National Park was back in his vision. He looked over at the ridge again. The guns were gone as were the horses and men in blue. The only sound came from birds singing their songs that told the world that all was at peace here now. He was standing there with his hands in the pockets of his black Harley jacket and the only smell in his nostrils now was the smell of new leather. He turned and walked passed Cindi and stepped down from the rocks until he reached a small grassy patch in between some of the formations.

He looked down the row of rocks and remembered the wounded and dying lining this bloody open air hallway. He remembered the look in the eyes of his friend, he couldn't remember his name but they were friends and his blues eyes smiled at him as he lay dying against the rocks. He remembered the blue eyes going blank with death. *What was his name?* He thought. *How can I forget the name of a man I fought beside for almost three years and who died here in front of me?* He felt ashamed of himself for forgetting.

He felt very strange. Still in one small corner of his mind he felt as if he were hiding there in the dark, watching himself with intense interest, but uninvolved. He looked down at his hands and saw them trembling. He had never felt this way before in his life, not even during the battles he had fought in. His legs shook and failed. The grass was slightly damp and his uninvolved self felt the wetness soak through his jeans to his knees. He felt the tears rolling down his face as his vision blurred. His uninvolved self suddenly was swept into the flow of emotion as it struggled to keep its distance.

Stewart struggled for sanity as reason escaped his grasp. Cindi's tiny dark hand fell on his left shoulder and with blurred vision he could just make out the beautiful old diamond ring on her finger which now rested against a custom made matching wedding band. He reached up with his own left hand and his new ring gently clinked against hers as he held on to her hand for dear life.

It was an anchor in a sea of insanity. Thoughts and images rushed at him and racked his body in sobbing convulsions. His mother's death, Julie's ruined body flopping into the river, the slave and his handler behind the two pretty young ladies, Gettysburg, his father clutching the wound where his bullet had pierced his heart, Doc and his spaceship from the future, the dead claim jumper, The Battle of Wilderness, Julie's death again, Doc trying to shoot Cindi, kill Doc, don't kill Doc, the internet, Gettysburg , motorcycles, Cindi's face, falling from the Red Lion Downtowner, Cecil's death, *Oh God, Cecil I'm so sorry*, Julie's face, *I'm sorry*, the three drug dealers in the desert, Gettysburg , Lieutenant Foster and his devastated platoon, the faces of all the men he'd killed screamed at him from his past, forty seven men, he had never counted before but now he saw forty seven faces, the number screaming at him in accusation, GETTYSBURG!, alone in a strange land…holding on to the hand of the woman he loved. The hand of his wife, who loved him, forgave him, cherished and adored him, accepted him for whom and what he was.

Cindi told him later that it had taken over three hours. She had feared that he might never recover his sanity from the episode

216

and had prayed over him the whole time. He remembered that it had seemed both like just a few minutes and an eternity at the same time. She had held him tightly as his past came spewing out of his soul as pus squeezed from an open boil. Of course he felt silly and embarrassed afterward as he stood up in the growing darkness and brushed himself off.

"I'm s…"

"Don't you dare apologize for this Greg," she said firmly, with her finger at the ready. "You've been running from yourself your whole life and you needed stop and face yourself for us to be able to move on. You needed to do this, and you need to forgive yourself."

"Yes, yes I did and I do. Thank you."

"How do you feel now?" she asked with a concerned look on her face.

"Hungry," Stewart replied.

"Me too!" She said with a big smile as she hugged him. "Now I know you're going to be alright."

They walked hand in hand back down to the bike and mounted up to leave.

"Hell of way to spend a honeymoon," Stewart commented sarcastically as he snapped his helmet on.

"It'll get better," Cindi replied, doing the same.

"Really? When?"

"Starting right now," Cindi replied as she pinched his butt. Stewart just smiled and swung his leg over the machine. Cindi hopped on and wrapped her arms around him and squeezed. The quiet of the nearly deserted park was shattered by the sudden roar as Stewart started the Road Glide's 103 cubic inch engine. The Samson pipes crackled as he rolled on the throttle and headed back into town. The sound gradually faded until the only sound left at the Devil's Den was again the sound of birds and crickets.

Doc tried to keep his head up but felt glum. The crude modulator thing seemed to be working fine and the ship was functioning normally in all respects except that it was drawing significantly more power during the time transfer than normal. It was still operating well within safety specifications though. He was now in a time path that would bring him back to his own time roughly seventy two hours from the time he'd left. The seventy two hours was a safety measure to prevent duplicity, the phenomenon of being in the same time period in two instances. No one was really certain what would happen if it ever occurred but no one was willing to find out either. All of the prevailing theories weren't good. It couldn't produce a desirable outcome no matter what theory proved to be correct.

He tried not to think about what would happen when he landed but found his mind continually rehearsing excuses, justifications and finally settling back on plan 'A' which was to just tell the truth and take full responsibility. He had never done that before in his life and he now saw why. It was hard. It was so hard for him to admit that he was wrong and that he had screwed up completely but he was determined to see it through. What good would his repentance be if he reneged when it really counted? He would do his best to stand with honor as he expressed his shame to his superiors. No doubt he would be fired and have to find some other employment opportunity that was completely unrelated to time travel.

He briefly thought about the errand that Stewart had asked of him in his note and smiled at the memory of the adventure of making that small delivery. It had been fun and he felt good about it even though it was yet another huge violation of protocols.

Doc checked his course again for the three hundredth time but the ship was still tracking true. Forty eight minutes to go before he dropped out of the time slip into normal space again. He wanted to eat or something but he couldn't leave the suit until the craft dropped velocity. He began going over the events of the past several weeks trying to make sure he had the details down. He found himself second guessing himself and trying to find his mistakes. He could have done this differently or that differently. He shouldn't have kidnapped the girl. He shouldn't have bought the gun that he found advertized in the Thrifty Nickel. It was driving him mad. He usually never seemed to mind the time alone in his thoughts when traveling but now he despised it. The suit was annoying him for the first time ever. He wanted to just pull it off, go home, jump into the shower for a few hours and go to bed.

He tried to nap in the wall lounge and sat up after a while.

"ETA?" he asked the ship.

"Forty three minutes," came the stony reply.

"Damn! Chess! Queen's knight... oh... cancel!" he said in frustration as the holographic board appeared and then disappeared just as quickly. He looked at the screen on the wall and stared at the continual image of the Earth and moon appearing and disappearing. Every iteration was a full year, more or less. Each one of them took only about thirty seconds to pass through. He only had about eighty years left to travel but it seemed to pass like the full eighty years to him. He felt terribly impatient and began to pace the cabin floor. He spoke to the ship in his mind and the stool raised from the floor in front the control consol. He sat down heavily and sighed. Then he leaned forward and rested his head on the console and began to pray. He had never really seriously prayed before as an adult but now seemed like a good time. He needed help and at this point in his life only divine intervention would be able to help him.

He awoke to the chime of the ship translating into normal space. He had come into orbit 70,000 miles above the North Pole. Exiting ships left from the South Pole while incoming came in at the North. It avoided collisions as well as the lunar orbit and no one had crashed yet. Exact times were difficult to adhere to when jumping back from the time slip drive so each ship was given a day of return and its own orbital entry level to avoid conflicts. It was programmed into the ship prior to departure and it would not, could not drop in at any other distance from the Earth. There had only been two close calls in history but that was when he was a child and no one had been hurt.

Doc began an auto search of the transmitting web to check for historical differences between his onboard data banks and the current worldwide transmissions. He then set his course for his home base on the North American Continent. The computer rejected the course and command substituted a new one. He had been intercepted by the authorities and his ship was set on a new course. His heart sank as he saw the location on the feed. It was still North America but instead of his home base on the Florida peninsula it was now New Washington in the center of the continent. He was going to the capital city of North America and he suddenly felt like he would throw up.

Frantically he called up the auto search and checked for anomalies. It was an optional feature that most travelers never bothered with including himself but now he felt desperate to find out how badly he had screwed up. The search was nearing completion with no discrepancies found as yet. It had to be bad if he had to go to the capital to plead his case. He might be arrested and jailed, he thought in horror. He had gone over the conversation he would have with his boss and the local authorities but never imagined that he would have to appear in the capital. He felt doomed and prayed again.

He stared at the monitor as the city of aqua domes appeared and grew larger. It was a beautiful city; he had been there as a young student, with numerous lakes surrounding the low, flat domes. The domes were layered plastic with water continually rising between the layers to the tops and then dropping through the interior air into the pools below to be recycled through the system. This simple procedure provided clean air at an over pressure to keep out impurities while also acting as a radiator for the community below. On the hottest days the interior was rarely above eighty degrees Fahrenheit and on the coldest days rarely below fifty. An ultra violet filtering film covered the interior layer which provided an environment which assisted greatly in human longevity. He was fascinated by the vast structures and their terrarium like beauty.

Of course he also lived under a dome like everyone else but the ones in New Washington were enormous compared to most others. They also had nightly rain showers programmed into the domes that cycled through in sections so that the greenery stayed watered rather than using the more traditional sprinkler systems. If one kept up with the schedule, one never had to get wet.

The ship settled down into the port and he felt the slight bump as it touched down. He reluctantly stood up from the stool and went into his personal cabin to change. He emerged ten minutes later cleaned up and dressed in his official directorate uniform. He checked the monitor for instructions. There were none. He then checked the auto search. No anomalies found.

He thought about that for a moment. No anomalies found. None. Zero. He felt even sicker to his stomach now. No instructions on the board either. He sat silently and waited, not knowing what to do next. A chime sounded and he saw that a vehicle was pulling under the ship.

It was unoccupied; he'd been sent for. He sighed again and slowly walked over to the beam lift and instructed it to take him down to the car. He sank into the floor of the control room, passed the lower hold and sat down in the car when his feet touched the floor. It was a very nice car; a Lincoln actually. He smiled as he recognized the stylized version of the old logo on the front dashboard. Ironic, he thought. He sat back into the cushions and felt the restraint system lock him into place. Only after the fake click sounded through the cars speakers did it begin to drive away from the ship.

He went right through all of the security gates without even slowing down. Apparently this car had all the right pass codes installed. The cloud of doom weighed even heavier as he realized that only those at the highest levels could arrange for such a reception. He was in really, really big trouble. He settled back and tried to relax. His throat felt dry so he ordered water and the vehicle immediately complied with a small chilled bottle rising into his left hand. He sipped on it slowly as he approached the city. The farm fields were full of greenery on the outskirts as he passed by them. It was spring and everything was growing. He saw the domes in the distance as the car sped along, passing all of the others.

"Speed?" he asked the car.

"One hundred sixty five," was that passionless response. That was pretty fast so whoever wanted to see him was in a hurry. He thought about the miles per hour the computer had just quoted him and briefly recalled from school the historical debate to reject the metric system because of its misuse by the communists who tried, and almost succeeded in taking over the world so many years ago. Scientists had fought the movement but popular sentiment had effectively rejected it for public use. Some scientists still used it but it was generally ignored by most people and using it was often viewed as subversive.

The domes grew large in the windshield and he briefly wondered which one he was going to. The white aluminum lattice that held the dome panes together shimmered in the bright sunlight. It was a very beautiful sight and he wished that he could enjoy it. He tried fantasizing that he was an important operative on his way back from a secret mission to save humanity and that this was the preliminary to his debriefing. It wasn't working. He still felt like throwing up.

It soon became evident as the car wound its way at high speed between the domes that he was heading to the largest dome which dominated the center of the city; The Great Dome. He wanted to swear. This was getting worse by the moment. No doubt anything he said in the car would be recorded and he would have to account for that as well. He remained silent as the car slowed and pulled inside the reception tunnel to The Great Dome. It wasn't the main entrance portal, Doc knew and it was almost deserted. Two men stood on the curb as he pulled up and he groaned slightly as he saw the security uniforms they were wearing. They were agents from I.T.M.S. and high ranking ones at that.

"Good afternoon sir, please come with us," one of the men said as the door swung up and open. He said nothing but simply nodded at them as he straightened his tunic. They turned and began walking and he followed close behind. He felt as though he might choke any minute on the lump in his throat. He tried to walk with his head held high, like a condemned man walking to his execution. It helped, a little.

They walked to a secure lift and one of the agents place his hand against the pad to open the door. The windowless box opened on their side of it and they all stepped in. The door closed and Doc turned to look out over the dome interior through the one-way walls. It was a beautiful view and he was even more impressed as the lift traveled up the curved inside of the seven mile wide dome. It wasn't hemispheric so it was only about three thousand feet high at the apogee but it was still very high. The lift stopped just above the halfway point on a small deck. The doors opened and they all stepped onto the deck which began to glide across the expanse to another deck on the top level outer ring. His escorts led him onto the ever moving ring where they traveled clockwise for a short distance. They walked off the ring and toward the inner ring. When they reached the inner ring they traveled counterclockwise for an even shorter distance until they were standing before the giant white and gold doors of the council chamber.

"The council, huh?" Doc gulped.

"Yes sir," the other agent now spoke. His voice seemed compassionate, almost respectful.

"Well, let's get this over with," Doc said quietly.

"Yes sir," the agent said as he pushed the door open.

The giant hall was full. Thousands of people sat quietly around the chamber as the twenty four council members sat wearing their hooded robes at their benches in a circle on the ground floor. The giant eight point gold star shone brightly in the center of the white marble floor as the sun beamed upon it from the dome above the chamber.

"To the center sir," the agent instructed, motioning with his hand.

Doc nodded and slowly walked into the bright light, stopping on the center of the star. He had only seen pictures of this place before and had never seen any of the council members before now. No pictures existed of them, and they were very secretive about their identities which were kept concealed by their robes. They served only in the public interest and no fame was allowed. The hall itself was named after one of his own distant relatives who was considered a hero by all humanity. He had never seen a picture of him either but he knew they existed somewhere. He had often thought about studying him but had always been distracted from it. Now he stood in his hall and faced a crowd of thousands for screwing up the timeline though he wasn't quite sure how yet. He cleared his throat and tried to speak but his voice cracked. The crowd laughed briefly and was shushed by the wiser members of the audience. He tried again.

"Members of the council, fellow human beings, I come before you today to take full responsibility for my actions," he began. "I have violated virtually every time travel protocol by engaging with primitives, sharing future knowledge, and failing to return them for mind-wiping and reinsertion. I have also violated our own social norms and customs by engaging in crude, thoughtless, and degrading behavior. I have lied, committed theft, kidnapping, and attempted murder. When confronted with adversity I chose to lower myself to a base mentality and rejected my enlightened upbringing in a pitiful attempt at self preservation. I have most certainly caused irreversible changes to the timeline and I am fully… fully prepared to accept whatever punishment that the council deems appropriate."

He felt better. He had confessed his sins and he now felt free. He would bravely embrace whatever they threw at him, even death. He should have died already anyway. The room was silent. He stared at the faces around him and he suddenly felt very strange. They were all smiling at him. The two agents came up and placed a chair behind him. He looked at them as one of them motioned for him to sit. He remained standing and looked around the silent room once again. One of the council members began to chuckle softly. Others joined him. Doc stared at the room as it erupted in laughter. He felt his face getting red with embarrassment and anger. He was the butt of a joke and everyone here knew the punch line but him.

"Quiet!" one of the council members shouted. The room became silent once more.

"I'm sorry, you have no idea what you've done, do you?" said the council member who had begun the chuckling.

"Not really sir. What exactly is going on? What have I screwed up so badly that I must report to the Council of North America's Elders?" Doc said, slightly defensive now.

"Oh no, quite the opposite actually. Why if it weren't for you and your 'mistakes' probably none of us would be here right now, especially not you!" the Elder explained. "Please sit down Doctor Stewart, and tell us all about your great, great grandfather, Captain Gregory Dean Stewart, formerly of the Confederate Army who helped to lead us all back to faith and sanity so long ago."

Doc's mouth dropped open and he suddenly felt faint. The two agents helped him down into the chair. He sat stunned for several minutes as he stared at all of the smiling, caring, loving faces around him in Stewart Hall. The full impact of all that he had been through began to hit him at once. It all came crashing together and it was overwhelming. Then one thing came into his mind and he smiled as he remembered, Romans 8:28; *'and we know that all things work together for good to them that love God, to them who are the called according to his purpose.'*

Made in the USA
Columbia, SC
15 August 2024

40093681R00124